RETUR...

CEN...

OF THE

EARTH

GREIG BECK

SEVERED PRESS
HOBART TASMANIA

RETURN TO THE CENTER OF THE EARTH

ISBN: 978-1-922323-97-2

ACKNOWLEDGMENTS:

Thank you to my test pilots: Jeremy Salter and Scott Erichsen. Your feedback was insightful, helpful, and allowed me to see through the forest to the trees.

"Those who descend into the dark find monsters.
Or become them."
-Jane Baxter, Krubera Caving Team

PROLOGUE

The frozen north of Georgia, Caucasus region, circa 102,000 years ago

The clan sat staring into the popping fire as if hypnotized. The flames were tiny now but at the fire's center the embers still glowed a searing red and it warmed their cheeks and filled the cave with the smell of resin infused wood smoke.

Their band comprised of four families, with seven hunters, ranging in ages from twelve to twenty-eight. There were also women, five young children, a single new baby, and two withered and toothless elders in their forties.

They had lived in the front chambers of the huge cave for several generations, had defended it against other family groups, and once had even repelled a towering cave bear.

But this time of year was always hard; snow fell day and night and the ground was frozen solid so there were no green shoots. And no green shoots meant game was scarce, and a good-sized animal was needed at least once a week to feed the clan.

Druga was only ten years old and was now of age to be able to go out with the other men. But it would be two more summers before he would be allowed to carry a spear.

When there was food it would be first shared amongst the hunters because without their strength the tribe would become weak and vulnerable. But it meant the old and very young were only fed if there was enough to spare. And in the cold of winter the old and weak always died.

And so it was that old Clee-ak finally succumbed. Little Druga quietly suspected his foul gas smells and persistent night-cough would not be missed.

As was custom, his body was sung over, dressed in the best skins and adorned with the finest bone jewelry and weapons for a day. Then they would all be removed, his remaining possessions shared amongst the tribe, and his naked body taken into the deep caves and left there in darkness so he could join with the ancestors.

Two hunters carried the near-weightless body into the cave depths

1

and Druga followed as the small procession's torch-holder. They went deep beyond their outer chambers to the place of the ancestors. They never usually went this far as it was eternally dark, and darkness had always been something to fear.

Druga thought it odd that the further they went the more the men became cautious and their eyes darted about. He always thought their ancestors would be adored, not feared, and he had always wanted to see them. So he kept his eyes wide open.

They eventually came to an opening in the cave floor and leaning forward the boy looked down into the pit, but the utter darkness gave nothing away except for a warming breeze against his cheeks.

The men carefully laid the body down and immediately Druga began to smell an overpowering stench like bad meat or old Clee-ak's breath when he leaned too close.

The trio backed away from the body and then began to creep away when from behind there was the sound of sliding. Druga immediately knew it was Clee-ak's body being dragged into the pit.

The three clan members ran. Suddenly, Druga didn't want to see his ancestors after all.

EPISODE 06

All was black, and such a dense black that, after some minutes, my eyes had not been able to discern even the faintest glimmer
— Jules Verne

CHAPTER 01

Harry Wenton was pulled from the cage. He kicked and thrashed, but his soft body was no match for the hard-shelled monstrosities that dragged him out.

The things clicked, squeaked and twitched their excitement as the last ragged remnants of his clothing pulled from his body. Harry screamed in panic but knew that no one would hear, no one would be coming to save him, and no one even cared as they had all abandoned him to be tormented in this hellish-red underworld.

He was roughly dragged by his long, matted hair to a set of logs that had been lashed sparsely together, and then bound to it by his ankles, wrists and neck. He begged, screamed and blubbered, but the creature's bulb-eyes on their quivering stalks were as dispassionate as blobs of dark glass.

Clawlike hands used small branches still holding their leaves to dip into a bucket and splash him with something that smelled of grease. He was lathered from the soles of his feet to the top of his head and he had to blink the oily liquid from his eyes and clamp his mouth shut.

He began to cry, knowing what it would mean. He was lifted then and carried toward the fire pit. The clicking and squeaking of the foul creatures reached a crescendo, and he wondered whether this was their form of laughing, or perhaps even singing.

"Help! He-*eeeelp!*"

He yelled until his voice cracked and only stopped when one of the nightmarish things leaned over him to peer into his face.

"Kill me first… *please,*" he begged.

It stared, inching closer and Harry saw the multiple mouthparts and feelers working furiously inside its maw.

"*Please,*" he whispered to it.

"*Eh-leee-zz,*" the thing began to mimic. The bulb-eyes shivered excitedly as the clicking and squeaking began again. The thing pulled back and Harry was lifted higher.

Behind them another creature loomed, and it was a monstrosity of mountainous proportions. All the things deferred to it, perhaps waiting on instructions.

Harry kept his eyes on it and then lay back. Even though he wasn't a religious man, he began to pray. He prayed this was all just a nightmare, he prayed he would be saved or spared, and he prayed that his heart would stop right now. But it didn't.

Then, Harry Wenton, Englishman, lawyer, multi-millionaire, and professional caver, was lifted and then laid over the fire pit for the cooking to begin.

Harry screamed, and screamed, and screamed, and...

"*Arghhh*." Jane sat up, holding her face.

She began to weep in the darkness of her room. *Please, no*, she thought miserably. *We left him to die*.

She swung her legs over the side of the bed and sat there feeling like her heart had turned to lead. She knew what Mike would say: *there was nothing they could have done*, and he was right. In fact, it had been her that had dragged Mike away from poor Harry.

She put the heels of her hands in her eye sockets and pressed, trying to erase the mental images. Even though the guy had been an asshole, he didn't deserve that. No one deserved that.

He might still be alive, her conscience whispered. But she knew that could be an even worse fate.

Jane looked at her bedside clock. It was just gone 4am, all was quiet, she was home, safe, and it was over a year since they had climbed out of the hole in the ground.

For the most part, the memories of their descent to the center of the Earth were now more like a lingering fever dream. Much of it was vague and felt like an old photograph left in the sunshine that was fading and fraying at the edges. She knew that psychologically it was some form of coping mechanism, and the only time she was really troubled was in her sleep when her mental defenses were down. And it was dark.

Straight after their escape she had dated Mike Monroe on and off but after a while he had become remote, obsessed with their adventure, and said he was still writing its history down. Then he had simply walled himself off from his friends, her included. She knew curiosity still burned within him, but he had promised her that there was nothing that could make him travel down there again.

She wanted to believe him. But he had also mentioned to her he had tried to contact Katya Babikov in Russia. But he found she was now gone from the medical facility in Krasnodar, and all he was told was that Russian government officials had taken her somewhere for some sort of special cancer treatment. And that was something else that gnawed at him.

Of their other team members who had survived, Andy had headed off surfing somewhere, and she and Maggie had finally gone back to their jobs. However, Michael, being independently wealthy, had been able to sit alone in his remote cabin in the woods, writing and brooding, and ruminating on a secret place at the center of the world.

She wondered if it was only her finding it difficult to slot back into a normal life again, but when she had spoken to Maggie, her friend had professed to the same. Everything seemed bland, colorless, and unremarkable since they had escaped from that red Hell.

Jane looked at the clock again; still way too early to get up, so she lay back down on her sweat-soaked pillow. She forced her eyes to stay closed and tried to think of azure skies over snow-capped mountains, birds singing, and fields of flowers.

And she refused to hear Harry Wenton screaming from the boiling-red center of the Earth.

CHAPTER 02

National Defence Command and Control Center, Moscow

Katya hated her room. The gurney-style bed was hard and the sheets tucked in so tight they bent her toes. But at least they were clean.

Surrounding her were gleaming white, hard ceramic tiles, walling a room that was far too big for just her. It was bigger than her entire apartment at the Krasnodar mental health hospital she had lived at for decades.

She sighed and let her eyes travel around the room's austere interior; the thing she hated the most was at night they turned out all the lights, and that terrified her, as there were pools of absolute darkness that her imagination conjured into steep tunnels burrowing all the way down to the center of the Earth.

When she had escaped the lightless caves nearly half a century ago, she never wanted to be in darkness again. Because things hid in the darkness. Things that could see and smell and find you even in blackness so complete it was as if you were blind.

Katya had tried to flee her room once, but outside she found she wasn't in a hospital at all, and there weren't other patients or doctors and nurses in the corridors, but instead military people and their joyless faces looked at her with stone-like empathy.

She had been quickly caught and now she had tethered wrist cuffs, for her own protection, the burly male attendant had told her gently as he strapped her down.

And then there were the interviews that had been going on for several weeks now, or was it months? They had wanted to know everything from the time she first dropped into the Krubera in 1972 with her friends, and when she had found the new passage that took them all the way to the center of the Earth.

They wanted to know about how they traveled, where they traveled, and what they found there. They wanted to know in detail about the entities they had called them, and how her friends had died; each one of them, and she wasn't to omit any detail no matter how gruesome or painful to her.

They spent days going over how she made it out by herself, and about her sister, Lena, who almost made it out with her. And then they had subjected her to all manner of tests to prove she was telling the truth, from injections of ice-cold liquid into her veins that made her relive the horrors all over again, to machines that monitored her heart rate and made scratchy lines on paper as she told her story.

They were rude to her, rough and uncaring, and acted with a mix of derision and disdain. She knew then that they wanted to travel there, and at first she didn't want to give up everything to try and stop them experiencing the fate her own team members had suffered.

Katya craned forward to look down at one of her strapped hands and at the bandages that were covering the ulcers all over her flesh. The sickness was on her skin and metastasizing deeper into her body, eating her away, one tiny cell-sized bite at a time.

And their tests continued. She lowered her head and sighed. After a while she began to hate them, and in the end she did tell them, everything, perhaps cruelly, because she wanted them to experience what she had endured to wipe those disbelieving sneers from their faces.

She knew they'd go and knew their exploration wasn't just for scientific reasons. The military presence was enough to confirm that to her. Whatever they were planning, it probably had little to do with science.

Then came the bombshell and the choice they had given her was the devil's choice. No more treatment for her cancers, and so to die here, in pain, alone and forgotten. Or come with them to act as their guide and become a national hero. And then the final promise: that they would make her well again.

In the end, she had no choice.

CHAPTER 03

CIA Headquarters, Fairfax County, Virginia, United States

Robert Lee Johnson worked for ISOD, the Central Intelligence Agency's International Surveillance Operations Division, and he was one of the dozens of agents responsible for collecting, assessing and analyzing, and then distributing the information they collected from their embedded foreign assets.

His brows came together as he read the latest data from a senior source within the Russian Federation: an exploratory expedition had been approved to travel to the deep Earth, with the objective of examining the viability of setting up a military base.

At first he thought it was to do with undergrounding yet more of the Russian military facilities, and it would have been of interest to the US armed forces' strategists. But then as more verifying information came in, it seemed so much more.

"You gotta be kidding me." If he didn't recognize the source's name, he would have discarded it. But this source was always accurate and was implanted at the highest level of the Russian military's administrative machine. If this agent said it was happening, then it was happening.

Johnson looked at the compiled information for another few moments before blowing air through his pressed lips, bundling the data, and then sending it upstairs to management.

CHAPTER 04

Blue Ridge, Georgia, United States

Michael Monroe jogged along his usual track out in the wilderness. He stayed in his getaway holiday home in the forest permanently now: no car horns, no exhaust, no glass, concrete and steel towers, and no shouting people on every corner. Just hundreds of miles of pine forest, lakes and rivers, mountains, and air so fresh he wanted to breathe it in forever.

Ever since he had emerged from the Krubera cave over a year ago, the thought of enclosed spaces made him feel anxious and agitated. But right now, he felt he was about as far from that as he could get.

He grinned as he ran; he remembered when he first came out here Jane asked him whether he was afraid of bears or wolves out in the woods. *Never*, he had replied. Given what he and his team had all faced down below, nothing on the planet's surface would ever scare him again, *period*.

He had finally finished his manuscript, complete with illustrations of the world within a world, and the weird, wild, and wonderful things he had seen. He described the gravity wells and how he thought they worked. He also included some of his theories about what else could be down there.

The finished document had ended up being quite large and disc-space hungry, so as he created it, he stored previous versions on the cloud instead of his local drive. *Thank heavens for new-gen anywhere Internet,* he thought.

Mike usually jogged for an hour and was halfway out when, for the first time in months, he heard a helicopter pass over him. He wondered whether a neighboring county was flying in some loggers. Or if some asshole poachers had rented a helo to drop them deep into prime hunting grounds out of season.

Mark growled deep in his chest. If that's what they were and he caught them, he'd send them packing. He had a rifle and knew how to use it.

It was on the homeward leg that he smelled the exhaust of the chopper. Ever since he had retuned from the center of the Earth he had found his senses seemed to have become super honed. Maybe it was being so close to death that had brought so much more awareness of his surroundings, and what it was like to be truly alive.

He came out of the last stand of trees and saw the helicopter, now with its blades fully stopped. It was insignia free, but looked military and possibly an MH-139. Mike could see in the cockpit a helmeted pilot, with obligatory dark, aviator sunglasses.

The man turned and then nodded to him. He then thumbed toward Mike's cabin, where the door was now ajar.

"You gotta be shitting me." Mike bounded up the few wooden steps, pushed the door fully open and stood in the frame.

Inside was a single man, seated at the table. He was about the same age as Mike, but extremely fit and tough looking. He smiled and stood.

He stuck a hand out. "Raymond Harris. Call me Ray."

Mike ignored him. "What are you doing in my house?"

Harris lowered his hand but the smile remained. "Door wasn't locked, and I'm here because I obviously wanted to see you."

"Why?" Mike stayed where he was.

Harris waved him closer. "C'mon Mike, sit down and grab a coffee. I only want five minutes of your time. And I just put your pot on." He sat and looked around. "Love your place by the way; I've got something similar outside of Boulder in Colorado." He nodded. "It's good to get away from it all now and then, right?"

"I thought I *was* away from it all. Guess I was wrong." Mike took a cup from his kitchen cabinet and poured a coffee. "You in the military?"

"Me, no." Harris waited until Mike finally sat. "Not really." He sipped his coffee, and then let his smile fade away. "You've been reclusive for quite some time now. Why is that?"

Mike shrugged. "Working."

"Working? On what?" Harris put his cup down.

"Private stuff." Mike didn't like the guy's over-confidence and was getting tired of his probing. He wanted something for sure. "Ray, was it?"

"Yes, Ray, Raymond, or just Harris." He shrugged. "I answer to any of them."

"Well, *Just Harris*, you now have four minutes left. Why are you here?" Mike sat back.

Harris nodded for a moment. "Came a long way to see you." He reached into his bomber jacket pocket and drew out some folded papers. He placed them on the table in front of himself.

Mike immediately saw what they were and shot to his feet with his fists balled.

"You thieving sonofabitch. Where the hell did you get those?"

"To the Center of the Earth?" Harris' eyebrows were raised. "Pretty cool stuff in here… if any of it is true."

Mike glared as his jaw clenched.

Harris sat forward. "Take it easy, Mike. I believe it. All of it." He clasped his hands together on the tabletop. "And your suggestion of one day being able to directly tap into all that fusion energy is inspiring." His brows were up. "Near limitless power."

"Near limitless. And clean," Mike replied suspiciously, suddenly suspecting the guy might be from one of the energy companies.

"An energy opportunity certainly worth investigating. But that's not my main concern." Harris spread his fingers on the table; they were large and blunt. "You upload things into the cloud." Harris shrugged. "And some branches of government programs that can access, search for, and collect data based on our defined trigger words."

Harris looked up. "And though they were looking internationally, your document popped up, right here in the good ole US of A. And it was just what we, *they*, were looking for."

Mike cursed through gritted teeth and glared back at the guy.

"Want to know something interesting?" Harris raised his chin. "Our missile defense shields cost us about three trillion dollars, including maintenance. Star Wars, where we'll be potentially targeting everything from satellites to incoming ICBMs with lasers and highspeed penetrator missiles, when finished, will cost many more trillions."

He laughed darkly for a moment. "Now imagine the brass finding out that after all that money has been spent and before it's even finished it's all a waste of money because someone could literally attack us from where we weren't watching or ever even suspected."

Mike frowned. "I have no idea what you're talking about."

"I think you do. But don't you want to know why I believe all the wild things you wrote? And enough to fly all the way out here?"

"I wondered."

"Picture this; someone fires a nuke up one of those deep holes, *ah*, what did you call them?" Harris clicked his fingers in the air. "Oh yeah, that's right, gravity wells. So, imagine someone fires a nuke up the ass of one of them that happens to reside under New York, or LA, or anywhere on US soil. Or maybe a hostile nation emerges from out of nowhere, and with an army."

"That's ridiculous."

"Is it?" Harris sat forward. "Here's the kicker: the Russians don't think so. Following weeks of interrogating one of their own people by the name of *Ms. Katya Babikov…*" Harris paused to watch him closely.

Mike couldn't help reacting to the Russian woman's name.

"Yeah, I know you know her, and met her in Krasnodar. Even though you left her name out of your notes." Harris meshed his fingers. "Anyway, Mike, let me tell you what happened to her. After interrogating her for weeks, the Russians must have believed what she told them because they decided to mount an expedition to the center of the Earth. It's a military mission with a small scientific appendage."

Harris continued to stare back at him. "This is not great news for us, and anyone else in the world. And I'll tell you something else, Mike; once they establish a beachhead down there, they're staying for good."

"I can't help you."

"You can't or won't?" Harris sat back in his chair, his mouth turned down for a moment. "Let me tell you a secret." He looked hard into Mike's eyes. "We already sent an expedition down there months ago to try and beat the Russians to the punch. Our team entered via the Romanian cave system."

He smiled as he slouched in his chair. "Never heard from them again. Even the people we had stationed as lookouts above the gravity well." His eyes flicked up at Mike. "Maybe they ran into those hairless dog people you described in your report."

"Hairless dog people," Mike spoke the words softly. He stared at the tabletop, taking in what he had just been told. Mike had received information back from the zoological hematologist months back and was told that someone was playing tricks on him. The sample he provided was mostly inconclusive, but the closest approximation they could get to a match was hominid DNA: a close relative, with a possibility of it even being human. Or once was.

He remembered what Jane had said to him in the deep caves and looked back into Harris' face as he whispered, *"Those who descend into the dark find monsters. Or become them."*

"Say what?"

"Forget it." Mike waved it away. "I would suggest you stay out of there, and I expect that the Russians will undoubtedly suffer the same fate as your first team."

"Can't just leave it to chance, Mike. National security doesn't work that way." Harris rose to his feet. "Let me cut to the chase. We're going back down and this time we need an experienced caver who's been there on that next expedition. Just as a consultant."

"Not happening."

"All we want to do is perform a little reconnaissance. Make sure our Russian buddies aren't going to do anything that threatens our geography, our people, or our energy future." He held his hands up. "Just a looksee is all."

Mike slowly shook his head. "Sorry you wasted your time."

Harris shrugged. "No, no, this wasn't a waste of time at all. You confirmed your report, and also validated my concerns. We're going, with or without you."

Mike remained pokerfaced and just watched the man.

"You never told me where you're from?" Mike said.

"No, I didn't." Harris smiled. "Well, my door is always open." He slid a card across the table. "Here's my number if you change your mind. But you'd better hurry."

He reached out to shake Mike's hand, and Mike accepted it this time. Harris then turned and headed out the door.

Mike followed. Once on the landing Harris circled his finger in the air, and the pilot started the chopper's blade rotation rate in preparation for immediate departure.

"That's it?"

"Sure, we're not the KGB bully boys," Harris said. "Besides, plenty more fish in the sea." He winked and then crouch-ran to the chopper and jumped in. He gave Mike a two-fingered salute and then they vanished over the treetops.

Mike stared in the direction they departed for many minutes until the sound of the craft vanished for good.

Fool, he thought and went to turn away, but then paused. He spun back. *Plenty more fish in the sea,* he'd said. *What did that mean?*

Mike went back inside and sat at his table for an hour, just thinking, with a leaden feeling growing in his gut.

*****

Ex-Special Forces Captain Ray Harris had the pilot connect him through to Jane Baxter's private number. It was answered almost immediately as if she was expecting the call.

"Hello again, Jane." His expression was deadpan. "I can confirm that Mike will lead the mission. He hopes you will join him."

He smiled as he heard her string together enough curse words to make a truck driver blush. He listened patiently to her blowing off more steam.

"Yes, yes, I know. But I also know he needs you." He waited a moment more as her anger abated a tad, and then went for the dunk. "He said he misses you."

He heard her exhale and whisper one more curse. But there was less venom in it this time. He listened some more and the corner of his mouth curved up.

"Good, he'll be delighted." Harris disconnected.

He then reached into his breast pocket for his phone as it buzzed, signaling an incoming text.

Right on time, he thought.

As expected, it was Mike Monroe. He read it: *stay away from Jane.*

He hummed as he tapped out a reply: *she's already agreed to lead us in.*

Harris mentally counted down: *5-4-3...*

And his phone rang.

"You sonofabitch. I knew that was what your '*other fish in the sea*' line was about," Mike fumed.

"She'll be with professionals, and safe. Your report gives us a good idea of what to expect. Plus she's experienced," Harris replied evenly. "Don't worry about us Mike, we'll be fine."

"You don't know what you're getting into. That place has a hundred ways to kill you. And that's before you even make it to the center. You have no damn idea," Mike said.

"But you do," Harris replied. "If you really want to ensure Jane has the best chance of surviving, then jointly lead our team in."

"You sonofabitch. What you need is the shit beaten out of you." Mike's voice was so loud Harris had to hold the phone away from his ear.

"Hey, get in line, buddy." Harris chuckled softly. "So, Mike, in or out?"

There was nothing for a few moments, and then:

"In."

Harris exhaled and nodded. "Good man. Tomorrow morning, 8am sharp, be ready, and-"

The line went dead as Mike disconnected, but Harris knew the man would be there for them. He seemed an honorable guy, and he hated that he had to manipulate the situation by using Jane Baxter. But this was critically important, so rules didn't matter much anymore. Harris replaced the phone in his pocket.

He checked his wristwatch; they had a lot to obtain and organize, but they'd be ready.

When he first read the document that Mike Monroe had produced, it read like a science-fiction story, and a small part of him wondered whether the guy was trying to engineer some sort of book deal. But then after they obtained the Russian, he now knew Monroe was telling the truth. And the look on his face and the real fear in the guy's voice told Harris he was really scared about going back down.

Therefore, if there was a chance that even only ten percent of what he described was real, then Harris felt he was right to take the precautions that he did.

Now, he was confident he'd be ready for anything.

CHAPTER 05

On route to the Bihole Mountains, Romania – the V5 Cave system

The helicopter lightly touched down but didn't even slow its blades as Mike was picked up out front of his house to be flown directly to the airport. From there he then had a direct flight to Romania, and after clearing customs, he had been trucked out to Fata Muncelului in the mountains, a paradise of green that was little more than a hamlet far out in the Romanian countryside.

His travel companions he had picked up en-route in Romania had spoken little, perhaps because they knew little, or just didn't want to share. The most they had done was introduce themselves. Ally Bennet was the color of burnt honey with straight black hair and large brown eyes that crinkled at the corners. Her travel buddy was Russell Hitch, solid and bear-like. Both experienced cavers, climbers, and he guessed by the look of their muscles, lumped knuckles, and obvious scars, either active-duty soldiers from some division of the armed forces, or maybe even mercenaries.

He wondered about that for a moment. If you were going to send a team down to confront a group of Russians, maybe even Russian military, and something went wrong, then you might want plausible deniability. A way to do that might be to use ex or off-the-books operatives.

Mike let his eyes slide to the two people again. *At least they didn't look like pushovers for what was coming*, he thought.

The truck let them out for the final leg on an empty hillside with just a small track to follow and all on foot to the small cave entrance that he, Jane, Andy and Maggie had crawled out from over a year ago.

Mike walked with Hitch and Ally and though he'd been traveling for around thirty hours and knew he should have felt beat, his heart rate was kicking up along with his trepidation the closer he got to the cave entrance.

As they came through the latest stand of pine trees on the emerald green hillside, the scene ripped open his vault of memories and he was wracked with a sudden bout of nausea. He turned to the side to vomit his last coffee onto the grass.

"Better out than in, *huh*, Mikey?" Ally slapped his back as she went past. Neither Ally nor Hitch were bothered in the slightest by him being sick and just kept on going.

Mike straightened, wiped his mouth and turned slowly. It was just as he remembered. The grass was cushion-soft with the occasional clumps of small bells of white flowers, and the air was clean and clear with a hint of wildflower and the humid scent of dew drying on grass.

"C'mon, Mikey boy," Ally shouted back at him as she and Hitch were about to enter the tree line.

It was only after another fifteen more minutes of hiking that he smelled the smoke and then coming out of the trees he saw a much larger group gathered around a good-sized tent with a fire blazing out front. He spotted Jane immediately and it made him feel good inside to see a friendly face, especially *her* face.

He waved as she turned to face him. She didn't return the wave, and he felt his heart sink a little.

What now? he wondered.

At least Ray Harris waved. "At last." He grinned. "We were about to leave without you."

Mike nodded to him but headed straight for Jane. He smiled warmly. "Hi."

She slapped his face, hard enough to swing his head. "Hey!" He rubbed his stinging cheek.

"You sonofabitch."

Mike heard Harris laugh, and he knew the entire crew was now watching them.

This wasn't the greeting he envisaged. "Jane, I came because..."

"Shut it, Mike. Just, shut it." She folded her arms.

He was only here because of her and she acted like he was intruding or something. "You could have told me, you know."

"Told *you*, what? And where, and who... told the hermit who lives out in the woods by himself?" She looked up at him from under lowered brows. "You sent us a copy of your half-finished manuscript, and then just dropped off the radar. It's been over six months."

He knew he had shut himself off, and thinking about it, and seeing her now, made him question why. "I was wrestling with... personal stuff."

"We were all wrestling with personal *stuff*. We were all there, remember?" She made a disgusted noise in her throat and faced away from him.

He lifted his chin. "I know, and I asked you to come with me."

"I remember, and you only asked me once. And you didn't sound all that convincing that you really wanted my company." She turned back and threw her hands up. "And then you were gone."

Mike exhaled and then looked around. "You make it sound like I really want to be here. I don't."

"Bullshit, I *know* you do. You've secretly wanted to return since we climbed out." She eyed him suspiciously.

"I came here to help, that's all. Nothing secret about it." He held his hands up. "We only have to get them to the gravity well. Then we can decide what we're going to do." He continued to watch her. "So why did *you* change your mind? You said you never wanted to go caving again. And you're about to take these guys into one of the deepest caves in the world."

"Lots of reasons." She stared off into the distance for a few moments, and then glanced back. "All of them dumb. One them the dumbest of all."

"So you believe Harris? I mean about the Russians going down there," Mike asked.

"Yeah, I do," Jane replied.

"That's why you came? Duty?" He tilted his head.

Jane seemed to think for a moment. "There's something else…" She gave him a broken smile and lowered her voice. "I keep having this dream, a nightmare, about Harry." She stared up at him. "That he was still alive down there."

Mike sighed. "I think that's unlikely."

"I know, probably, but…" She turned to look into the fire.

He looked at her profile for a moment more. She was still as attractive as ever, but now looked a little haunted around the eyes—lack of sleep from those nightmares, he bet.

He decided to change the subject. "Anyway, how've you been? Still doing biology classes?" He smiled down at her.

"Not now; got a job at the university doing research. After what we experienced, I felt I needed to know more about life, lifeforms, and evolution. But a holiday would be nice," Jane replied.

He moved closer. "Can I recommend somewhere with long black, sandy beaches, tropical jungles, and all under a warm, red sky?" Mike grinned.

"Not funny, Mike. And in answer to your earlier question, no, I don't want to be here, and if it wasn't for you, I wouldn't be within a thousand miles of this damn place."

"What?" His brows shot up. "Then why did…?"

She strode away.

Shit, he thought. He really wanted to convince her he didn't want to be here either. But a strange thing started happening on the way over to the Romanian cave. In amongst his trepidation and nervous palpitations, there was excitement and anticipation building.

It was true that he always dreamed about returning and what he'd need to do the job properly next time. And now all the resources seemed to have all been handed to him on a plate. He suddenly realised he was secretly delighted.

Mike looked around the camp and saw that in amongst the groups of milling people were several cases stacked up. Harris noticed him looking them over. He waved again and sauntered closer, his face riven with mock concern.

"Trouble in paradise?" Harris asked.

"It's nothing."

"Don't worry about it. She'll get over it as soon as you apologize." Harris grinned.

"For what? I didn't do anything wrong," Mike insisted.

"I didn't say you did anything wrong; I said you need to apologize." Harris chuckled. "*Sheesh*, never been married, *huh*?"

Mike got it. "Very funny." He nodded toward the crates. "What did you bring?"

"Well, your manuscript was very informative, Mr. Monroe. Though my superiors are treating a lot of the imagery as science-fiction and perhaps brought upon you all by your extended time trapped below the ground, we thought the underlying substance meant it wise to have adequate protection."

"So, I dreamed most of it, *huh*?"

"I didn't say *I* thought that." He led Mike to the wooden crates and flipped open the lid. There were rifles all stacked in rows. Harris pulled one out. The dark metal gleamed and what was amazing was the weapon was flat. Harris telescoped it out.

"Cool." Ally Bennet wandered closer. "Steyr AUG?"

"Close." Harris grinned. "Steyr AUG P *variant*; top of the line Austrian manufacture. Nice and light, flat packing, polymer grip, laser sights and magazine can take a variety of rounds. Should do the job in tight spaces."

Harris handed it to her, and Ally immediately pulled it into her shoulder, focusing on objects as she looked through the scope. She turned it sideways for a moment and then looked back to Harris.

"There's no rail for a launcher."

"That's right, only because they're too bulky, same as their rounds. We've got to travel light and skinny. These babies will do it while retaining lethality." Harris grinned. "But don't worry, we brought a few extra surprises as well."

He opened more crates and lifted out what looked like small fishing tackle boxes. Mike saw there were bullets inside, but some color-coded.

"We've got standard rounds, but red tips are incendiary, and black tips are explosive. All are armor-piercing." He turned and winked at Mike. "For some of those big-shelled bastards you mentioned."

Jane had been standing back with her hands on her hips. "Much as we wanted some of those horrors dead, we've got to remember it's their world and we were the intruders." She came closer. "Or are these for starting a war with Russia?"

Harris gave her a nod that was almost a small bow. "We won't be doing either, Jane. All I want to ensure is we all come home in one piece. Frankly, I hope we never fire a shot. But if our backs are to the wall, they won't be for long." Harris straightened and turned to Ally. "Plus we have some miniaturized frag grenades; just for luck."

"Cool." Ally nodded her approval.

Jane groaned. "So you're onboard with all this firepower, Mike?"

Mike nodded. "Yeah, I guess. Better to have it and not need it, than need it and not have it."

"Bingo, sir." Harris pointed at his chest.

Harris turned slowly. "We have a range of knives, plus handguns for you." He saw Jane about to protest and held his hand up. "Jane, if it never comes out of its holster, that's fine with me."

Her mouth drew into a line for a moment, but she finally nodded.

Mike watched her and knew she was only acting prickly because she was pissed off. She knew they needed to be protected and what against.

"Good." Harris turned to the group and clapped his hands a couple of times to get their attention. "Listen up people. Tomorrow morning, six hundred hours sharp, we are entering the V5 cave system, and then making our way to the G-well that our friendly caving consultants here will be directing us to. Tonight, I want you all to familiarize yourself with your equipment, weaponry, and caving suits. All of them will be your best friends and your safety nets for however long we are below ground."

Harris folded his arms, the muscles straining his shirt as he looked along their faces. "You've all read Mr. Monroe's report. We work on the assumption that we will encounter various forms of large, aggressive indigenous lifeform. We will try and avoid them as our first option, but we are here to do a job, and nothing must be allowed to get in the way of that. Understood?"

"*HUA*," they replied as one.

Mike knew then that his suspicions were correct and their traveling companions were no mere cavers.

"You said you were here to do a job. Remind me again what that actually is?" Jane asked.

Harris' gaze was unwavering. "Defend the United States of America, its allies, interests, and you and your families." His expression softened. "And don't worry, we're not going there for a war. We just want to see what our Russian friends are up to and stay alive while we're doing it."

Jane looked briefly back at all the firepower and then back to him. "I wish you luck."

Harris nodded and turned away. Jane moved closer to Mike and raised her eyebrows. "I don't know whether I feel safer or more scared."

"Safer," Mike replied confidently. "The last time we were extremely unprepared, so this means we can defend ourselves quickly.... if we even decide to go all the way," he added.

The pair wandered over to the kitout area. There were caving suits, all manner of climbing equipment and Mike was delighted to see it was all top quality.

"Spared no expense," Mike said.

"Top of the line, and that's government for you." Jane then reached into a box and pulled out a weird-looking headset with four lenses on the front.

"What the hell is this thing?"

"Quad vision, and the best in the business," Ally Bennet replied without looking up from her tasks.

"There are only two sets," Mike observed.

Ally looked up at him. "That's right, Mikey. And at sixty-five grand a piece, we're lucky to get one, let alone two."

"That's more than my car's worth." Mike turned it around to examine the piece of equipment. "One problem: night vision relies on light amplification; down in the caves, there is no light to amplify."

"You would be right if that set was a standard FLIR Forward Looking Infrared unit." Ally rested on her haunches. "Those guys rely on image intensification, which gathers incoming low-level light, converts the photons into an electrical signal, amplifies the signal, and then displays the boosted light-level image on a green phosphor screen."

Jane nodded "I'm familiar with light amplifiers. I've used them before." She smiled. "The green on green is the best color because the human eye is adept at differentiating between shades of green compared to other colors, right?"

"Very good." Ally pointed at the quad set in Mike's hands. "But those bad boys don't need to boost anything, because the internal software generates a false-color display of the observed infrared radiation, or IR, from whatever you're looking at. When combined, the two technologies prove a potent pair. The night vision allows for long-range spotting under normal conditions while the IR augments that capability when ambient light levels are either non-existent or the target is obscured by fog, dust, or whatever."

"We've only got two eyes so what's with the four lenses?" Jane asked. "What do they do?"

"One-eighty degree vision side of the eye is captured." She grinned. "Almost impossible to sneak up on someone in the dark if they're wearing a pair of those."

Mike hefted it. "It's light."

She took it from him. "Lightweight, robust, and best of all, they're mine." She grinned. "Don't worry kids, I've got your backs down there."

Mike looked at Jane. "Not bad, I guess."

From behind, Harris spoke up as he stood beside the fire. "Ladies and gentlemen, everyone please take your radiation meds before sleep, and see you bright-eyed and bushy-tailed at six hundred hours." He turned away to converse with one of the other soldiers.

Another woman approached with a couple of small cups and bottles of water. Mike immediately saw there was a softness about her rather than the abrasive toughness of the soldiers.

She smiled and handed them a cup each. "Hi, you guys are obviously Mike Monroe and Jane Baxter, right?"

Jane nodded. "Yes, and you?"

"Penny Gifford, doctor, surgeon, and part-time caver." She pointed over her shoulder to another youthful-looking, patchy-bearded man talking to Harris. "That's my buddy, Alistair Peterson. He's a scientist, specializing in biology, entomology, and also dabbles in primitive languages." She turned back. "So you can expect he has a thousand questions for you two."

"Not sure we'll have a thousand answers," Jane said and frowned down at the small paper cups they'd been given that were half full of tablets. "I'm assuming they're not all vitamins."

Penny smiled and slowly shook her head. "Potassium iodide, called ThyroShield, a non-radioactive form of iodine. Plus Radiogardase, which will bind cesium and thallium in your system and allow you to excrete it. And finally, Diethylenetriamine penta-acetic acid, a substance that collects heavy metals." She smiled. "Closest thing to internal radiation armor plating we got. At least for up to a year."

Jane looked at the tablets for a moment and turned to Mike. "Only need them if we go all the way."

"That's right." Mike reached out for the little cup and bottle. He looked at the mix of blue, white and red pills for a moment more, then tossed them back and quickly gulped water.

He half smiled and shrugged. "They take a while to infuse throughout the system so, just in case."

"*Argh.*" Jane grabbed hers and did the same.

Mike looked at the small woman. "You said you've caved before?"

"Yes, a little. But I've done plenty of cliff climbs. That's why I was called up," Penny replied.

"Called up?" Jane asked.

"I'm National Guard. So is Alistair. National security duty calls, so here we are." She smiled.

Mike tilted his head toward Ray Harris and his group. "They don't look like National Guard to me."

Penny turned momentarily. "They're not. Some branch of Special Forces I think. Or maybe once were." She turned back.

Mike looked at Jane and shrugged. "Doesn't matter, I guess."

"I've read the report you produced." Penny lowered her voice. "I just want to say I'm glad you both decided to come. We'll certainly need your experience and help if even half of what was in there is real."

Mike and Jane shared a glance, and then Jane scoffed. "Penny, let me give you some free advice straight up. If you want to survive, then work on the basis it's *all* real."

"Okay." Penny took the empty cups from them. "I'll let you two get some rest. But look out for Alistair, Jane, as I know he's going to bug you about that arthropod evolution theory of yours." She bid them farewell and went back to what looked like a simple bedroll near the fire.

Mike and Jane were offered the luxury of sleeping in the large tent, but they declined. For the next few days, they'd be sleeping on cave floors, so might as well start the acclimatization process now.

Mike sat beside Jane and saw her looking up into the night sky.

"The stars?"

She nodded. "Just want to remember what they look like." She turned. "And promise them I'm coming back."

He smiled and reached out to lay a hand on her forearm, but she moved it away. He dropped his hand.

"We're only consultants this time."

She snorted softly. "Then why do I get the feeling when it comes time for us to leave, they won't let us."

"I won't let that happen," Mike said, and meant it.

She turned to him. "And I promised myself I'd never go back down.

And yet, look where I am." She lay down but kept her eyes open. "Good night."

CHAPTER 06

The Romanian V5 cave was also called the 'pothole' for good reason. The opening at the surface was easy to miss and barely more than a small rip in the ground. It was narrow and dropped straight down for several hundred feet so for countless millennia it had a tomb for unobservant animals.

Jane stood at the top all rigged up and started down into the impenetrable darkness. *Here we go again*, she thought.

She turned to look over her shoulder at the team. "Ready?"

She stared back down; though the cave was open to the spelunking public in the dry season, the notifications stated that it could be dangerous. Jane knew that was an understatement as there had been numerous fatalities and also several cavers simply vanishing within its dark and twisting labyrinths.

"Let's go."

She dropped down with Mike right behind. And as they reached the first major hall at eight hundred feet down, she exhaled and inwardly shuddered. The smell of rock dust, ancient mustiness, and just a hint of the sharp tang of some mineral pools somewhere brought back the memories of when they walked these last few passages in near-total darkness as they fought their way back to the surface over a year ago.

As the team caught up with them, Jane saw that one of the largest of the group, a man appropriately named Bull Simmons, began to plant small devices about, and his pack looked full of them.

She later learned that they performed two functions: the first was a radio relay that took a signal burst, boosted it, and fired it on to the next relay device. Theoretically, they could send a signal right around the globe, so it was hoped they could fire one back and receive response all the way to the Earth's center.

The other function was they acted as Light Emitting Diodes, LEDs, which converted minuscule amounts of electricity into light, and with full batteries could work continually for months.

It was obvious that Harris had taken onboard their comments about their fluorescing crystals not making it to the surface and wanted to ensure that there was other illumination seeded about, waiting for them on their return to the surface.

The lights were off for now, and when asked, Bull had mumbled that they were sensor operated, so their life was extended for years.

The other failsafe Harris had applied was they all carried flashlights, with plenty of extra batteries. Simple, but great idea, and Jane would have opted for batteries over bullets any day.

Jane was still only thirty-three years old, had been caving since she was a teen, and had never been afraid of the dark. That was until that last terrifying climb out. Now shadows within shadows made her jumpy as hell.

They hadn't yet made it to the hidden part of the caves where the sightless had pursued them and that would take them many more hours yet. Jane reached down to feel the small gun sitting snug on her hip. She hated firearms, but she hated those pale, skinless-looking creatures even more.

Mike took his turn at the lead and she walked at his back, still angry with the big oaf for shutting her and everyone out, and just as angry at herself for still caring enough about him to undertake this insane cave drop.

Enough time had passed where she had finally managed to blank out most of the horrors, but now as she smelled the odors of a deep cave, saw the paths they had traversed, and felt the oppressive weight of the countless tons of stone above her, her stomach fluttered as the memories came flooding back like a recurring illness.

Once they passed through the known caves it would then take a further two days before they arrived at the hidden, small, horizontal wriggle hole. It was this that led to the colossal rift that dropped down toward the passages that took them to the Romanian gravity well. She just wished it would take them longer as she needed more time to think, and to decide.

Her mind worked overtime: would Mike want to continue? Jane wondered. She bet he would. And then what? Would she go with him? She felt the knot of indecision twist in her stomach a little tighter.

Mike had said that he'd go with them until they got to the gravity well. They should be safe, *after all they've got guns, and these guys are pros*, she reminded herself. Also, Mike wasn't leading the team, Harris was. She was going to try and ensure that she and Mike stayed at the center of the group. The military guys had read Mike's report and they had the weapons, so let them do the heavy lifting.

Jane saw their caving expedition in three sections: the first was the known caves that had been mapped before. They had all the usual risks associated with a deep cave. But these were manageable for anyone with caving experience.

Then, secondly, there were the new caves, the unexplored rift zone that they had broken into, that were unmapped and were a vertical drop for thousands of feet. Following these meant continuing on to places where she knew the creatures in the dark lived. She shuddered just at the thought of their greasy, skinless look.

Then finally came the gravity well to the inner world. At this time, she felt she wouldn't be heading back to that boiling red, hellish place, no matter what they offered or threatened her with.

Like Virgil she had climbed out from the ninth circle of Hell, and she had no plans to return.

Jane sucked in a deep breath of cool, dry cave air. She still had time to make a decision so she shoved it aside for now.

*****

Miles below them, all the way down the rift wall and across into the nesting cave, the creatures stirred. One of them lifted its head, sightless eyes and its mouth and nasal slits wet as it inhaled the air, tasting it. Vestigial ears that ran all the way up the side of its head and were little more than exposed tympanic membranes, turned toward the cave entrance.

It felt the stone, sensing for the most minuscule of vibrations. Hunting in the stygian dark caves meant using senses a surface creature could never understand. And competition for food was fierce, even amongst its own kind. It would have crept out of the cave by itself, but its kin were already stirring.

Outside, it reached out a long taloned hand and grasped the rock wall. It turned its face upward and bulging totally white eyes stared. It was not vision it relied on, but a tiny section in its brain that collected all the information of its senses together and created an image of what the caves were telling it.

Beside it, more of the pack joined in. Together they started upward.

CHAPTER 07

Forty hours later the group arrived at an unmapped staging area that was an offshoot on the V5 cave system. This particular system was not the deepest cave by any means but its labyrinthine side caves ran for dozens of miles, and many were still unexplored.

Jane knew that to their west the cave continued on down to its traditional known basement, just another five hundred feet below them. But what they sought was a secondary passage. One Jane, Mike and their team had discovered by accident over a year ago, and one that allowed them access out onto the face of the towering rift wall.

Harris tilted his helmet back and wiped his brow. "We're now at five thousand, two hundred and twenty feet." He looked one last time around the broad cave and then turned to Jane and Mike. "I think this is where experience needs to take the lead. Ladies and gentlemen, over to you." He waited.

Mike lifted his light and panned it around. The cave was bone dry and filled with dust that was like silky powder coating every surface.

Jane turned slowly and then found what she sought. "Here, this way."

She turned side-on and slid into an almost invisible crack in the rock wall. The team followed with some of the larger members having trouble sliding through and to exhale and push their packs ahead of them as they wriggled after her.

When they emerged, Jane was waiting for them. She pointed. "There."

Under a lip of stone was a small hole near floor level that was no more than eighteen inches wide and high.

"Got it," Mike said and crossed to the hole, getting down low, holding his light before him and sweeping it back and forth. He stopped dead.

"Hold it."

Jane pushed in beside him, and the rest closed in but stayed a few feet behind the pair.

"What is it?" Jane asked.

He kept his light on the cave floor. "Remember when we emerged?

It was me that came last from the hole." He pulled back a little and shone his light over the cave floor in front of them.

"Yes, that's right, we waited on you." She watched his face.

"Then the cave floor here should have been undisturbed since we crawled out and the only thing showing was our boot marks, or what was left of them." Mike exhaled through his nose. "But look now."

Jane turned her beam of light to the cave floor. "Oh."

Over the year-old boot marks and all around them was what looked like stretched naked prints.

"It followed us up," Jane said softly.

"We didn't seal the cave. So of course it followed us," Mike replied. He moved his light around. "I also think there was more than one of them."

Harris crouched beside Mike. "Your cave dogs?"

Mike stood. "They're not dogs." He turned to face the soldier. "I think they're what happens when hominids get trapped in caves for tens of thousands of years and need to adapt."

"Hominids, *huh*? You don't know that," Harris said. "And you don't know if the creatures, the humanoids you referred to, that once lived down below were even human beings. That DNA evidence of yours was inconclusive, remember?" He turned away. "As far as I'm concerned, they're animals."

Harris turned to wave over the female soldier. "Ally, get in there and check it out."

"You got it, boss." With zero hesitation, the woman immediately got down on her belly, shone her light into the small hole, and then in the next second wriggled in.

Harris rested on his haunches and faced Mike. "Bottom line, whatever those things are, if they don't bother us, I won't bother them. Maybe." He smiled flatly and then turned to his team. "Everyone stay alert, and get skinny. It's gonna be a squeeze."

Jane looked up at Mike. "I think we've gone far enough. They can find their way to the well."

Mike winced. "Not easy. Even though I created a map, it's still a tough and winding descent. A single wrong turn and they'd be lost."

"Mike, please, I don't feel good about this," Jane whispered.

"I understand your fear, Jane." Harris, overhearing, nodded sagely. "You underwent a terrifying experience and now you've bravely come back down. But look at my team..." He waved an arm out to the men and woman behind him.

Jane and Mike looked along their faces, all sweat-streaked with dust and cave grime. They were all chisel-chinned and steely-eyed, only

Alistair and Penny looked like kids amongst them and the female doctor gave Jane a small wave.

Harris continued. "Think about it: are they going to be safer if you came with us or not?"

Jane rolled her eyes. "Cut the emotional blackmail, will you?"

"No, I won't apologize, but you know we have a better chance for a successful mission with you guys with us. That's way I wanted you here." Harris hiked his shoulders. "C'mon, get us to the gravity well. Like you said you would." He reached out a hand to gently lay his fingers on her elbow.

Mike noticed she didn't shrug Harris off like she did to him.

Jane looked away, but Mike slowly nodded. He looked down at Jane. "Just to the well, okay?"

Jane tilted her head back on her neck and shut her eyes. She then exhaled loudly and seemed to think about it for a moment more. "Just to the well, if…" she pointed at Harris, "you give us one of your men to accompany us back up. If those creatures are roaming around in the upper caves, I don't want to have to sleep with one eye open."

Harris rubbed her arm and nodded. "Fair request; at this point I can't see a problem with that."

Ally came sliding back out of the hole and got to her feet. She dusted herself down. "No sign of life and all clear, but there's an almighty cliff wall up and down and well beyond the range of the scanners."

"The rift wall," Mike added.

"Down is where we want to go," Harris replied. He turned to the group. "Think thin, people, we're going in."

*****

Harris watched as the group squeezed into the hole one after the other. He knew he needed one or both of Mike and Jane. He also knew that if one of them agreed to guide them all the way to the center, then the other would follow.

Harris smiled confidently. *Now who's the weakest link?* he wondered.

CHAPTER 08

Mike stood on the ledge, the toe of one boot right on the lip and first looked upward, holding the beam of his light straight up and slowly moving it over the sheer rock face. Then he angled it down.

Jane came and stood beside him, also one foot on the edge and sucked in a deep breath. "And here we are again."

"Yep." He smiled. "Guess that's something else we have in common: we're both mad."

Harris came up beside Jane, snapped a glow stick and dropped it. Mike leaned forward to watch the glowing ball of light as it traveled down into the black void.

It continued on for many seconds before the dot vanished into oblivion. As it traveled, Mike watched like a hawk, not the light but the cave wall. He was looking for any trace of the pale, skinless-looking figures clinging there. Thankfully he saw none.

"How long to the next pitch?" Harris asked.

"Took us three-quarters of a day to scale up," Jane said. "But that was free climbing."

Harris turned to her and whistled softly. "That's some badass stuff."

Jane smiled crookedly. "You'd be surprised what you can do when your feet are to the fire."

"Ain't it the truth?" He stared back down. "But going down is faster, and by rope, three to four times as fast. So, I'm thinking about an hour, one and a half, tops. Sound about right?"

Mike nodded. "I think so. Then if we can find the right passage, maybe another six hours to the gravity well."

"Good." Harris turned.

The rock shelf they were on got crowded once their group came out onto it, and Harris looked them over for a moment.

"Okay everyone, grab a coffee and take five. Then we go over the edge." He looked back to Mike and Jane. "You too; we're getting to the sharp end now."

Mike and Jane sunk down with their backs to the wall and sipped from their canteens. Penny stepped over people and brought the young entomologist with her.

"Knock knock." She even pretended to knock on a wall as an introduction.

Mike grinned up at her. "Who's there?"

Penny dragged the young guy forward. "Penny and Alistair."

"The annoying bug guy you mentioned?" Mike grinned.

"Guilty."

He looked to be in his mid-to-late twenties and probably right out of university, and even through his sweat-slicked and greasy complexion he looked to be blushing.

He put a hand on his chest. "I'm Alistair Peterson, Dr Alistair Peterson." He remained standing, eyes wide. "I was wondering...?"

"Yes of course, sit down and ask away." Jane chuckled. "And you too, Penny."

Alistair sat close, legs crossed. "I read your report, Mr. Monroe; three times." Alistair's eyebrows went up. "Terrifying, but also very exciting. For a bug guy, I mean."

"I'll go with terrifying," Mike replied. "And call me Mike."

"Thank you, and *Alistair*." He nodded. "But as an entomologist, the description of the realization of Ms Baxter's evolutionary suggestion is the most amazing thing I've ever heard. We've always wondered what a world would have been like if the arthropods won the race to colonize the land."

"Race?" Penny asked. "What race?"

Alistair beamed. "Probably the first and most important race on the planet. Especially as far as human beings are concerned." He turned to her. "Back when life was young on our primeval world, say around 400 million years ago, amphibians were the first to leave the water. In effect, they were in a race because the arthropods were also evolving to the land, and getting real big. At that time, the amphibians only won because they were quicker at developing efficient lungs and also creating egg cases that didn't need to be laid in water. But it was so close, only a few million years in it."

"So the shrimp lost?" Penny said.

"Shrimp, yeah." Alistair chuckled. "It was a time when evolution was in overdrive and our primitive planet had things creeping around like the giant sea scorpion nine feet long. Also, *Arthropleura*, a centipede nearly ten feet long, plus carnivorous dragonflies the size of crows. The amphibians won, *just*, and thank god they did because they eventually became us."

"It must have been a-*mazing*." Penny grinned, open-mouthed.

"I can't wait to see it." Alistair closed his eyes for a moment as though conjuring the images into his mind.

"Did you not read the report?" Mike asked. "It was a damn nightmare. And if there were only ten-foot long centipedes then most of our team would not have got killed, and quite horribly."

Alistair nodded vigorously. "I know, I know, I didn't mean it was going to be a paradise, just that from a scientific perspective it would be an extraordinary experience."

"Don't be in such a hurry to get there," Jane added. "It might be the last thing you ever see."

Alistair sighed. "I think the first Europeans to enter the Congo or the Amazon would have found a place that was deadly as well. But you can't hide from reality."

"Why are you here, Alistair?" Jane asked. "I mean I understand the requirement for having your skillset, but why did they bring you given we're supposed to be looking out for Russians?"

The young scientist held up a finger. "Because of something I do." He sat forward. "Let me explain. All arthropods have a basic design: exoskeleton, bulb or compound eye, segmentation, and simple brain and stem. Even though they come in thousands of different shapes, sizes, and forms, they all have the same characteristics, and therefore have primarily the same strengths and weaknesses."

"Makes sense," Mike agreed.

Alistair smiled. "I'm a bug expert. But I also work with primitive languages." He shrugged. "Something I studied prior to specializing in entomology."

"Okay." Mike half-smiled. "And, how does that fit?"

Alistair's grin widened. "Well, over the past decade there have been significant advancements in communicating with insect species. And I..."

"Say what?" Jane's laugh was like a bark. "You're going to try and talk to them? You're insane. There are some arthropods down there that have intelligence, and they don't see us as their intellectual peers, but instead as walking food parcels."

"I didn't say *talk* as in actually use a spoken language, although that is the end goal. But rather communicate via scent, sound, mimicry, and visual cues." Alistair shrugged at their expressions. "If you click your fingers just the right way, you can fool a male cicada into thinking you are a female cicada ready to mate. If you have a small flashlight and blink it on and off, you can pretend to be fireflies of either gender without much trouble. And if you have a test tube full of different ant pheromones you could theoretically make a group of ants do whatever you want."

Alistair sat forward, his eyes shining. "You see, our brains, human brains, are uniquely wired for what I call, *symbolic communication*, and the majority of our language skills are acquired through learning. However, insects communicate through a form of language that is totally inherent. It's like an inbuilt code they're born with and all we need to do is find a way to decipher it."

"Wow." Jane glanced at Mike.

"How the hell does someone end up in that field?" Mike asked.

Alistair shrugged. "Language, communication in all forms, has always interested me. I started out as a linguist, but then my love of bugs meant working with the human tongue stopped interesting me." He grinned. "And then *hey presto*! Here I am."

Penny looked a little sceptical. "Well, from a medical perspective, I can tell you that the human tongue and voice box is not really geared up for making the range of sounds an insect can."

"My professor always said to 'think outside the box.'" Alistair hiked skinny shoulders. "But what if there is no box? What if the insects had true intelligence? Like Mike just said. Then they may want to communicate as well. What I've found with first meetings with primitive cultures is that if both parties want to communicate, it'll happen."

Mike clicked his tongue in his cheek. "Yeah, good luck with that buddy."

****

Mike lowered his canteen and took a moment to look along the team that Harris had brought with him. He had met Penny and Alistair, and also two of the soldiers on the ride in. There was Russ Hitch, who was large, taciturn, and with a goodsized biker's beard going on. Also Ally Bennet, the black female who caught him looking at her and returned a half-smile and wink.

Then there was Ray Harris, who seemed more like some sort of cross between a CIA operative and a Special Forces squad leader, and was the oldest by a good ten years. However, he had proven to be one of the most athletic and experienced of all of them. There was also something about him that hinted at danger, and he definitely didn't like the way he looked at Jane. Or for that matter, she back at him.

Pete Andreas was the youngest and Mike wasn't sure he had ever heard him say a word. But the other guy, Brice 'Bull' Vincent, was planting another LED and signal booster on the cave wall, and he was loud, jovial, had large hands, lantern jaw, and prominent tomahawk-like nose, and would have been right at home on the deck of a fishing trawler, hauling up hundred-pound tuna one after the other.

They seemed a good bunch, and the upside was they could all climb, even Alistair and Penny. On balance, he was pretty happy with the team Harris had brought with him.

His only nagging worry was he wondered how many of them really believed what they read in his manuscript, or if they had even read it all the way through.

Time will tell, he knew. He also knew that those that were prepared might just make it back home.

If he didn't descend all the way again, Mike initially wondered whether he and Jane would wait for them at the entrance to the gravity well. But given the team could be gone for weeks, months, or forever, that'd be a stupid idea. Besides, he knew there was no way that Jane would descend all the way again or wait in the cave depths, and he didn't blame her. To even get here he knew she was pushing back hard against her own fears.

Mike snuck a glance at her. He admired her a lot. And for the life of him he couldn't work out why he had shut her out. He had her, and let her go. *Dumb*, he thought, *but that's been me all my life*. He sighed and turned away.

In minutes they were ready to descend into the rift, and Harris came and waited beside Mike and Jane as they stood on the lip.

Harris stared down into the nothingness for a moment and spoke without turning his head. "This is where you said you had your encounter, right?"

"That's right," Michael said. "With one of the creatures. Damn things can basically crawl up the walls."

"They were blind, but have extraordinary hearing, smell, and also had sensory hairs. Plus they had a highly muscled but sinuous, long-form body," Jane added. "They've totally adapted for living in places that require wriggling, squeezing, and climbing."

"Just like in caves." Harris grunted, and then turned. "Well, like I said, if they leave us be, we'll let 'em live." He slapped Mike's shoulder. "So let's get this party started."

In minutes more they had several bolts fired into the rock wall, and then Harris sent Bull Vincent and Russ Hitch over the edge first. Maybe sending his two biggest guys was like a warning to whatever was down there: here come some real predators.

Mike noticed that both men had their rifles over their backs, side arms plus multiple blades strapped to their waists and thighs, and grenades on their belts. No one could accuse them of going in underprepared, he guessed.

Two by two the group descended. They'd used a ring on the bolt, and doubled their rope, so when the final person had descended to the end of their length they shot in another bolt, added a ring, and then released the rope to slide it through their upper ring for recovery.

In caves, rope was critical, and a limited resource. They could climb without it as they had proved last time when they scaled back up. But then Michael and the rest of them had lost twenty pounds, and though he had been weakened from the muscle loss, it meant he had less overall mass to haul up or down a rock face.

Jane, Penny, and Harris went next, and that left the last four: Alistair, Mike, Ally, and Pete Andreas. Mike stood on the edge watching Jane's descent, as the others joined him.

"Two by two?" Mike asked. "Who goes last?"

Ally looked out along the sheer and seemingly never-ending rift wall. "Screw that, Mikey." She pulled her bolt gun and fired in another bolt. "All four at once."

In seconds all four of them were roped up, and Ally gave him a small nod.

"Okay turkeys, let's do this."

She gripped the rope and leaned back, sliding down the rope a good forty feet before she struck the wall, and then hopped again.

The others bounced down as well. In a while they came to a rock perch only a few inches wide but the first of their group down had shot in two bolts about fifty feet apart and rigged a rope between them. It acted as a hammock-like temporary ledge and gave them time to rest and prepare for the next drop.

They'd continue to do this until they touched bottom, still hundreds of feet below them. Mike estimated they were down at about twelve thousand feet now and there was a hint of a warm breeze blowing up into their faces that carried smells of dank water, rotten fruit and he also couldn't help thinking it smelled of body odor.

Harris organized them again, and the first two went over the edge for the last few drops that were to be the longest and deepest.

Alistair, Mike, Ally and Pete had once again agreed to descend together. The four watched as the last team disappeared into the blackness, and Ally, close to him, spoke without looking up.

"Your girl is a good caver."

Mike snorted softly. "She's very good. But not my girl."

Ally looked him up and down for a moment. "Her loss." She hooked her ring up to the drop-line. "Ready?"

He nodded, and then over they went, separated by about ten feet on either side of their fellow cavers.

It was about fifty feet down that Mike eased past a vertical split in the rock face and saw what looked like greasy matting deep within the fist-sized opening.

He paused, staring into the hole: maybe some sort of unknown plant growth but probably more like a common form he'd come across before that was an obligate troglobitic fungi like *Acaulium caviariforme* or maybe *Aspergillus baeticus.* He looked along the wall and for the first time noticed more of the pockmarks having the same matting around their edges.

Because of their fading glow stones, they'd obviously missed these on the climb up. Mike lifted his hand with the flashlight on his wrist, pushed it into the hole and shone it around.

"*Shit.*" He jerked his hand back. *What the hell. Did something move in there?* he wondered.

"*Argh!*"

Andreas' yell snapped Mike's head around to where the man hung on the wall.

Mike's brows came together as he tried to make sense of what he was seeing in his light beam. With his free hand, Andreas punched at something that extended from the rock face and looked like a long arm complete with hand on the end that was scrabbling to get a hold of his belly.

"Goddamn get off me, you motherf..." Andreas hung on tight with one hand and used his other one to grip the thing around its, what...throat, neck, wrist? It was impossible to tell.

"Hang on. I'm coming at you." Ally began to walk to the side and then swing back toward her colleague, and Mike did the same from the other side, while Alistair just stared with wide eyes and open mouth.

"*Argggh.*" Andreas threw his head back as the thing finally managed to get a grip on his belly. "Goddamn, biting into me..."

"Clear," Ally yelled, with enough momentum on her swing to reach him. She held onto her rope with one hand while holding up a long-bladed knife with the other.

Andreas' face was screwed up in pain but he pulled his hands free and in one smooth movement, as Ally reached him, she swiped the blade down hard, completely severing the thing.

Dark blood splashed, and Andreas was left with the stump still clinging to his belly.

"Freaking monstrosity." He ripped it free and held it up, squeezing it as though trying to choke it to death. "*Bastard!*" Andreas exclaimed as he stared at it.

Mike was close enough to see that the end of the thing that had been trying to burrow into his stomach was a fleshy pipe with a hole in the end that was surrounded by three long claws or teeth he had thought were fingers. It was basically a mouth on the end of a column of muscle.

Andreas lifted his arm.

"Don't," Alistair yelled.

Too late; Pete Andreas flung the thing far out into the darkness.

"Now we'll never know what it was or get a chance to examine it," Alistair complained.

"I don't give a shit what it was; I just wanted it dead and gone." Andreas turned his red-hot glare on Alistair. "You get one of those things trying to eat their way into your belly and see if you want to play with it a while."

"Okay, big guy?" Ally asked.

"Yeah, yeah, fine now." Andreas wiped his brow roughly with his forearm. "Hey, Ally, thanks, owe you one."

"No sweat. Let's all get on down." She began to drop again.

Mike sucked in a deep breath and still felt a bit shaky. "There are more holes in the rock face. Avoid them if you can."

"No shit," Andreas retorted. He checked his belly one last time and then began to slide down his rope.

Mike began to drop as well, this time avoiding any crevices or holes in the rift wall.

In another half hour they had all reached the bottom of the sheer rock face, and Harris was waiting for them.

"What the hell happened up there?" Harris demanded.

"Something attacked Andreas," Mike replied.

"Came right out of the wall." Andreas pointed at his belly where the shirt was torn and bloody. "Tried to eat me."

"Get that cleaned up, now," Harris ordered.

"On it." Andreas rapidly started to remove his shirt as Penny gathered some iodine and gauze.

Harris turned back to Mike and Alistair. "What was it?" he asked.

"Looked like some sort of lamprey. Came out of a crack in the wall and tried to fix itself to Andreas' belly. We didn't encounter them before," Mike said.

"Lucky you." Harris shook his head. "I don't like surprises, Mr. Monroe."

"No one likes those sort of surprises. Maybe those things didn't hear us before, or maybe the blue light of the crystals didn't rouse them. What do you want me to tell you?"

"My job is to keep everyone alive. Your job is to help me do that by giving me a heads-up when there could be trouble. Sounds simple, right?" Harris' gaze was unwavering.

"Can only do that if I know there's danger." Mike stared back just as hard.

"Lamprey, did you say?" Alistair asked.

"Yeah," Mike said out of the side of his mouth.

"They're one of the oldest life forms on Earth." Alistair nodded slowly. "Some have a protein coating that is waterproof, so if their lake dries out, they can ride it out until it refills, days, weeks, or even years later."

Mike turned away from Harris. "You think it was a cave adaption?"

"Why not? You said your hairless creatures walked up these walls. So makes sense that an ancient parasite adapts to preying on them. That thing bit right through Andreas' tough shirt; imagine if it latched onto the bare skin of one of your wall climbers. Never get it off." Alistair raised his eyebrows.

Jane scoffed. "Every predator has its prey, and sometimes, every predator has its predator."

"Yeah, very interesting." Harris called his group in and immediately sent one of his soldiers in each direction of the cave they were now in. This time the men had their rifles held out in front of them and lights emanated from their helmets and gun barrels.

Mike and Jane walked a few feet along one end of the cave, and Jane stopped and then crouched.

"Cave floor is churned up. I'm sure this is the direction we took but I was expecting to see our footprints still marking the dust," Jane said.

Mike got down beside her just as Harris loomed behind them. The man lifted his light over their shoulders. "Looks to me like there was a lot of activity after you guys departed. This is an out-there question, but as the V5 cave is open to the public, could there have been other people down here after you guys?"

"I'd never say never, but it's unlikely. We would have heard about it on the speleological grapevine if someone found new, deep caves in the V5." Mike nodded to the cave floor. "Besides, do they look like bootprints to you?"

"No sir, they do not," Harris replied.

"I'm not a tracker, but these are like the prints we saw above. And I see no heel or toe marks from caving boots on these either," Mike said.

"Then let's have a closer look." Harris got down on his haunches and held his light up. "Look here." He used a finger to draw a broad box in the dust, and then scraped some of the excess debris away from within it. Sure enough, there were prints, or rather some sort of animal pugmark.

"Like a dog or big cat," Jane said softly.

"Toe walker," Harris said. "Animals like dogs are what's called digitigrade animals, meaning that their digits—toes, not their heels—take most of their weight when they walk. Because of this, dog toe bones are very thick and strong."

"These things might have been people once," Mike said softly.

"Humans usually walk with the soles of their feet on the ground." Harris stood. "But that's not much use if you live in caves, right?"

"*Boss.*"

Harris half turned. "Yo." He turned back to Mike and Jane. "Duty calls." He headed back toward the main group.

Mike lifted his light in the opposite direction that Harris had taken and stared down along the dark cave. There was no dust in the air and his beam of light was able to travel far. But still the cave kept on until it finished in a black nothingness.

"You know, I think we came from that way."

Jane looked about. "I can't remember. Our lights were fading and so was I. But maybe you're right." She turned to him. "So you think these things are what happened to the race of people from the cave city below? The ones that escaped up into the caves?"

"Maybe. The zoological DNA analysis was inconclusive, but the probability was high. De-evolution, inbreeding, cannibalism, plus for all we know the effects of the long-term radiation. In ten, twelve, fifteen thousand years, they might have reverted back to become primordial savages."

"C'mon Mike, you've seen them; they're more than just savages. They looked like an entire new species," Jane replied. "Horrible."

"Inbreeding creates deformations." He shrugged. "So does radiation-forced mutations."

"You're right, but all of the changes were selective adaptations, perfect for living in a cramped, lightless environment." She lifted her light. "The only way to evolve and keep it beneficial to the environment a creature is living within is to bring in new blood now and then, rather familial inbreeding that can result in debilitating physical distortions."

"*Mike, Jane.*"

Harris' voice came out of the darkness.

"Sounds like he found something." Mike allowed Jane to step ahead of him, as he didn't want her behind him and out of his sight. *The old protective urge kicking in again,* he thought. Even though she'd probably reject it if she knew what he was doing.

In a few minutes they found the group standing around the outside of another cave mouth, one no more than three feet around and Harris was crouched at its entrance. He waved them closer.

When Mike and Jane joined him, he turned. "Smell that?"

Mike sniffed and got the musty acrid scent of an animal's den. "Yes, might be where the creatures came from, or their lair."

"You never went this way?" Harris asked.

"Nope, never saw it. I'm fairly sure we came up from way back that end of the passage." He thumbed over his shoulder.

Harris peered into the dark hole a moment more and then stood. "Bull, take a look."

"Seriously?" Mike's mouth dropped open.

Bull quickly checked his weapons, adjusted his light and pulled the communication set over his head and the bead in front of his mouth.

"Check, one, two," Bull said.

"Receiving." Harris nodded, and then slapped the large man on the shoulder. "Stick 'em, big guy."

Bull crouched, shone his light around for a few seconds and then went in fast.

Mike couldn't believe the guy's courage. But guessed that was his job, and also he'd never actually seen one of the creatures.

"Fifty feet in, all clear," came Bull's first message.

Harris had pulled the receiver from his ear so they could all hear the interaction in the quietude of the caves.

"Proceed," Harris said.

"Branching at eighty feet, all clear," Bull said, out of breath.

"He shouldn't be in there by himself," Jane said.

"He knows how to handle himself," Harris said without turning. "Besides, if the crap hits the windmill, he'll be able to back out a lot quicker if he's got no one behind him."

"*Phew,* reeks in here," Bull whispered. "I'm now in the main cave; looks like no one's home. Looks like a freaking nest in here." And then. "But they were definitely here."

Harris turned to Jane. "Think we scared 'em off?"

"Unlikely," Jane said. "Ask him how many does he think were in there?"

Harris nodded. "Bull, how many dog people were in there, you think?"

"*Ah...*" Bull seemed to do a quick count. "Lots; fifty maybe." He grunted. "Hard to breathe with the stench; methane and ammonia."

"Okay, you can wrap it up," Harris said.

"Hold that; got an alcove, looks weird, I'm going in." Bull grunted again and there was the sound of scraping as he obviously jammed himself in somewhere tight. "Got a body, or what's left of it. Human skeleton. Hey, it's wearing something around its neck."

Mike frowned and leaned closer.

"Lana," Bull said softly.

"*Lana.*" Jane gripped Mike's arm. "Katya's sister; who went missing." She turned to Harris. "I need to see that body."

"Me too." Harris turned and snapped his fingers at Penny. "Doc, you're coming with us." He put a hand to the mic button. "Bull, stay where you are, we're coming to you."

"Roger that, I'll be here," Bull said.

Jane, Mike, Harris, and Penny crawled into the small and narrow cave. In just a few minutes they could see Bull's bobbing lights. But he'd been right about the smell; as they got closer to the main den it was miasmic to the point of being eye-watering. The odor was a combination of rotten meat, faecal matter and urine, and something like old sweat, all hanging in a cloud of ammonia vapors.

Bull waved them on. "In there."

"Stay on point," Harris said to him.

Mike and Jane went into the smaller side cave first, followed by Penny and then Harris. The small alcove was no more than eight feet around and only four high. But at its rear there was a skeleton stretched out on the ground. Jane got closer and lifted the small gold chain from around its neck.

She turned to Mike and nodded. "Yes, *Lana.*"

"Take it; for Katya," Mike said.

Penny moved her eyes over the bones, her hands hovering but not actually touching. "This young woman suffered." She grimaced. "Both arms and legs had been broken while she was alive."

"To stop her crawling away," Harris replied. "They immobilized her."

"They kept her hostage?" Mike asked.

"There's partial healing in the bones, so she was kept like this for several years." Penny brought her light closer to the groin area and indicated a discolored patch underneath it. "Poor woman, in pain, lying here in her own filth for all that time."

"Why? Why keep her alive?" Jane asked.

"I think I know," Penny said softly and leaned over the bones. "See here?" She pointed. "See these shotgun pellet-sized pockmarks along the inside of the pelvic bone? They're caused by the tearing of ligaments..." Penny straightened, "...during childbirth."

"Oh, they raped her." Jane squeezed her eyes shut. "A nightmare."

"Worse; they used her to breed." Mike turned to Jane. "It's how they got that new blood into the pack."

"I'm going to be sick." Jane turned away and threw up.

"Let's get out of here," Harris said. "Bull, you bring up the rear."

Mike took one last look around. "Katya had said coming down here was Hell for her. But it was nothing compared to what happened to her sister."

"This would never bring Katya closure." Jane wiped her mouth with her forearm. "It would only torment her guilt even more."

"We're done here, people." Harris turned away and the group followed.

*****

Bull waited a full minute for the group to exit. He then shone his barrel light around one last time, illuminating the skeleton, material that looked like piles of hair or fine roots that had been pulled together as some sort of bedding or nest, and also peered into any nooks and crannies he could locate.

Creepy as fuck, he thought.

He turned away, about to exit.

Tock.

He froze.

Tock.

He turned back. *What the hell is that?*

Big Bull Vincent angled his head, trying to get a bead on the noise. The problem was, in a cave sounds bounced around all over the place.

He lifted his rifle and panned it around, ready to deal death to anything that even looked at him sideways.

After another moment of all quiet, he lowered his gun. He then exited the cave. Double time.

CHAPTER 09

"Don't let them take me."

"What?" Mike turned to Jane who walked with her head down.

"I said, don't let them take me." She glanced up at him, her face drawn. "Kill me first."

"What's that supposed to…?" He suddenly understood. "*Aw*, Jane, stop thinking like that. We'll be fine."

Jane had dropped her head again, and Mike lifted his arm, about to loop it over her shoulder, but didn't know if she'd like that. Instead he just laid a hand lightly on her shoulder. "We'll get them to the gravity well, and head back, with an armed escort. Our job will be done."

She shook her head. "It'll never happen, something will stop us; you mark my words."

He sighed. *She's just depressed*, he thought. Seeing Lana's fate would have been enough to bruise anyone's spirit. Plus, sometimes going days without sunlight can bring on a malaise in even the most experienced cavers that can cause everything from flashes of out-of-nowhere anger to bone-deep depression.

Mike also knew that cave darkness seemed to magnify idiosyncrasies: if you come into a deep cave feeling low, you get depression. And if you come with fears, you end up with dark terrors and jump at every shadow.

But Jane was a strong person and he bet she'd snap out of it. He *hoped* she'd snap out of it.

Harris dropped back beside them and kept pace for a while. "How much further?"

Mike glanced at the soldier. "Should be another vertical chute a few hundred yards ahead. We drop down a hundred feet or so, pass through a few caverns and then simply head along another passage until we come into a larger cave with the gravity well."

"Very good," Harris replied.

"From there, you guys simply fly all the way to the Earth's center. Piece of cake," Mike added.

Harris turned to him. "Still really like you guys to come with us."

"Not a chance," Jane shot back.

"Okay, Jane." Harris nodded. "But remember, last time you guys were there you were unprepared, on the run, and..." He bobbed his head, "...this time, you'll have hard muscle and firepower all around you. You can enjoy it a little more. Study it and learn about it. They'll be talking about this expedition for generations to come." He shared his most disarming smile with them. "This is big, and you're already part of it." He moved a little closer to her. "Guide us, we need you."

Jane just made a sound of disgust in her throat, and Mike slowly shook his head. "*Nah*, we'll pass."

Harris straightened. "We'll pay you a thousand bucks a day, tax free." He raised his eyebrows. "Even backdate it from when you first got on the plane, how about that?"

Jane simply sped up and left them behind. Mike shrugged. "I think that's your answer."

Harris chuckled as he watched Jane leave them behind. "Strong willed; I like that."

"Very. And eyes off," Mike said as he sped up to catch her.

"Why? You two aren't dating," Harris called from behind him.

*****

After several more hours of walking in winding, featureless passageways, the line of cavers had strung out with about fifty feet between soldiers Russ Hitch, the lead person, all the way back to Pete Andreas at their rear.

The passage they now moved along had steep walls on either side and nothing but darkness above. It was a huge crack in the rocks and Mike recognized it as the passage where they first decided to head upward instead of moving horizontally along the pathways. That meant that they were only an hour at best away from the gravity well cave.

Jane walked quietly, lost in thought. Alistair had tried to engage her in conversation about evolutionary biology a while back but her one-word answers had eventually warned him off.

The team made use of multiple lights each on their helmets, on their wrists, or for the soldiers, on the barrel of their guns, and all provided good illumination in the inky blackness.

Up ahead the team entered a huge cathedral-sized cave with a lip of stone over one side creating half a ceiling just a dozen or so feet above their heads.

Mike frowned as he concentrated. It was hard to hear with the constant mumble of conversation going on, plus the scuff of so many feet. But after a moment he stopped dead.

"Quiet."

Harris put a hand up to halt the group and turned. "What have you got, Mike?"

Mike tilted his head, concentrating, as Jane moved in closer to Harris. Mike didn't like that she sought him out for protection but guessed one of the heavily armed soldiers was better than him right now.

"Everyone be quiet and listen," Mike said.

The sounds died away. Caves were rarely empty of all noises, as there can be the drip of water somewhere, the trickle of grains of sand, or even the creak of old stone trying to get comfortable like an old man who has sat in his favorite armchair too long. And the solid rock carried sound, so something that happened half a mile away might seem like it was just over your shoulder.

The group had all stopped moving and some even held their breath as they all listened now. Lights criss-crossed in the darkness, but everyone mostly had their eyes on Mike.

Tock.

Mike slowly turned his head.

Tock.

He changed angles to now focus on the direction behind them.

Tock, tock.

"I hear it," Harris whispered.

"That's them," Mike said.

"Them?" Alistair asked. "You mean… the cave creatures?"

"Yeah, I heard that same noise in the skeleton cave," Bull said.

"What? Why didn't you tell us?" Mike asked.

Bull shrugged. "Didn't know what it was then."

Tock, tock, tock, tock, tock…

The group looked one way then the other, but there was nothing, even though the sound seemed to come from all around them.

Then there was silence again.

They waited.

"Have they gone?" Penny asked in a small voice.

Her answer came fast from out of the dark, a greasy-looking white body slammed into Harris. He went down with a grunt. Then another came at Bull. Gunfire erupted from all around them, and when Mike looked up, he saw their cave ceiling was full of scuttling near-translucent bodies, clinging there like hairless, upside-down dogs with gargoyle faces.

There were too many, and they moved in amongst the people fast and confidently. Squeals came out of the darkness as bullets smacked into flesh, and in a few moments, the cave seemed to get even darker as lights began to go out.

Mike pushed through to Jane, throwing his arms over her as one of the things landed on him, grabbed his helmet and ripped it free. And then vanished.

Then he realied what they were doing. "*The lights.* They're taking our lights."

Sure enough, helmets, wrist lights, and guns with barrel-mounted lights were roughly pulled from hands or heads.

In seconds more it was all over.

Harris yelled, "Sound off."

For a moment it seemed they had escaped unharmed as people replied from within the darkness.

Almost all of them.

"Andreas, sound off." Harris looked about. "Where's Andreas?"

The few remaining lights flicked about the cave.

"*Andreas!*" Their shouts now filled the cavern. But there was no response.

"He's gone," Hitch said from the darkness. "And so have the creatures. I damn hit one, I know it; I saw it go down. But it's gone now as well."

"*Andreas!*" Harris yelled again. He went to his mic and tried to locate his man on the comms link. "Pete, can you hear us?" He waited, and then, "If you can't speak, make a noise or use Morse."

They waited, but nothing came back.

"They took their own injured and dead away," Mike said. "They only wanted to blind us, take our lights."

"How? How did they even know they were lights when they're cave blind?" Alistair wailed. "Or even know *we* needed them to see?"

"Maybe they could detect the electrical current. Or the heat, or who damn well knows. I don't think these things are just dumb beasts at all." Jane growled as Mike helped her to her feet. "And you know what else them taking our lights tells me? I think they've hunted us sight-reliant people before."

"Oh." Alistair grimaced, making his white teeth stand out in the darkness.

"We need to find him," Harris said.

"We don't even know where to look," Jane said.

"We shouldn't run off into the dark," Alistair said. "They'll pick us off one by one." His voice was getting higher and he jammed a fist over his mouth. "No, no, no, this is bad."

"Calm the hell down, we've got more lights," Harris yelled.

"No, leave most of them out for now. We need to save them," Mike said.

Harris turned to Ally. "Bennet, we go to headset."

"You got it." Ally pulled on the infrared quad-goggles, and Harris did the same.

"Ah, shit," Ally said softly. "You see'n this, boss?"

"Oh yeah, we got several dozen hostiles hanging in the cracks and crevices way up in the rift above us." Harris lifted his gun.

"Are you sure they can't see? Because those suckers are all looking right down at us," Ally whispered.

"I'm betting they're seeing you like you're seeing them: thermal images," Jane said. "Except their sense of smell and hearing will be much more acute than ours."

"Any sign of Andreas?" Hitch asked.

"Nothing. Just them. And lots of them." Ally slowly turned. "Do you think they know he's a male? You know, so they can't breed from him."

"Yes, human males and females give off different pheromones. They're carnivores, so they probably took him for meat. Just like they took their own dead," Jane said.

"Oh." Penny looked about. "We need to get out of here."

"I agree. This place is not defendable," Harris said. "Mike, Jane, which way to the well?"

"Wait a minute," Hitch demanded. "What about Andreas? He's still out there."

"He's dead," Harris shot back.

"You don't know that, boss." Bull's voice was deep and low. "Maybe a few of us should head back to that nest we found; you know, take a looksee."

"And then you'd be dead too." Harris looked up. "We're on their home turf and those things outnumber us about ten to one. And there's probably many more." Harris straightened. "We all knew the risks and what's at stake; we complete the mission."

Ally scanned the ceiling. "I count about thirty bodies up there and more comin' in. All waiting for something."

"Maybe us chasing after Andreas is exactly what they're waiting for," Mike said.

"I said these things have probably hunted people before for a reason," Jane said softly. "Dozens of people go missing in these deep caves, sometimes whole spelunking teams just vanish. We think they've fallen off a cliff or got lost, but maybe they haven't."

"*Shee-it.*" Bull blew air through puffed cheeks.

"We need to be out of this cavern; they knew to blind us and they did that for a reason. And my bet is that they wanted to blind us so an attack would be more effective when they had more numbers." Mike looked down along the passage.

"This is a damn kill-box."

Mike spun back. "We need to go, *now*."

"You heard the man," Harris said and took a last look upward.

Mike wished he had a pair of the goggles but couldn't decide whether seeing the threat made it easier to deal with or worse.

"Ally, lead 'em out," Harris said. "Everyone stay one arm length to the guy in front, nice and tight. And do *not* use your lights unless I give the word. *Go*."

Mike grabbed Jane's hand and she took it. He led her on. He knew the passage eventually led them to the gravity well chamber. But then what would he do?

From up ahead there was a grunt and then a scream.

"Fuck it," someone yelled as lights came on.

Then the gunfire erupted again. And no one held back. It was as if all the pent-up fury of the previous attack, Andreas being taken, and raw fear was spewed forth in waves of bullets.

The chamber was filled with deafening noise, and smoke, and ricochets. Greasy-looking bodies moved fast, mostly evading the aim of the soldiers, but a few taking hits and falling to the cave floor where they squealed and thrashed like landed fish.

More and more of the long, translucent creatures seemed to come from all around them, and Harris roared.

"Keep moving."

Ally led them into the well chamber and the group fanned left and right around the dark void of the gravity well. Hitch and Bull still fired back into the narrow cave they had just emerged from.

"Cease fire." Harris leaned back into the passage. "Damit, they're still in there. Maybe waiting for us." He turned to the two soldiers. "Keep covering that opening."

The men took up positions either side of the entrance, and Hitch got down on one knee while Bull stayed high, both with the barrels of their guns pointed down into the darkness that was lit now by the lights on the gun barrels.

"Mike, that's it?" Harris asked.

"That's it; it'll take you all the way to the center of the Earth," Mike replied.

"This is as far as we go," Jane announced as she glanced up at Mike. "Right?"

Harris' head jerked back on his neck momentarily. "Are you shitting me? Where are you going to go? Those goddamn things are waiting for a chance to either come charging in here, or us to go out there."

"We're not going to the center; we told you that." She pointed at his chest. "You promised we could have an escort to the surface if we wanted it."

"Did you not see what just happened back there?" Harris shook his head. "Lady, those things just entered our defensive line when we were at full strength. You two plus a guard would be overwhelmed in 10 seconds, maybe 20, tops."

"We'll take our chances."

Mike knew Jane was digging in, and no amount of logic was going to dissuade her now.

"The mission dynamics have changed." Harris' expression became stony. "You want to commit suicide, that's fine. But I'm not throwing away the life of one of my soldiers, end of story."

"I knew you'd go back on your word." Jane shook her fist in the man's face.

Harris folded his arms and spoke softly. "I'm now down one soldier and do not have any spare resources." He then turned to Mike. "Mr. Monroe, you know, and I know you know, that if you leave the security of the group, you'll both die."

"Boss, we got a lot of movement," Hitch said from behind them.

Harris turned back and pointed at Mike's chest. "They'll eat you." He then turned to Jane. "And you saw what they do to their female captives."

"You sonofabitch." Mike surged forward, fists up. He threw a straight right.

Harris easily blocked it, moved to the side, and used Mike's momentum to knock him down. Mike sprawled and Harris pointed into his face.

"Raw truth, Mike. It sucks, I know, but there it is. Come with us, and live." He turned away, leaving Mike on his ass. "Listen up people, we are going to jump. Pair up. Ally and Penny, Hitch and Alistair, I'll take Mike, and Bull gets the lovely Jane Baxter."

He turned back to Mike and Jane. "Sorry Jane." He sighed. "If you want to hate me for wanting you to stay alive, then so be it."

Mike, still sitting, turned to Jane whose eyes glistened in the light of their flashlights. "No choice," she whispered.

After a few seconds she nodded.

"Good." Harris held out a hand. "Mike, we get to go last."

Mike ignored it and got to his feet himself.

Harris went to the passage mouth, pulled his goggles down and peered in. "Oh yeah, getting real crowded in there." He lifted them to his forehead. "I'm going to give them some push back, and buy us some time. Ally on the count of five, and everyone else at five second intervals: 5-4-3-2-1…*Go*."

Harris got down on one knee and began rapid firing into the passage. Ally and Penny, roped together, dived in. Then they all began to peel out, diving head first into the hole, as they had learned to do from reading Mike's manuscript.

Harris emptied his magazine. He stood, professionally changed his magazine and then backed up. It was just he and Mike remaining.

"Ready, big guy?"

Mike nodded. He felt like shit, as Harris' comments to them were like a slap in the face and hurt more than the knockdown he just took. They were raw and ugly, but they were the truth: go, or stay and die; horribly there was no sane choice.

"I'm ready," Mike said.

Harris got to the edge. "Count of 3-2-1, *go*."

In they went.

EPISODE 07

If there were no thunder, men would have little fear of lightning

— Jules Verne

CHAPTER 10

On their voyage down there were no landmarks, only sporadic flashes of blue light, and a never-ending vortex of darkness. Jane remembered nothing from her previous time coming up in this gravity well, perhaps because they were physically and mentally exhausted and they mostly traveled while unconscious.

She noticed that the soldier she was with, Bull Simmons, constantly looked back over his shoulder to see if they were being pursued. But there was nothing other than the dots of lights signifying her colleagues.

For the most part, Bull's mouth hung open in wonder, and after another few hours, he pulled her closer, undid his belt and lashed it to her wrist.

"Get some rest; I'll keep watch." He nodded and smiled and let out some of the belt length so she floated free. It also allowed him free hands to throw more of the communication relay lights against the cave wall.

Thank you, she mouthed and closed her eyes. She didn't think she'd be able to sleep knowing she was headed toward a place she had promised herself a hundred times she'd never go back to.

But here she was, headed back down to where her previous team had been decimated and she had seen Harry Wenton dragged away into the darkness by some sort of thinking arthropod creatures from the center of the Earth. Yep, here she was, and already the deaths had begun again.

Jane kept her eyes pressed shut but didn't find restful sleep; instead she simply slipped into a gloomy unconsciousness.

*****

She was grabbed and felt her body be eased to the ground in the tomb-silent cave. It seemed the one thing the team had practiced was preparing for their arrival, and being able to protect themselves and their equipment, instead of coming in like a fleet of crashing dirigibles like Mike and Jane had done on their first arrival.

Bull released her and unstrapped her wrist. "All good?" he asked.

"Yeah, I'm good," Jane replied, rubbing her arm where the leather strap had been attached, probably for the past twenty-eight to thirty hours.

In minutes more they all assembled, with Hitch staring back up into the gravity well to make sure nothing followed them down.

Penny buzzed around checking everyone for abrasions, cuts or skin lacerations, and expertly treating and covering them with iodine and bandages. Bull and Ally were dispatched to check out the perimeter just in case the former occupants had decided to leave guards for when they returned.

Mike spoke softly to Harris, and Jane watched the pair for a moment more. She wondered whether Mike ever really planned to go back to the surface at the well, or push on as he had done. And for that matter, whether Harris had decided long ago that they were coming all the way, and the attack was a convenient excuse to keep them hostage.

Drop it, that's dumb, she thought. *I'm just feeling blue and looking for someone to blame.* Besides, she was here now, so she'd better deal with it.

She cast another glance at the soldier. For some reason the guy intrigued her. He saw her looking, waved, and sauntered over. She noticed he had his rifle cradled in front of him now. "You okay?"

"I'll live," he said, and though she was intrigued, she didn't fully trust the guy.

"That's the spirit." He continued to watch her. "I'm sorry it worked out like this. I hope you see it was unavoidable."

"Yeah, maybe." Her mouth set in a hard line.

"Well, it's true," he said softly, and then stepped a little closer. She saw Mike watching over Harris' shoulder. "I would have been gutted if anything bad happened to you. Just want you to know that, Jane."

"I…" She began.

Harris turned away. "Listen up people. I'm sending a scout team down the passageway. The rest of us will wait here until they report back."

"And if they find it's guarded?" Mike asked.

"Yes, what do we do?" Alistair asked. "Head back up and straight into the jaws of those things in the dark?"

Harris shook his head. "No, Mr. Monroe and Mr. Peterson, we eliminate the threat by evolving our tactics." He turned. "Hitch, Bull, scout ahead, and see what we're going to encounter. At this time, do not engage."

The men nodded and headed off in the darkness, and Harris turned back to the group. "Our estimations are that the Russians will be several miles to the west of us. We need to see what it is they are doing, observe them, gather information, and that's it."

"Then what?" Jane asked.

"If their work is benign then our job is done." He gave her a flat smile. "We have no plans to set up a base here, or even be here any longer than we have to."

Jane stared for a moment, trying to discern any subterfuge in the man's expression. But there was none. She couldn't really tell whether he was stating a fact or he would just be a damn good poker player.

Harris smiled and held up a hand with three fingers together. "Scout's honour."

She had no choice but to believe him. "Fine." And she couldn't help smiling back.

The group sat, sipped water, and ate some of their protein bars. Mike sat next to her, but for the most part they sat in silence. On the other side of them, Harris pulled a cigarette pack-sized box from a pouch and typed in a brief message.

"The comm system?" Mike asked.

Harris nodded as he finished typing. "Should allow me to send and receive very short messages letting them know we've touched down. But no idea how long it'll take them to go point to point as they're bouncing along all the relay boosters."

He sent it and stared at the box for a moment more, before sighing and sliding it back into the pouch. "Guess I'll know when I know."

It was in another thirty minutes that Hitch and Bull jogged up from out of the darkness and announced that the cave had been walled up down at what they thought was its exit.

It seemed the creatures had decided to cover off the entrance, and that gave Jane an indication of who had done it the first time. "They rebuilt it," she said.

"Well then..." Harris got to his feet. "Why don't we take a looksee on what's waiting for us on the other side of that wall?"

As they headed down the passage, Mike pointed out familiar landmarks to Penny and Alistair: the groups of tiny, ancient skeletons, some in family groups in the alcoves. Also the remnants of dropped weapons, urns and bowls that might have once contained food, and piles of clothing, all now turning to dust.

When they arrived at the cave's end, Jane could see the new wall that had been built was a lot more formidable than the last. And different. Her brows knitted as she approached it.

"Mike, look; the stones seem to be glued in place. Some sort of resin mortar."

She reached a hand out and touched the rocks. Between was an amber-colored mixture that was set hard, and trailing her fingers over it, she felt it was glass-smooth, like some sort of hardened wax or plastic.

"Secretion," Alistair said.

He reached into a small bag at his waist and pulled free a small folding knife and plastic vial. He scraped some of the material from between the cracks and into his container. He held it up to his light and jiggled it.

"Most arthropods can secrete different sorts of mixtures to create nests, exoskeletal shells, hives, or different structures for their protection." He stepped back. "This is amazing; they've actually used this extruded biological matter to cement the rocks together." He turned to them. "Could indicate intelligence."

"No shit." Mike scoffed. "They knew what they were doing. We think they'd sealed it once before, just rock on rock. But this time they've added a little glue to make it difficult for us to return."

Harris thumbed toward the wall. "Hitch, make a hole, quietly if you please, and stick a pipe through."

"On it." The soldier withdrew a few tools and started to slowly corkscrew a long, slim blade in between two of the rocks. The material was hard but not like cement and more like fibreglass resin as it tended to flake when Hitch put his shoulder into it.

After ten minutes he had dug out a small pile of the stuff and jammed his blade in all the way.

"I'm through." Hitch slowly pulled his blade out, put his eye up to the hole for a moment, and then pulled back. He then unwound a cable from a box, plugged it in, and handed the small device to Harris.

Hitch then stuck the cable end into the hole and fed it through. Harris turned on the device and an image was displayed on the small screen. Mike and Jane crowded in closer to see.

Mike squinted down at the images, but the first thing he noticed was the darkness on the other side.

"Where's the crystal glow?" Mike asked.

"Was going to ask you the same thing," Harris said.

"Could they have faded?" Jane asked.

"We've only been gone a year or so, and the crystals were still glowing after the city had been abandoned for what we estimated was over ten or twelve thousand years." He turned to her. "More like destroyed or removed."

"But there was tons of the stuff," Jane replied.

"We don't know how many of the creatures there were. An army could have done it," Harris said without looking up. "Pan left."

Hitch used his fingers to angle the cable camera.

"Now right." Harris' face was dead calm as he studied the images. "Up." After another moment he shrugged. "Well, looks all quiet in there now." He switched the screen off and tossed it back to Hitch. "Wrap it up."

"We're going in?" Penny asked.

"That's why we're here." Harris clicked his fingers at Ally. "Ms. Bennet, take that wall down."

"On it." Ally dropped her pack and removed a single foil-covered package the size of a block of soap, plus a smaller box. She unwrapped the foil and then peeled off some of the soft plasticine-like material. She rolled the portion out into a long string, which she then placed around the outside of the blocked doorway. She stuck a silver pin into it and finally calibrated a small timer.

"Thirty seconds," Ally said and fast-walked back up the passageway.

Everyone else took cover and placed hands over their ears. Mike hated the idea of explosives, especially the thought that they might be ringing the dinner bell for the weird arthropod people.

"5-4-3..." Ally counted down, "2-1..."

The explosion happened right on time and was more a muffled *thump* than a sharp and hot *bang*. It finished with the sound of tumbling rocks and filled the cave with dust.

Ally stepped out. "Mr. Harris, your wall is down."

Harris rose to his feet and waved some of the clouds away. "Good work," he said and approached the tumbled wall.

He had his rifle in his hands, and the other soldiers had done the same. *At least they were taking it seriously*, Mike thought.

Hitch and Bull stepped over the rubble and planted themselves on either side of the tumbled debris. Harris and Ally came in next and rushed forward, guns up. Both found some cover and just dropped low in the dark cavern.

"Hot as all in here. And just as dark," Ally said. She panned her arm around that held the motion sensor. "I got nothing, nobody's home."

Harris cracked several glow sticks and tossed them out into the darkness. Their yellow glow illuminated the ancient and desolate ruins. He slowly stood and turned. "Okay people, come on through."

Mike and Jane, followed by Penny and Alistair, scrambled over the rubble.

"Wow," Alistair said softly, and then grimaced. "Warm."

It was as hot as Mike remembered. Leaving the cool of the cave behind and entering the world below meant they were drawing closer to the boiling-red sky.

"This is nothing compared to what you'll experience outside," Jane added.

"Where's all that blue light you promised us?" Ally said.

"We wondered the same thing." Jane looked to where one of the huge columns of rod crystal used to be: the one she remembered had been thicker than a light pole and just as high. Now there was nothing, not fragments or even crystal dust. "It's all been removed. Someone or something obviously knew we needed it to see," she replied.

"We don't know that for sure," Harris said. "For all we know that raiding party you mentioned came here to mine the stuff. Maybe they valued it as well."

Jane scoffed. "Whatever you say."

Harris lowered his gun. "Well, the party is over here. Whatever group had come is now gone. I suggest we get moving and pick up the Russian trail."

They walked single file down along the broken pathway and entered the ruins of the ancient city. Penny stopped and grabbed Alistair's arm.

"I never expected this. It's all so old." Her mouth hung open. "It must predate the first Egyptians."

"Even the Sumerians, I'd say," Alistair replied.

Mike turned. "We thought maybe about twelve thousand years, give or take a century."

"This was a mature civilization. The architecture is quite sophisticated." Alistair walked toward a broken column and brushed away some dried lichen. "There's writing here, but, it's difficult to understand." He looked up. "Your manuscript said there were pictoglyphs?"

"Hey." Harris kept his voice low but forceful. "We're not on a walking tour. Get moving."

Mike nodded but turned back to Alistair. "Yes, and it told the tale of the war and their demise. The survivors split up, some marched out into the jungle, some took to the sea, and some headed up into the high caves."

"And you think those things in the caves are what became of those who went up in the caves?" Penny grimaced. "Those poor people."

"If that's what they were, people I mean," Jane added. She turned back to the open area she was in and walked slowly around for a moment before she stopped. "Hey, Mike, where did we leave Saknussov's skeleton? I'm sure it was here, *right here*." She pointed at a flat area of ground.

Mike joined her and frowned. "Hey, you're right, it was propped against *that* plinth, remember? Pointing up toward the doorway. It's gone now."

"They took it." She shook her head. "Why take the bones?"

"Erase all trace, maybe?" Mike said.

"Or to study," Alistair said softly.

"They had Harry Wenton for that," Jane added bitterly.

"But he was alive. And maybe that's the way they wanted him." Alistair looked up. "We often take active and inactive specimens, and study both."

"Oh." Jane turned to Mike. "Do you think...?"

Mike shook his head. "No, no I don't. Forget it, Jane, he's dead."

Alistair wandered around a little more and then crouched. "Look here."

"Hurry up," Harris yelled.

"Wait, we must learn more," Alistair pleaded. "A few moments, please. This is important."

Mike held up a hand to the glaring commander. "One minute."

Mike, Jane, and Penny followed Alistair, and he pointed at the ground. Mike could only see scratches and divots in some of the cave soil and on the bare rock.

"What is it?" Mike asked.

"Maybe footprints of your arthropod people," Alistair said and indicated some grooves in the lichen on one of the tumbled rocks.

Alistair crouched on his haunches. "There's an order of arthropods called Decapoda or it literally means ten-footed. It's a broad order and covers everything from crayfish, crabs, to lobsters, and shrimp. But it's one of the oldest, and the earliest known specimens date from the Devonian Period some four hundred million years ago."

He ran his fingers along a few of the grooves. "Sharp pointed tracks, and usually have ten legs, but can have as many as thirty-eight appendages. The actual legs for locomotion are called pereiopods, found on the last five thoracic segments."

Mike nodded.

Alistair looked up. "Was that something like them?"

"They were more upright, but we didn't get a good look. And maybe the legs were working together instead of separately," Mike added.

"Possible." Alistair nodded. "They also have large ones at the front that have enlarged pincers, called chelae, as well as multiple pairs of maxillipeds which function as feeding appendages; like little hands to feed the food into their mouths."

"Yeah, that sounds like our guys," Jane said. "Horrifying."

Alistair looked back down. "These deep marks indicate the pointed, spiked legs of a pereiopod of considerable size." He looked up. "And you said intelligent?"

"Yes, they carried weapons," Mike replied.

"I believe it," Alistair replied. "There's only been a few studies done on some arthropod species, but one, the mantis shrimp, are highly intelligent. They exhibit complex social behavior, fighting techniques. And most extraordinarily, they have a great capacity to learn and retain knowledge. They have very efficient brains."

"Now give them a few hundred million years to evolve and grow." Jane's eyes seemed devoid of life.

"Then they'd be very formidable indeed." Alistair rose to his feet.

"*Move* it," Harris' yell echoed in the dark cavern.

Alistair cupped his mouth. "I need more time."

"No," Harris began. "You'll…"

"This race lived here for thousands of years. We must spend a few moments learning from them. It might help us later on." Alistair backed up.

Mike hiked his shoulders at the soldier. "This hominid species also encountered the creatures that scattered them, so might be worth knowing if they mentioned them or anything about them. It's important."

Harris bared his teeth, his breath hissing through them undoubtedly at the challenge to his authority.

"You can always leave me. Pick me up when you get back." Alistair had already turned away.

"Give him a few hours," Jane added.

Harris shook his head, and then pointed at the young man's chest. "You got one hour, Mister, sixty minutes, to have a quick poke around. Then we're moving out. *All of us.* Confirm?"

"Got it, confirm one hour." Alistair grinned and hopped up onto a slab of lichen-covered rock and headed into the ruins with Penny at his heel.

Mike turned to Jane. "Why not? Might answer some questions."

The pair followed Alistair and Penny, and Harris organized his team, sending a few out as scouts and Ally to follow the civilians as their guard.

Penny pointed things out to Alistair, marveling at the ancient structures, but Ally was more on edge as she tried to see into every dark crack, crevice or corner all at once.

Mike sighed; not having the crystals meant the huge cavern was filled with shadows and silence, and it was like one giant mausoleum. He knew that archaeologists would give their right arm to spend just a few minutes here, and one hour wasn't going to be enough time to learn very much at all.

Another time, he thought, as this place was an expedition all in itself.

Alistair hopped from fallen column to broken wall, as Penny scaled behind him. Mike turned slowly, holding his flashlight out straight. There were tumbled blocks the size of cars, and boulders of shattered crystal with everything having a coating of moss and lichen giving it a patina of Verdi Gris. It looked as ancient as it really was.

"I can't believe the beings that created this magnificence might have devolved into those things in the caves above us." Jane pushed slick hair back off her face.

"Not all of them I hope." Mike then cringed and shook his head when he heard Alistair lifting and toppling rocks to see what was underneath them.

Ally scolded him for the noise that bounced around in the gargantuan cavern for many seconds.

"Got a body here. Well, a skeleton anyway." Alistair crouched beside a fallen slab.

"Saknussov? Let's check it out," Mike said. Jane held out a hand, and Mike quickly grabbed it to help her up on a fallen plinth.

"Jane." He held onto her hand.

She stopped and turned.

"I wanted to say I'm sorry." He gave her a broken smile. "About you being here. About me not calling you." He shrugged. "I wanted to, but..." He trailed off, not sure how to say what he wanted.

She squeezed his hand back and smiled. Then nodded. But that was all. "Come on." She dragged him toward Alistair, Penny, and Ally.

"Poor little guy was crushed. He was male, and young." Penny pointed to a large flat stone that Alistair had lifted off the body. "He was alive for a while." The figure's hip was crushed in several pieces and the thighbone was also shattered.

"Poor guy." Mike crouched. "Looks like he didn't make the exodus."

"Is that a weapon?" Alistair reached for the footlong clear rod in its hand. He held it up. "Is it crystal?"

Mike took it from him and then frowned and held his light closer. He snorted softly. "No, I think it's diamond. And it's no weapon; looks more like a key."

The end was sharp: no wonder that Alistair had thought it a weapon. But it was four-pronged, and the other end had a loop, perhaps to hang on something.

"Was he running to open something, or running away after already locking it?" Mike handed it to Jane.

"Must be worth a fortune," Ally said, looking down over their shoulders.

Jane took it and used a thumb to rub some of the moss from it. "They might not have valued diamonds as we do. Down here they might be abundant and no more interesting than river stones." She weighed it in her hand. "But this thing had other value; it was strong and near invulnerable to time and weathering. It was meant to open something big and enduring."

Mike stood and shone his light around for a moment and then back to the small skeleton. "By the angle he's lying, he was headed that way, but came from back there." He pointed into the darker recesses of the cave.

"Thirty minutes, people," Harris yelled to them.

"Which way?" Mike asked, knowing they probably wouldn't have the time to explore both unless they split up which he didn't want to do.

"Well, if whatever it was, was unlocked, then we can expect it to have been already raided thousands of years ago." Jane looked to where the small being had been running from. "And if he did manage to seal and lock it, and he had the only key, then..." she handed him the key.

Mike took it and grinned. "It might still be sealed." He held up the key, looking for a keyhole that looked like a plus sign. "Could be in a door, wall, or the floor. Let's spread out. You too, Ally."

"Sure, Mikey." She nodded at the diamond key. "But if there's any more of those, I'm having one."

The small group spread in a line and walked back through the ruins in the direction they thought the small person had been fleeing from.

They quickly burned ten minutes and Mike knew Harris would be on at them again to return. If they didn't find something soon, or anything they could use to buy more time, they'd never know if something had been hidden here that was a real clue to what these people valued enough to die for.

They soon came to a once-mighty collapsed building and all that remained standing was a huge wall, or rather single slab of white stone that was covered in writing.

"Their language," Alistair said, walking forward.

"It reminds me of Egyptian hieroglyphics." Penny shone her light along the rows of characters. "Pictures as well as symbols."

Alistair frowned. "Yes, but it's weird: to me like there's two styles of writing; the first is more stylized and then the lower form seems more rushed. You know, I think one was done earlier, and the lower script much later." He turned. "And in a damn hurry."

"I don't suppose your language skills extend to hieroglyphics?" Penny asked.

Alistair grinned. "This is not Egyptian, even though some of it is a similar pictoglyph style. But…" He blew air through his pressed lips. "It's possible to draw out its meaning by doing a quick count of the different signs."

"Signs?" Mike frowned. "You mean symbols?"

"Something like that." Alistair lifted an arm to point and then moved his finger along the rows. "You see some writing systems with less than forty different signs may be alphabetic. And then, a writing system with one or two hundred signs may be syllabary, in which each sign stands for a syllable." He turned. "Get it?"

"Sort of," Mike replied.

"But some writing systems are logographic, with thousands of different signs, and each sign might represent a single word or even an entire sentence. It's also useful to look out for strings or signs that repeat, as these may be names of things."

"That sounds promising," Jane said.

"Don't get your hopes up too much. There are still some ancient languages that have never been deciphered to this day, even by experts. An example is the Indus Valley script that is still a mystery. I heard that not even the great Professor Matt Kearns of Harvard has unlocked that one." Alistair clicked his tongue in his cheek. "A Rosetta stone would really help right now."

"Hurry it up here, people," Ally said.

Alistair ignored her. "I can only give an impression of what I think it *might* say. But to fully translate it, you'd need a specialist forensic linguist trained in ancient languages. Oh, and probably a few years."

He backed up and began to shine his light around. "Do we move on?"

"Yes, we do," Ally said.

Mike shone his light down at the ground. "Not yet, we were led here; this is a path. And it ends at this wall."

"So maybe it doesn't end at all," Jane said.

Mike nodded. "That's what I think. It might be some sort of doorway."

"Okay." Alistair turned back. He pointed to the top of the wall. "This major symbol is repeated, so I'll assume it's a place name. Maybe the name for this city or kingdom or the land."

"Call it Lemuria; the lost continent," Jane said. "It's what Katya called it."

"Lemuria it is then. Okay, bear in mind I'm doing little more than providing an educated guess." Alistair began. "*Lemuria, the blessed land of three monarchs. Those that tamed the jungle,* something, something, *and protect us from the…* something that might say: *hard-shells or skins.*" He turned and flicked his eyebrows up. He turned back and then pointed to a small image of a being with multiple arms and what looked like feelers. "Your shelled friends?" asked Jane and Mike.

Alistair's lips moved silently as he tried to draw out the meaning. Occasionally he shook his head or his brows knitted. "There's a name here and a reference to something that might be god or deity, or even master, and some sort of worship."

He stood back. "There's pieces missing, but then down here the new writing starts. "*The war goes on, but we have ended* or *lost.* Something else I can't understand and then: *we must choose our way* or *choose to go forward.*"

"They were at war, and were losing," Mike said. "Their choice was to stay and fight, or maybe it was to flee, and then which way to go: the sea, the jungle, or the caves?"

"The three monarchs each chose their own path," Jane said.

"Time's up." The roar came from down in the cave depths.

"Okay guys, the boss calls. We're done here," Ally said.

"That's all," Alistair said and quickly rubbed his hand over the stone, causing a shower of fine particles to rain down. He was about to stand back when he stopped, and then stepped forward again. He dusted away some more of the loose grains and stuck his finger in a hole.

"Hey, you said the keyhole would look like a plus sign, right?" He stood aside. "Like this?"

Jane grinned. "*Exactly* like that." She turned to Mike "Go on, quick, try it."

Mike held out the key and eased it into the hole. "It fits." He gently turned it. Nothing happened.

"*Soldier, get those people down here now.*" Harris' voice was rising to an incendiary level.

"Sir." Ally turned back to the group. "You're gonna have to park this for another time." She grabbed at Alistair and pulled him back. She did the same to Penny.

Mike frowned and placed his hand on the turned key. He then pressed it. It sank in another few inches, and then there was a deep clunk from inside the stone.

"Something's happening," Mike breathed.

"I'm coming up." Harris bounded up and across the ancient, tumbled architecture.

There was a grinding that they felt right through the soles of their feet, and just as Harris arrived, a huge portion of the wall in front of them swung inward on some sort of pivot.

"What did you do?" Harris demanded.

A gust of foul air blasted out at them.

"Stand back." Mike stood in front of Jane. "The air inside might be rotten. Let's give it a minute." He turned to Harris and grinned. "I think you'll allow us a few more minutes now, right?"

"A few," Harris said, his gaze flat. "We're not on a damn treasure hunt."

After a few more moments they crept forward, and with the illumination of multiple lights, saw steps leading downward.

"They're clear; no debris. This place has been sealed since whatever happened here all those millennia ago." Alistair chuckled. "There's a light down below... *hey, it's blue.*" He turned and his eyes gleamed. "Some of your glowing crystals."

"Seems not all of them were taken after all," Jane said.

They came to the bottom of several dozen steps and began to fan out.

"Stay in sight," Harris said.

"Beneath the gaze of the god," Mike said softly as he stared up at the huge idol carved into one wall.

The single statue was fifty feet tall, with blue glowing eyes. In its hand it held a staff, and the other was outstretched as though offering something.

"Human," Jane said.

The face had normal human features, and there was no sign of any extra limbs or carapace plating. It was also painted a deep red.

"*Ah,* damn." Penny shook her head. "This is what our fleeing guard must have been protecting." She pointed. "Their children."

They crossed to Penny who stood before several mounds. Tangled together were dozens of skeletons, tiny, some no more than a few feet tall. They looked as if they were hugging each other.

"Children, babies, their most prized possessions. They locked them in, and probably hoped to come back for them when the attack was over." Penny sighed. "Damn."

"They never came back. So the children just waited here until they died." Jane's mouth set in a hard line. "Terrible."

Harris grunted and turned. "We're finished here. Let's go." He spoke over his shoulder. "Grab some of those crystals; we may need them."

The group gathered a few of the smaller glowing rods, and Alistair pushed the lid off a stone receptacle. He peered in.

"Looks like ashes," Alistair said.

Mike pocketed some of the crystals and also looked inside. "More like old paper. Might have been books or some sort of written texts:

unreadable, long turned to dust."

Alistair groaned. "We're too late. For everything."

"Almost but not quite." Jane looked up at one of the walls.

There were mostly carved alcoves with small statues depicting aspects of the life of these Lemurian people, but one wall was totally flat for several dozen feet.

"A map."

Harris stopped at the bottom of the steps. "Say what?" he turned back.

"Has to be," Jane said.

They gathered in front of the huge image; it was like an ancient mariner's drawing where the world was spread flat. There were seas, jungles, and mountains. All had the Lemurian script across different areas.

Mike pointed to a circle at the bottom. "That must be us, here. And look, the huge column mountain containing the gravity well is depicted."

Sure enough there was a column drawn with a dark stripe up in its center.

"They always knew about the wells," Jane said.

"If that's true, then they've picked out others." Harris stepped forward. "So, they knew about *all* of them."

Mike pointed again. "Across the ocean and back through the jungle, there's another. Might be the one we came in through: *the Krubera*."

"There are others; good to know." Harris nodded. He pointed to Ally. "Take some pictures. This will be very useful."

"Yes, yes," Alistair agreed. "Close in on the writing as well."

"And also get a picture of that." Jane turned to Mike. "Any ideas?"

"Holy crap." Mike felt his scalp prickle. "I don't..."

He lifted his light closer as Jane also held her light on the far section of the map. If an artist could take every nightmarish creature imaginable to meld them all together, it might come close to the depiction on the edge of the land and water that was in one quadrant. There was a monstrous, hulking beast with blazing red eyes, a face hanging with tendrils or tentacles cascading down over lumped shoulders, and with muscular, scaled arms ending in clawed hands.

"Could it be real?" Penny whispered.

"A nightmare!" Mike stared.

"I dreamed this thing," Jane said.

"I think there's a name for the city in the shadow of the monster." Alistair mouthed the words for a moment, attempting to pronounce it. "It says something like..." He chuckled. "No idea. But if I had to guess, I'd say *Y'ha-nthlei*."

"That name rings a bell." Jane turned to Mike. "Did Katya mention that?"

Mike shook his head.

"*Y'ha-nthlei*; home of the deep, old ones." Alistair's eyes narrowed.

Mike turned. "The what?"

"You know what I think?" Alistair's eyebrows went up. "Ever read any Lovecraft?" he asked.

Mike frowned. "No, but I've heard of him."

Alistair turned back to the image. "He wrote of a huge ancient god, or elder being called DAGON, 'one of the great dreamers from the beyond'. It was said to slumber in the depths in the city of Y'ha-nthlei. Everyone assumed it meant the depths of the ocean. But what if…" he thumbed toward the map.

"They meant the depths of the planet," Mike finished.

"Coincidence," Jane said. "How could he know?"

"Because this elder god was supposed to haunt the dreams of certain people who were sensitive to it, like Howard P. Lovecraft apparently was. And maybe you are too." Alistair looked back up at the titan. "We just don't know much about our world prior to the Theia impact event when a large celestial body slammed into the Earth and the moon was created. But there was about a billion years of lost Earth time we know nothing about that something could have evolved and lived that bore no resemblance to what exists today."

"Maybe it is the god-king of the crustacean people. They're Y'ha-nthleians." Alistair raised his brows.

"Sounds like bullshit," Harris announced. "You do remember that ancient mariner's maps contained images of sea dragons, as in 'there be monsters' right?" he snorted. "Probably the same thing." He turned away, but paused. He turned back, his face split by a grin. "But we'll try and avoid that quadrant, just in case." He chuckled and waved them on. "We're out of here."

Jane turned to follow and Mike noticed she hugged herself, perhaps feeling gloomy about the children's bodies. He saw her stop, look down and then bend to retrieve something. She held it flat on her hand as she stared.

"What have you got?" Mike asked.

She held her hand out. On it were two coins, gold, and on one side a head, human male, regal-looking but with three faces, and when she flipped one, the other had an image of the monstrous beast from the map.

"Keep them," Mike said.

She nodded and stuck them in her pocket.

Harris led them back up the steps, and at the top, Mike lifted the diamond key. "What'll we do with this?"

"Bring it," Jane said. "Close the door, and let's keep it as well. This place was sealed to keep the arthropod creatures out. Let's make sure it stays that way."

Mike stuck the key back in the lock, pulled it and then turned it back the other way. With a deep grinding the door swung shut. He placed the key in his pack.

"There's so much more to learn," Alistair whispered.

Mike nodded. "Another time," he replied, and then followed Jane and the others down through the ruins.

*****

Ray Harris led them out to the mouth of the colossal cave. He checked his long-range comms device and saw he had an answer. He quickly read it: *message received. H*e snorted softly; *nice to hear from you too*, he thought.

But then he guessed that as the messages took so long and needed to be super-compressed, and then bounced across hundreds of relays, then huge messages were never going to cut it. *Emergencies only*, he thought.

They slowed as they approached the exit. And then the red glow became their entire world. Most simply stood and stared, with others gaping, open mouthed, at what they beheld.

"Holy crap." Harris sucked in a deep breath of the hot air and then let it out with a hiss. The primordial-looking forest was a land of giants. Everything was oversized, with some of the tree trunks being as wide around as a house.

He noticed in their leafy canopies that spread wide and actually merged together creating a dense umbrella-like cover that they moved and were teemed with hidden life. All manner of chirps, squeaks, and clicks emanated from deep inside, with now and then something taking flight, gliding, or leaping from one tree to another. There was also the far-away boom of an animal trumpeting as if coming from the throat of an elephant the size of an office block.

There were gossamer vapors of a humid heat mist curling through the tree trunks and limbs, and he looked upward and squinted. The sky was like a cauldron of boiling-red liquid that made the very air seem red.

He remembered from Mike Monroe's notes that the theory was there were miles' thickness of volcanic glass shielding them from the worst effects of the seething liquid that generated this world's heat and light. It was a sobering thought that just a few miles over their heads was untold trillions of tons of molten metal and magma being held back by a thin transparent skin.

He turned away from it. Harris was chosen to lead this mission because he had the skills, and also nerves of steel. But right now, he felt creeping self-doubt and that made a tingle of fear run up his spine.

"*Ho. Lee. Shit.*" Bull shook his head. "It *is* real."

"And at last before me I behold the hot red from my nightmares." Harris turned to Mike and Jane and raised an eyebrow.

"Very prophetic; who said that?" Jane asked.

"I did, just then." Harris chuckled and turned back to the glaring vista.

"Well I'll be damned; they were right." Hitch grinned. "It *is* goddamn red."

"And hot," Bull said. "Reminds me of the Congo. Same sort of jungle too." He squinted. "Except this looks bigger and meaner."

Harris stared out at the jungle for a moment, and then carefully walked forward out from under the lip of the cave mouth. He turned, looked up at the rock above them and squinted. "Nothing. Looks like your giant wasp critters are gone."

Mike came forward, put a hand over his brows and also looked up. "Maybe when the war party came, they killed them all. Overwhelmed them."

Harris walked back up to the cave entrance. "Shame, wanted to see 'em." He then pulled out a small box and switched it on. He angled it around, until he got a fix on what he was looking for. "Well I'll be damned; found them." He looked up and then indicated a place along the cliff face and toward the coast. "That way."

"What is that thing?" Jane asked.

"Well, we were lucky to get a heads-up on the Russian mission before they left. One of our deep cover operatives managed to get one of their team to carry a tracking tab. And we're homing in on it."

"You bribed them?" Jane asked.

Harris chuckled. "Nope, got him blind drunk, and then our female operative inserted it under his skin." He grinned. "I said he was carrying it. I didn't say he knew he was."

"Ouch." Jane frowned and then looked out at the jungle. "If they came from the Krubera then they should have come from that direction." She pointed out toward the towering trees.

"Maybe they came a different way; trying to avoid some of the landmines they stepped on last time," Harris said.

"The last time?" Mike asked. "What last time?"

Harris turned. "You do know they dragged poor old Katya Babikov with them, don't you?"

"You're kidding? She's in her seventies... and with multiple cancers." Jane scowled. "Those bastards."

"That they are." Harris looked at her. "Anyway, they're in that direction now. And if they're that way, then that's the way we're going."

Jane peered along the cliff face. That wasn't a direction she knew and so they had no idea what lay ahead. She had thought that seeing as they had Katya with them they would have retraced her steps, and Harris could have simply met the Russians somewhere midway.

She let her eyes move along the massive wall of rock; the column mountain ran for another half-mile and then there was the beginning of a small line of flat-topped mountains. Following that just through the rising heat mist she thought could just make out a distant coastline.

She and the team had removed their helmets and replaced them with foreign legion-style hats that had a brim and also covered their neck and ears: a form of wrap-around sunglasses like goggles.

Harris pushed his goggles up and then lifted a small set of binoculars to his eyes. He panned it along the far coastline for a moment and then handed them to Jane.

"No sign of our friends, but what do you make of those things a few miles out on the waterline?"

She took the glasses and focused on the objects. "Could be something washed into the shallows. Or could be some sort of animal. Or maybe boats," Jane said after a while. "But whose?"

He turned and grinned. "Maybe it's how your lobster people arrived."

"Maybe," Mike said. "We never ascertained whether they lived in the water or totally on the land. We were a bit preoccupied with getting the hell away from them."

"Probably in the water, if they're like, you know, lobsters and stuff," Bull announced.

"Not necessarily." Alistair frowned into the distance. "On the surface we have many terrestrial crustaceans. Ones like the giant coconut crab, the *Birgus latro*, also known as the robber crab. It is the largest land-living arthropod in the world and grows to three feet across. Plus they're fantastically strong. They can tear open a coconut."

Alistair opened his hands wide. "They're big and tough, and have one of the thickest exoskeletons on the planet. They also have branchiostegal lungs, which are used instead of the vestigial gills for breathing. In fact, in their adult form, they'd drown in water. Did you know that?"

"Yeah, stop talking, Professor." Harris rolled his eyes. "A simple: *yes, they could live on land*, woulda been just fine." He then pointed.

"That coastline is in the direction we want to go, so guess we'll find out what those things are soon enough." Harris circled a finger in the air. "Load 'em up and move 'em out, people."

"Harris." Mike took a quick look back over his shoulder. "Should we guard the cave?"

"Against what? Who?" He raised his eyebrows, but then shook his head. "At this point there is no threat. Best not to split our forces." He raised his chin. "You two good to go?"

"Okay, and yeah we're good," Mike replied.

Jane stayed silent.

CHAPTER 11

Center of the Earth – 10-miles North East of the Monroe Team

Dmitry Varanov, the Russian expedition leader, raised a hand to stop his team. He turned about slowly and then looked up at the seething, red ceiling above them.

Right here, must be by now, he thought and then clicked his fingers to one of his men. "Mr. Chekov, take a position fix. This will be it."

Leonid Chekov nodded and immediately set to unfolding the positioning pad and its pulser. The device fired a signal pulse through the layers of the Earth, all the way through the mantle and crust, and then continued up to the orbiting Sokolov, Bird of Prey, satellite system.

In turn, the Sokolov would immediately return the pulse and give them a position in relation to the surface that was accurate to within ten feet. *Brilliant technology*, Dmitry thought, *and more advanced than anything the Americans had.*

As he waited, he surveyed his surroundings and his jaw set. He loathed it here: dripping foliage that seemed to exhale heat and humidity like the breath of a dragon, and everything they encountered seemed alien, from the oversized vegetation to the colossal geology, the waterways, and even the weird smells. And the worst was the animals that were like something conjured from a mad artist's insect nightmare.

He'd seen gargantuan creatures like moving skyscrapers pushing aside mighty trees on elephantine legs. Also flying things as large as jetliners that had stiff and veined bat-like wings. And once they encountered a living hole in the ground, fifty feet across, and lined with inward-pointing teeth as if some monstrous worm lay hidden there just waiting for some blundering thing to fall into its red maw.

Dmitry also hated that there was no nighttime, and therefore no respite from the constant hellish light and heat. Plus the continual glaring red light affected his and his team's mood: everyone was sleep-deprived, on edge, and understandably so.

When he was young his mother used to tell him about good and evil, heaven and hell, and how good people ascended to a blue paradise in the sky, and the bad people's souls were sent down to a hot, red Hell.

He now knew this was where they went, and perhaps each of these nightmarish creatures they encountered were actually the souls of wrongdoers, their true face finally exposed, as they were banished from the Earth's surface.

And here I am as well. But am I just passing through, or trapped like those others' souls for eternity? Dmitry wondered morosely.

He held up a hand and saw on its back the familiar faded military tattoo of a snarling wolf holding a dagger in its mouth, and underneath, the motto: *Death or Victory.*

At least for now I'm still human, he thought and exhaled. He squared his shoulders before turning. "Well?" he demanded of his man.

Chekov read the returned pulse information as it presented as a grid map on the tiny screen he had laid out. He began to nod as he looked up.

"This is it. Estonia, directly under Ämari Air Base." He began to pack the positioning equipment away.

Dmitry squinted as he looked up toward the fiery ceiling above them. It swirled and raged like liquid anger with its furious heat. And thousands of miles above that, their goal.

In Estonia, and right on Russia's doorstep, the Americans had constructed an airbase. It had been tolerated in the past, as it was a lesser-grade, low-traffic airfield complex and could only service lighter craft and helicopters.

But that was now due to change. The new American president had approved a multibillion dollar budget to increase the base's size and capabilities so it could accommodate a tactical fighter aircraft parking apron and taxiway to support the new F-35 strike fighters, and worse, bombers.

Dmitry ground his teeth. If that wasn't enough of a provocation, they were also planning Special Operations Command training and barrack facilities at the base. It had now turned from a minor political irritant, to a major military headache.

Attacking the base overtly or even by one of its proxies would provoke significant economic sanctions plus possible military retaliation. Neither, Russia was ready for. Something more clandestine was required and that was where he and his team came in.

Dmitry turned and smiled at the frail old woman. Even though she wore a hat with a veil over the front to shield her from the blazing red heat, and perhaps hide her visage from the group, he knew she watched him.

Dmitry went and knelt beside her. She didn't move a muscle as he placed his hand over hers that were folded in her lap.

"Have you got everything you need?" Dmitry asked softly.

He could just make out her features underneath the veil and was sure her eyes shifted toward him. She remained still and mute.

"You're very brave." He squeezed her hand that felt like a small bundle of sticks wrapped in parchment. He smiled into the veil. "And we appreciate you being here to help and guide us." He waited another moment, but there was no response.

Dmitry couldn't really blame her. The government officialdom had basically threatened her with solitary confinement and restriction of her medicines to force her to come with them. And any reward she may experience on return would only be if she or any of them survived.

So far she had refused to be a burden on them, and he felt ashamed they had brought her, a woman that reminded him of his grandmother, on this perilous expedition.

He lowered his head to look under the brim of her hat. "And so Katya, this is where your hard work and advice pays off."

The old woman just sat still as stone. Dmitry gave her hand one last squeeze and rose to his feet. He turned to nod to his team, who watched him like hawks. There were nine of them, including Katya, and himself. He had brought together military specialists, engineers, and scientists.

Leonid Chekov, a military engineer, was his second-in-command, plus there was Mila Golobev, Nadia Zima, and Oleg Krupin as his scientists. They brought with them a mix of geology, biology, and medical expertise. And then there were his soldiers: Pavel, Viktor, and Sasha, as his brute force.

Together they had all already been in the center world many weeks and had mastered the tough scale down into the Krubera cave as they followed the instructions of the old woman.

Katya had been allowed to climb down some of the easier drops herself, but most times she had to be strapped to the back of one of the bigger soldiers like a child.

Her eyes had been saucers of fear on their way down. But other than the darkness, and the sheer drops, they had encountered nothing of the goblin-like creatures she described that plagued her own trip.

Maybe they had just been ghosts conjured by a tired and tortured mind and never really existed at all, Dmitry wondered.

But then on arriving via the fantastical gravity well, and then blowing a hole in the collapsed cave entrance, he had been left speechless: the world here was astounding, and amazing, and horrifying all at once. His scientists had been spellbound, no more so than Mila, the young evolutionary biologist who just in her first few minutes had a hundred theories as to how this world began and how the denizens had evolved.

And now they were ready to begin phase one of their true mission.

Dmitry clapped his hands together and then rubbed them. "And so, we execute our mission objective." He sucked in a deep breath and let it out. "Viktor, Sasha, prepare the HERP."

The two men immediately set about constructing the base generation unit, and then added a long tubelike structure over a tightly packed coil. The High Energy Resonance Pulser, or HERP, would direct a compressed-energy resonance beam upward, like a laser, but instead of focused light, it would deliver focused vibrations.

Dmitry watched his men construct the weapon. *So much power for something so small*, he thought.

He knew that vibratory or sonic-directed energy weapons had been in use for decades and spanned the infrasonic, ultrasonic, and audible ranges. The key was in the ability to produce directed resonance, and an infrasonic pulse generator could induce that electromagnetically.

Lower-grade weapons, already in use for crowd control in France and China, were successfully able to target a person's inner organs by resonating in their chest area or in their head. If the power level is low, the person may experience migraine, stomach cramps or palpitations as their organs were vibrated. But increasing the power level would turn their organs to jelly: total destruction at a cellular level.

And now Russia had taken it to the next level and increased the power a thousand-fold while also improving the targeting ability and its compression technology. The result was a militarized infrasonic generator that could theoretically be as destructive as a nuclear weapon. In computer simulations it worked perfectly. And it was his job to take it from the laboratory to the battlefield.

The men finished and sat back on their haunches, waiting. Dmitry stared upward for a moment. He would not even know if it worked until his command told him of the results.

There was no need to delay any further. Dmitry nodded.

"Fire."

Sasha pressed the button and an electronic whine filled the air and a glow emanated from within the stout canon-like pipe. The air around the pulser began to shimmer as the beam of highly agitated air moved upward, entering the glowing red sky and then racing through the thousands of miles of solid stone to the surface, all the way to Estonia and the American base.

"Pulse delivered, sir," Sasha said.

"Good." Dmitry nodded. "And so, we wait."

CHAPTER 12

Ämari US Air Base, Harjumaa, Estonia

Major Fred Lawrence stood with his hands on his hips and surveyed the state of his base. Tomorrow, U.S. Air Force Brig. Gen. Robert Agustin was paying a visit to inspect the new infrastructure and deterrence air fleet.

The long, newly widened and significantly reinforced runway now held twenty-four strike fighters all lined up. In addition, there were new maintenance shops, and below ground in reinforced bunkers were the barracks and repair workshops.

As far as he was concerned the upgrade wasn't a minute too soon. Just across the border was a massive geopolitical adversary, and one that was growing increasingly belligerent by the day, conducting probing intrusions into Estonian airspace, launching cyber-attacks on their radar systems, and even trying to plant agents as laborers onto the build sites.

Well, now he had some muscle to stand up to them and stop them from rolling right into Europe. It would keep Russia in check, so the US could focus on other adversaries flexing up further south.

Lawrence waved, acknowledging the chopper pilot: he'd do a last swing over the site to make sure everything was shipshape. The general would do the same, and if there anything out of place, he'd prefer to see it first.

Lawrence jumped into the cockpit, placed the earphones over his head and nodded to the pilot who immediately lifted off. They rose at a forty-five degree angle and firstly headed north. They'd do a few loops around the base, in ever-widening rings. He didn't really expect to find any issues, but he wanted the general's visit to go off without a hitch.

Congress had invested hundreds of millions into the upgraded Estonian base, and he wanted to ensure they thought they got their money's worth.

When they were around two-fifty feet in the air, Lawrence stared down at the orderly structures and the magnificent fleet of his lethal flock: A-10 Warthogs, F-15 Eagles, F-16 Falcons, F-22 Raptors, and F-35 Lightning Strike Fighters, all lined up in a criss-cross nose-to-nose pattern. Their beauty and lethality made his chest swell with pride. *Own the air, own the war*, was a maxim as old as military flight itself.

Lawrence squinted and then blinked several times. His brows knitted together as he tried to focus. The ground seemed to blur a little, and he lifted his sunglasses to rub his eyes with thumb and forefinger, before focusing again.

But the ground still blurred.

"You seeing this?" He asked.

"Yes, sir. Thought it was just the cabin vibrations," the pilot replied.

"Drop us down fifty feet," Lawrence requested.

The ground shimmered. Lawrence then saw people coming out of barracks and maintenance shops to turn one way then the other, obviously confused.

"What the hell..." He sat forward.

The ground seemed to swell upward, cracks appeared in the runway, and then they shot through the light.

"*Lift, lift,*" Lawrence shouted.

"Taking her up," the pilot replied and began to raise the chopper another hundred feet in the air over the base.

The cracks were in a circular pattern and running all around the base as if someone struck a pane of glass with a hammer. Light started to show through the cracks in the ground that still rose in the air like a pregnant belly, and then what looked like magma began to spatter onto the tarmac from within the scars.

"Good God." Lawrence's eyes widened. He knew if he were closer to the ground he would hear the screams as people fell flat, dropped into the fissures opening up, or became caught by the magma and then burst into flames like bugs on a hot skillet.

"Get them out," Lawrence whispered. But he knew he'd said it to no one.

The helicopter pulled back some more so they watched now from half a mile, as the radiated heat was becoming a risk to their craft.

In the next instant the huge blister had risen to a hundred feet in the air, and then burst, as magma and boiling gas vented. In the next second the entire base dropped into the collapsing crater.

The base comprising of two hundred and twelve people, massive infrastructure, and billions of dollars of air strike power, simply vanished as it dropped into a molten hole.

Lawrence lowered his hand from the mic button and sat back. He knew he was in shock, as the sights and sounds of the catastrophe seemed a million miles away.

"It's all gone," he whispered, his eyes blurring with tears. "Everything."

CHAPTER 13

Mike smiled at Jane who returned the gesture, and it immediately made him feel warm inside. *She's thawing*, he thought.

He looked up momentarily and felt the heat blast his cheeks and nose.

But how could anything *not* thaw in this damned heat? He squeezed his eyes shut and waited until the red dots stopped floating behind his lids.

They had set out along the face of the monolithic column mountain on a flat, rocky path. Hitch was out at point with the large Bull Simmons bringing up the rear. Harris came next, followed by Mike, then Jane, and Ally who had been ordered to keep an eye on Penny and Alistair.

In just an hour they were all soaked through with perspiration. Penny wiped a forearm across her brow and eyes.

"We're going to need to take salt tablets every second day if we keep losing water, salt, and minerals like this," Penny said. "I know we took the tablets, but not sure why we couldn't wear some sort of radiation skin-block as well."

"The smell," Mike replied.

"He's right," Alistair agreed. "Arthropods, especially the land-based ones, have exceedingly good senses of smell, and can detect single atoms of some chemicals for miles." He lifted his arm. "We're already taking perspiration bacterial blockers to keep the smell of our sweat to a minimum. But the odor of perfumes, deodorants, and lotions will stand out like a beacon."

"And ring the dinner bell," Jane added.

"Oh, yeah," Penny said. "I get it." She looked up. "Then hopefully we won't need to be under this blazing inferno for too long." She paused as she stared upward with one eye closed and the other crinkled. "Simply amazing."

They had to deal with the heat and constant bombardment of the glaring red glow for hours until they entered a stand of tall bamboo-like plants that seemed to have a path beaten between them.

Harris held up a hand. He looked over his shoulder to Mike and Jane. "Natural pathway or game trail?"

"Probably one turned into the other," Jane said as she looked up at the plants and then rapped on one. Just like bamboo, it sounded hollow.

Their woody toughness and closeness to each other created biological cage bars that would have made the going impossible if they tried to burrow through them.

Harris stared in at the dark trail. "Some of your beasties were experts in camouflage, *huh*?" he said.

"Near invisible," Mike replied. "Imagine a *T-*,rex armor-plated, and standing still as stone. And worse, you don't see it until you're right in front of it."

Harris began to chuckle. "Worst pep talk ever." He turned back to his team. "Hitch and Ally, two by two. And freaking eyes out, we might have a bogie in the brush."

"Yo." Both soldiers stepped forward now with their rifles tight in against their shoulders.

The trail they moved along was about six feet wide, but the towering bamboo-like stalks either side of them created a long corridor that closed overhead as the plant's canopy foliage joined up about fifty feet above them.

The upside was it gave a respite from the light and the heat. The downside was the gloom. Just a few dozen feet in, the thicket became dark and secretive.

Ally and Hitch slowed their progress and moved in a crouch like a pair of coiled springs with their guns at the ready.

Harris let them get a couple of dozen paces ahead out at point, and after a moment Hitch raised a hand and then said something out of the corner of his mouth to Ally. She nodded and tilted her head as though listening. Then she pointed out into the shadowed thicket.

It was then Mike noticed that the surrounding jungle that was once filled with the constant thrum of life had fallen deathly silent.

Ally held up a hand, fingers spread, and then changed to holding up just one finger before easing through the bamboo bars and into the thicket. Harris spoke over his shoulder to the group.

"Stay here." Harris moved slowly up to Hitch's position.

"Stay here," Mike repeated to Penny and Alistair as he and Jane also eased forward.

"What've you got?" Harris whispered, sighting along his gun at the forest of stalks.

Hitch kept his eyes on the thicket. "Heard something weird, just in there. Ally went to check it out."

Harris bared his teeth for a moment. "You remember that little speech I gave about no one goes anywhere by themselves?" He shook his head. "Idiots."

Harris took a few paces toward where Ally had left the trail. And then back, he cocked his head.

Mike and Jane were halfway to the soldiers but paused. Mike slowly turned; from the other side of the trail and from deep within the thicket came a sound, low but constant.

"Hear that?" He concentrated, trying to place it. "Celery." He turned to Jane. "Like when you're munching on celery."

Russ Hitch scoffed. "Hey yeah, that's the sound, like munching-crunching. But it was over there before." He pointed to where Ally left the trail.

"Contact," Harris yelled and spun with his gun up.

From out of the thicket sprinted Ally. Her eyes were wide and she sucked in her breath, hard. "They're coming; damn eating everything."

"Say again?"

"Things; grub things." Ally wiped her mouth. "Coming across the ground like a wave, like a wave of maggots, except big. Eating everything, plants and anything too slow to get out of their way." She turned about. "We do not want to be in front of them when they get here."

"Okay people, let's..." Harris went to wave them on, but then stopped dead. "*Ah*, shit." He stared. "They're coming in from that way as well."

"And in front," Jane said. "We need to go back."

Harris looked one way then the other. "Let's backtrack and go around."

"Look." Penny pointed down the track.

About two hundred yards back along the way they had just come, a rippling blanket of bodies undulated and squirmed toward them.

"Oh gross." Penny grimaced and backed up.

"Mike, Jane, what are they?" Harris pointed his weapon at the mass.

"We've never seen them before," Jane said. "Alistair?"

"*Huh*?" The young man seemed momentarily mesmerized. "Some sort of larval stage of fly or beetle."

The large grubs were a milky-yellow and bulbous-looking, exactly as Ally described: like giant maggots. Except these were nearly three feet long and had a hard, shining head and pair of scythe-like pincers that they used to cut down anything biological in front of them, and then feed into their mouths: plant, fungus, gastropod, or small animal. Their foraging and consuming was the source of the crunching noise they had heard.

"They've got us hemmed in," Bull said. "We need to make a hole. Burn 'em."

Harris shook his head. "There's too many. We'd exhaust our

ammunition." He looked about. "And we're not starting a fire while we're in the center of a damn bamboo thicket."

Harris spun to Jane and Mike. "I know you've not seen them before, but now would be a good time to hear from those voices of experience."

"Climb," Mike said. He dropped his pack and removed a length of rope that they all carried. "They're not touching the bamboo. So everyone do what I do. And hurry."

Everyone did as asked and had the rope in their hands in seconds. Mike cut two four-foot lengths, walked to one of the stout pole-like plants and tied one end around his left boot front. He then looped it round the long trunk and tied the end to his other boot. He then used the second piece of rope to loop around the trunk at shoulder level and wrapped it around his hands.

"We use gravity and we climb... like this." He pulled the rope tight in his hands and it gripped the bamboo-like pole as a demonstration. He then lifted his hands and dragged the looped rope higher and pulled. The rope tightened and locked on as his weight came down on it, gripped the trunk, and he pulled himself up a couple of feet. When he was up, the rope around his feet tightened against the trunk, allowing him to rest his arms or use them to move the rope higher and scale up another few feet.

"Like New Guinea coconut tree climbing," Mike said. "Our weight locks the rope against the trunk."

"I get it." Harris had already tied his ropes and began to climb by Ally, Hitch and Bull. Penny was also making slow progress, and Jane was already five feet up from the ground.

Only Alistair couldn't quite get the hang of it.

Penny turned, frowning. "Hurry up, Alistair."

"I am. But I just, can't..." he looked over his shoulder. And probably shouldn't have. The grubs were now only a few dozen feet from him, and Mike could see the jungle being mowed down around them with the only thing untouched the obviously inedible trunks of the bamboo.

The giant, voracious bug larvae were consuming anything below three feet. They'd make short work of a soft human being.

A small creature that looked like a kangaroo with a hard shell tried to leap over the grubs, but only managed to land amongst them. Before it could leap again, it began to squeal and was pulled down. The grubs in its vicinity flushed a brilliant red as they gorged themselves on the poor creature's shell, flesh and blood.

No matter how many times Alistair tried, he just couldn't get the concept of pull, hang, climb, and then repeat. And the more nervous he got, the more he fumbled.

"He's not going to make it," Jane said from twenty feet up. She turned to look down at Mike.

"Damn it." Mike grimaced as he watched the near-panicking entomologist. "Alistair, untie yourself."

"What?" Alistair said. "But..."

"Shut up and do it, quickly. And then run to the bottom of my tree-trunk." Mike relaxed his feet and handgrip on the trunk, and the rope loosened, causing him to slide the dozen feet he had scaled back down the ground.

The young man even struggled to get his shoes out of the rope-locks, and just watching him gave Mike a knot of tension in his stomach. The grubs were now just five feet from him.

"*Hurry up,*" Mike yelled.

Alistair stepped out of the rope loops, tripped, and fell flat on his face. He crawled forward and then got up to run the last few feet.

Mike was waiting for him. "Climb on my backarms over my shoulders and around my chest: *not* my neck. Then wrap your legs around my waist." Mike looked over his shoulder. The grubs must have detected them, as they had turned and all were swarming toward their tree. "Ready?"

The grubs were just a few feet from them and Alistair clung onto him like a giant monkey. Mike sucked in a huge breath, threw the loop of rope about two feet up the pole-like trunk and then heaved himself and Alistair up.

Even though Alistair wasn't a big man, the strain was more than Mike expected and the rope slipped as it tried to grip the trunk's smooth, woody texture. Mike rested his feet in his rope stirrups, and then threw the handheld loops higher again.

Behind him he could hear the crunching of the grubs' jaws and didn't want to look back as he knew they were right behind them now. Over the noise of the grubs he heard Alistair's fear-filled rapid breathing.

He pulled himself up another foot, knowing he was still far too low. His hands were becoming purple as the blood was being cut off by the strain of the weight on the rope tightening around his hands.

He used his feet to rest a second, and then dragged himself and Alistair up another foot. Mike looked across to Jane who was twenty feet up and staring down, not at him, but at what was happening below him. He knew he must have been only about three feet up by now.

"They're... here," Alistair wheezed into his ear.

Mike agonizingly dragged himself up another foot and chanced a look down. He felt his skin crawl as the grubs were actually climbing on top of one another and with each layer it brought them closer to his ankles.

His hands were now numb as he tried to lift another foot higher, but his shoulders rebelled and he knew he didn't have the strength.

I just need to rest for a few seconds, he thought, and rested his damp forehead against the rounded trunk.

With his skin in contact with the plant he felt the vibrations against the wood and jerked back to look down. A few of the things had taken to chewing into the tough bark: not on any of the other bamboo-like stalks, but just on his. The objective was clear.

"They're cutting us down." He looked up to the others perched on the other stalks, safe. "A little help here, guys."

Hitch and Ally begin to fire into the squirming mass, but even striking two of the grubs at once left hundreds to carry on the climb and also the cutting.

Harris leaned back, using just one hand to hold the straps and reached into a pouch pocket. He drew forth an incendiary flare, bit the top off, punched it against the trunk he was on so it flared to life, and tossed it down at the base of Mike's tree.

The effect was instantaneous. The creatures boiled over each other like glistening mud and pulled back from the flare. Harris dropped another one on the opposite side of the trunk, causing the rest of the maggot-like things to create some space around Mike's perch.

Mike looked up and nodded to Harris who winked in return.

The flares would only burn for a few minutes, and Mike knew it was now a race to see whether the grubs would wait just outside of the ring of heat and smoke as the flares burned out, or if they gave up and continued on in their locust-like devouring of everything in their path as they crossed the jungle floor.

Alistair shifted on his back, and Mike slid a few inches. "Keep still, or we're dead," Mike hissed.

Mike looked out over the jungle and saw that the moving carpet extended as far as he could see into the twilight-dark thicket. The flares had already burned for several minutes, and from his recollection, modern heat flares burned for anything from three minutes to ten depending on their brand, storage, and price.

Alistair shifted again, getting restless or sliding.

"Sorry, I'm slipping," Alistair moaned.

Mike just closed his eyes and counted off seconds, trying not to think about the agony in his hands, fingers, shoulders, or his back where Alistair dug in. Alistair started to slip a little more, and a small voice in his head whispered to just let him go.

In another few minutes, he heard Jane calling his name. He looked up into her shocked face and knew the strain was twisting his features.

"I can see the end of the swarm," Jane said and looked out to where the creatures had appeared. "Just a few more minutes. Hang in there."

He nodded slowly and lowered his head to the trunk and shut his eyes again. Below him the first of the flares sputtered and went out.

It was about thirty seconds between flares, so the next would be burned out then. With his eyes closed he counted down from thirty, and every second he expected to feel the nudge on his boot as the first of the worm-like things reached him.

The crunch of the devouring horde continued on, and then it became everything, as the fizz of the flare was suddenly not there anymore.

Time was up. He opened his eyes. The grubs were back at the base of his tree stalk.

Harris fired his handgun at a few that were beginning to gnaw on the wood again, but then in their revolting peristaltic wave-like motion they moved away across the ground. The bulbous and slimy-looking moving carpet had scoured the Earth and continued on.

And then they were gone. Mike saw that the jungle had been cleared of everything organic as effectively as if it had been swept clean. He continued to look for a moment more and then allowed his hands to loosen. For a few seconds nothing happened as his fingers were swollen like fat, purple sausages. Then he fell back and collapsed to the ground that was only four feet below them. Alistair, still clinging to his back, cushioned his fall.

Mike lay there sucking in huge breaths and holding up his ruined hands as he watched the others slide down their bamboo poles. Harris sent Bull, Hitch and Ally out to scout the area and he came and crouched beside Mike.

He grinned. "Bravest and dumbest thing I've ever seen." He nodded and then turned to Alistair. His expression hardened. "Son, you won't live long unless you learn to do the basic things right. Next time, Mr Monroe might not be there to pull your ass out of the fire."

Alistair just nodded.

Jane came and squatted beside Mike. She leaned down to kiss his forehead, and then handed him her canteen. "Having fun yet?" she asked.

He took the canteen in two hands, as his fingers still wouldn't bend. He sipped. "That was close." Mike held out a throbbing hand and Jane took it and rubbed it for a moment to try and push more circulation into his throbbing fingers. Then she used it to haul him to his feet.

"What were they?" Harris asked. "Looked like giant maggots."

"Maybe they were," Jane said. "We never encountered them when we were down here. Maybe we encountered the adult form, but..." She shrugged.

"Could have been a lot of things," Alistair said, dusting himself off. He got to his feet and looked to Mike. "Thank you, Mike. I, *ah*, kinda froze up there."

Mike nodded, but felt he needed to repeat Harris' warning. "You can't do that here. You can't just freeze up. You just have to act." Mike patted the young guy's shoulder. "Do better next time."

"All my life when I get scared everything just stops working properly." Alistair shared a lopsided grin with them. He then turned in the direction of the horde. "This, swarm, is not unprecedented; there's a carnivorous caterpillar in Hawaii called *Eupithecia*, from a large genus of moth. Those things looked like some sort of beetle larvae, and there are plenty of those on the surface that are meateaters as well, but..." He looked up.

"But we're not in Kansas anymore," Jane finished for him.

"Exactly," Alistair replied. "It's undoubtedly something new, and they could grow into something very different from what we know or expect." He grinned. "It was amazing."

"Oh yeah, you looked like you were having the time of your life."

"Okay people." Harris slid his rifle over his shoulder. "That's enough excitement for now, and we've still got a job to do; let's keep moving."

Jane turned to Mike and then snorted softly. "We've only just begun."

CHAPTER 14

Dmitry waited and watched as Chekov pointed the receiver's antenna toward the flaming red ceiling. The information squirts were super compressed but still took up to an hour to arrive. As usual, they would be short and to the point.

In another moment, Chekov's brow creased as he read the short sentence. He turned, his smile wide.

"Complete success."

Dmitry exhaled and closed his eyes. *A complete success*, he repeated the words in his mind. Very few soldiers get to play such a significant role in their country's future. And his role may well be to see Russia become the world's new leaders.

Chekov quickly turned back to the device as more words started to appear. "New target being assigned." He held up a hand and slowly his eyes widened and then he whistled softly. He sat back and turned to Dmitry again.

"Kosovo... *Camp Bondsteel*."

Dmitry worked to keep a straight face. He simply nodded and turned away. He knew Bondsteel very well; it was the largest US base in Europe and their bulwark against any threats in that area: namely Russia.

The huge camp held nearly fifteen hundred soldiers: six hundred and fifty of America's best from North Dakota Army National Guard and more than eight hundred regular soldiers from across the states in Task Force Falcon.

In fact, the site was so large it was basically a small, militarized American city with the best hospital in Kosovo, three gyms, recreation facilities, football and softball fields, a film theatre, and its own police and fire stations. In addition, it even had a Taco Bell and Burger King.

Dmitry exhaled slowly through his nose. Taking that out would render the Americans weakened to the point of irrelevance in that theatre. And they would never know where or how it happened.

He rubbed his chin making a rasping sound against the stubble. And if they managed to destroy that, then what would be next: Fort Bragg, Eglin Air Force Base, or even USSTRATCOM itself?

He smiled; they, *he*, would change the power dynamics in the world for a generation. Or perhaps forever.

Major Dmitry Varanov straightened his spine and checked his bearings. The distance between Estonia and Kosovo was thousands of miles and would take months to reach. But that was only in surface distance time. Down here, it would only take them around a week, *if* Dmitry pushed them.

He turned, his eyes alighting on the old woman. He knew he didn't need her anymore and wished he could somehow send her home. A more ruthless leader would simply abandon her. Or mercifully, put a bullet in her head.

But Dmitry was a man of honor, and he would do his best to get her home. He clapped his hands once.

"Rest time is over. Heading is south-southeast. And we will be moving at double time."

EPISODE 08

The globe began with the sea, so to speak; and who knows if it will not end with it?

— Jules Verne

CHAPTER 15

The group emerged from the bamboo thicket, and Harris spread his team either side of him without venturing out from the overhanging growth.

"Well I'll be damned." The ex-soldier snorted softly. "It's like a sea of blood."

Jane looked out over the vista and inhaled the scent of brine, drying weed, and baking sand. She placed a hand over her eyes and looked over the near-endless expanse of water.

Harris was right, it did look like blood, and she had thought the same thing when she first saw it.

There were vapors rising from the glassy water like tiny wraiths, and it lapped in little waves on midnight-black sand. She already knew the water was tropical warm, and other than the vapor ghosts there was nothing above the surface: no boats, no floating debris, and no reefs. But she knew that below that calm facade, things lived, big things.

"You brought us here because you wanted our counsel," Jane said. "So here's some real strong counseling: avoid the water." Her smile was flat.

Harris nodded. "I remember your notes." He looked back at Mike. "The sea spider thing." He turned back to the sea. "We can follow the shoreline, staying close to the cliff face."

"What happens if the land runs out?" Mike asked. "We get to the end of the coast, and it simply ends at the water?"

Harris nodded. "Fair question." He grinned. "But that will all depend on where the Russians have gone, won't it?"

Harris suddenly put his hand over a pouch at his waist as it vibrated. "Got a blip." He retrieved the small box from within a pouch, and he began to access the data. "Coming through now."

The group waited and watched him as his brows came together.

"What the f…" His eyes began to blaze and he growled deep in his chest. He slowly looked up, his gaze almost volcanic. "Ämari in Estonia… it's gone."

Ally frowned. "Say again, boss?"

He turned back to the screen. "Command says our base there has been completely destroyed. Some sort of underground and targeted destruction through vibration waves."

Harris stared for a moment more, just a small vein pulsing in his temple now. He spoke softly. "Now do you see?" He stared into Mike's eyes. "Now do you see why we are here?"

"How many dead?" Mike asked.

Harris shrugged. "There were over two hundred military and civilian personnel at Ämari base. No idea how many lived or died. But assume all of them died."

"Those sons of bitches."

"Thank you, Ms Baxter and Mr Monroe." Harris lifted his eyes to them. "If not for your work, we would have no idea why or how this occurred. It would have been a mystery." He spoke through his teeth. "But now we do."

"How are they able to do that?" Penny asked.

"Some sort of new technology," Jane replied.

"We'll find out, what and how." Harris' jaw was set as he turned to look along their faces. "This is what they're doing down here. And this is why we are here. They are obviously planning more than scouting for sites or performing scientific explorations; they are enacting their covert war plan. Right now. That means our observe-and-report mission also needs to adapt and evolve. Our job is to stop these guys and if possible, capture that technology."

"So we *are* going to war?" Alistair said. "At the center of the Earth."

Harris' eyes slid to the scientist. "They've already declared war with the destruction of our military base. They just don't know that we know yet. And that is our biggest military advantage right now." Harris' jaw jutted for a moment. "And in fact, sir, our job is to *stop* a war." Harris looked from Alistair to the rest of the group. "Does anyone here think for one New York minute that these guys will now all just go home?"

"No sir, they're goddamn going to move it up the scale."

"That's what I expect, Hitch," Harris replied. "They'll already have another target in mind, and Estonia was just a test run. Next site will be bigger, more destructive, and even more deadly."

"Oh my..." Jane whispered.

"They think our military leaders don't know what's going on. But they do. And that means, if we can't stop their next act, then our military will respond. With everything they've got."

"World War," Mike said.

Harris just stared for several seconds. "Now do you see why we need to find those bastards and stop them?"

"Do you think we can capture them?" Penny asked.

Ally burst out laughing. "Lady, these guys just killed around two hundred Americans, probably without giving it a second thought. You really think they'll let us take them prisoner and walk them out of here with their hands on top of their heads?" Her face hardened. "We kill 'em all. Or they'll kill us."

Harris turned away and lifted his field glasses to his eyes for a moment. "I estimate they've got a week's head start on us. We need to close that time and distance lead, run 'em down." He lowered the glasses, and then paused. He turned to Ally. "They're headed southwest; what bases have we got in their path?"

"Dozens," she replied. "Italian, German, and shared NATO bases in most countries."

"Now tell me the biggest and most formidable." Harris waited.

"No question, Bondsteel, in Kosovo," Ally replied.

Harris exhaled slowly through his nose and began to nod. "Yeah, that'll be it; one of our largest and most advanced bases in Europe." Harris' mouth turned down. "Plot me a course, and we'll see if we can get in front of them."

Harris looked briefly at Alistair. "Time to stop a war."

CHAPTER 16

Dmitry turned and clicked his fingers to get Katya's attention, but she ignored him.

"Pavel, bring her," he said to his soldier and then waved Katya to the front. Pavel tried to help the old woman toward him, but she swiped his hands away.

He grinned; even with her advanced age and her illness she still seemed athletic and feisty. He leaned forward.

"Are you okay, Ms. Babikov?" Dmitry asked.

She nodded, but under her veil he saw she was sweating profusely, and even though they had been instructed to give her cortisone to boost her metabolism and appetite, and he was personally making sure she got plenty of food and water, he still saw she was wasting away. There were ulcerated cancers covering her exposed skin, and he just hoped they weren't spreading inside her body to then destroy her internal organs.

Dmitry took her hand. It felt like a small bony bird; he patted it. "Do you remember this place?"

"My team… never came this way." She coughed for a moment and then shook her head. "But I don't like the look of it."

"I don't either." Dmitry smiled and turned back to the gloomy path forward. "Then it seems we are the first. Unfortunately."

The area of forest he stood before was so dense it was dark as night just a dozen feet in. And worse, between them there were barbed vines with hooks like cats' claws, and woven so tightly together, they were near impassable.

There was one way through them, and disconcertingly the tunnel-like pathway was covered in some sort of webbing; not the gossamer of spider silk, but thicker and glistening like veins of spilled varnish. And it coated everything.

Dmitry reached out to break a piece off. It was only slightly sticky and was a little like fresh amber. He called over his shoulder to his senior scientist.

"Oleg."

The man came to the front of the line. Dmitry held out the substance to him. "Your opinion."

Oleg took it and held it up, worked it in his hands a moment, held it to his nose for a second more, but then just shrugged.

"Like *Iriska*, toffee," he said.

"Yes, but could it be from the plant, like hardening sap or resin?" Dmitry asked.

Oleg rubbed his thumb hard against it, looked at it and then sniffed it. He frowned and then sniffed again. In a flash he drew his long knife and slashed the end of a tree branch hanging close to them. Milky sap ran like blood and dripped to the ground. He dipped a finger in it, and then sniffed that as well. After a few seconds he wiped his hands on his pants and looked to Dmitry.

"I don't think it's from any plant. At least not this plant. If I had to guess, I think it's something that was excreted. Biologically."

"Excreted?" Dmitry asked.

"Like bees make the wax for honeycomb, or the lac beetle creates something very similar to this that is turned into shellac – hard but also smooth." Oleg handed it back.

Dmitry looked around slowly. "So, maybe from a bug, *huh*?" He exhaled. "Either a very big bug, or a lot of bugs."

Dmitry knew that going around this section of jungle would cost them a full day. He didn't want to do that, and besides, the sooner they got their job done, the sooner they'd all be home.

He turned to the group, all watching him, and he pointed at his eyes with two fingers and then to the trail through the dark forest. He then circled a finger once in the air and led them in.

Dmitry watched his foot placement, because some of the resin mixture crackled when he placed his weight on it. Looking up, he saw it was woven right throughout the tree limbs, creating tunnel-like structures, or simply hanging from branches like huge amber shawls. Once in amongst the web tunnels he could smell the overpowering scent and understood why Oleg said it was not resin; there was no sharp tang of sap, but instead a chemical sweetness that was cloying and unpleasant. It made him a little queasy and reminded him of something from his childhood but he couldn't quite remember what.

Chekov eased up beside him. "You notice? There's no sound."

"Quiet as a tomb." Dmitry half-turned. "But we're being watched, I can feel it. Can you?"

Chekov nodded. "Ever since we entered."

The group eased forward, carefully placing one foot in front of the other. There were nine in the Russian team, including Katya, who was like a small ghost in amongst the bigger men and women.

He had placed her in the center of his group, and Pavel and Sasha flanked her. Also toward the middle of the group were his scientists, Mila Golobev, Nadia Zima, and Oleg Krupin, and Viktor at the rear. His friend

Chekov walked at his shoulder.

The air became thicker and more cloying the deeper in they traveled. The resin-like matter glistened in places, and where it was still wet it was sticky, reminding Dmitry of Oleg's comment about it being like caramel toffee.

Also, in amongst the tree limbs and resin webbing were things that looked like dark balls all crowded together like massive puff balls or grape bunches except they were easily four feet across.

"What are those, some sort of fruit or fungus?" Chekov asked.

"Like big mushrooms, maybe?" Dmitry replied in a hushed tone.

Up ahead there was something else. A long bundle of something stuck to one of the enormous tree trunks. Dmitry held up a hand to stop the group and he carefully crab-walked forward. When he was within a few feet of it, he saw that it was some sort of creature, swaddled up inside the resin netting.

He leaned forward and saw the thing was roughly twice as big as a man, and looked like a giant cockroach except with an elongated face like that of a horse with jagged teeth. It would have been a formidable animal when it was alive. And yet, it had been subdued.

Dmitry reached for his flashlight and shone a light on the thing. He could then see that all along its body there were holes roughly the size of his fist, and by the way the carapace of the animal seemed to have been broken open, the holes looked like they started from within the creature. Dmitry turned and waved Chekov closer.

He lifted his light again. "What do you make of this?"

Chekov frowned. "Looks like something came out of it and punched its way right through the exoskeleton." He turned, looked around and then up. "Look."

Above them, hanging like ghastly Christmas ornaments, were more of the webbing sacks stuck to the mighty limbs or hanging from them by cords of the tough and sticky resin.

"I think this is a nest," Chekov whispered. "And we are right in the middle of it."

Dmitry suddenly remembered what the smell reminded him of: when he was a child, he crawled under his family house and saw what he thought was a large ball of cottonwool stuck to a beam. He pulled it free with his bare fingers and as soon as he did it exploded into hundreds of tiny spiders running everywhere at once and especially up his arm. The smell had been like this: sweet and nauseating.

Dmitry grimaced and tugged on his friend's shoulder. "I think we should hurry."

In a few more minutes, where they walked was now completely

covered in resin, and the air was so humid a mix of perspiration and water dripped from his chin and nose.

Dmitry gripped his gun tighter. The grape bunches were everywhere now, but he had no desire to see if they were any sort of fungal, animal or edible fruits as the acrid smell was making his eyes water.

Passing through another aperture, they entered an even larger space that might have been in the center of three huge tree trunks, but there was so much of the material strung about it created a cave that glistened like honey and amber in the light from their flashlights. In another time it might have been beautiful, but here, now, it was ominous as the entire ceiling was crowded with the bulbous objects.

Dmitry halted the group as they surveyed the multiple exits and he decided on their next move. A humid, foul-smelling mist was at ground level rising just to their knees, and poking up through it were several of the large greyish bulbs.

Mila Golobev, the biologist, carried her gun awkwardly. She was a scientist who had been given some basic weapons training before departing and never looked comfortable with it in her hands.

She carefully approached the bulbous growth and when just a foot from it, prodded it with the barrel of her gun. It shivered and seemed to pull into the ground a little tighter.

"Maybe some sort of fungus growth rather than a tree seed pod or fruit. But displaying thigmotropism reaction to touch, more like a forest puffer ball." Mila looked around. "It's certainly humid enough in here to support a range of fungal species."

"Doctor Golobov, please get back in line," Dmitry replied.

"Okay. Just one more thing." Mila looked it over one last time, her gun barrel still pointed at the large orb as though she wanted to give it another prod. But instead she held the gun in one hand and reached out with the other.

She gently laid it on the bloated thing. She grinned and spoke over her shoulder. "It's warm."

"Touch *nothing*," Dmitry insisted.

She was about to turn when the thing shivered again and made a squelching noise. Instead of pulling in tighter to the ground it suddenly lifted several inches. Mila went to step back, but her foot had become glued to some of the sticky resin.

She fell back onto her butt. And as her finger had been within the trigger guard, when she hit the ground, her rifle discharged a single round.

The noise was excruciatingly loud in the tomb-silent space. Everyone froze, but when the echoing boom finally fell away, they weren't left with silence anymore.

There was a sound like a breeze in unseen trees, a rustling and sliding noise.

"Where's that coming from?" Dmitry whispered.

"All around us. Everywhere," Chekov replied, turning slowly.

"Form up, get in tight," Dmitry said. His soldiers herded everyone into a close group with the scientists and Katya at the center.

Mila tugged at her glued feet. She froze when the bulbous dark ball rose up before her. Her mouth dropped open and she could only stare as the thing turned toward her. It wasn't a fruit, giant seedpod, or even some sort of giant mushroom, but instead the bulb was an abdomen, and its front half looked like a long and spiked skull with massive pincers each side of a constantly moving mouth.

The skull-like face that was crowded with too many dark and pitiless eyes fixed on her, and it began to lift itself on long shining legs. Mila screamed, long and piercing, and tried to scuttle backward on her backside, but her feet were still stuck fast.

She lurched forward to try and untie her boots as the creature loomed over, but Pavel fired, blowing a hole in the center of its cluster of eyes. It shrieked, insanely loudly and its legs drummed madly on the ground.

And then the hive woke up. From all around them the bulbs lifted on long spindly legs and turned from their resting or hibernating positions to gaze at the small soft animals within their hive.

Dmitry felt the weight of a thousand eyes on them, and then like an army that had been ordered to attack, they began to climb and drop down toward them.

"Fire," he yelled and opened up with deadly accuracy.

The soldiers had formed up in a defensive ring and their guns filled the nesting chamber with hundreds of blistering rounds, puncturing many of the bulbous abdomens and blowing long legs from bodies. But for every creature they hit, more appeared from out of the glistening amber tunnels.

"Move it." Dmitry began to edge back and then turn to run, using his gun to clear a path. From behind him a percussion blast meant one of his team had fired a grenade. Immediately the room was filled with heat and more smoke.

Dmitry heard Mila scream again, but this time it seemed further away, and when he spun to her, he was in time to see her being dragged into one of the amber tunnels, and then gone. In seconds her voice became fainter and fainter until their gunfire, his team's roars, and the hellish squeals of the attacking horrors swallowed it entirely.

Dropping from the ceiling, and emerging from the tunnels in the resin hive, hordes of the creatures attacked them. The smoke from the now red-hot guns and blasts created a thick fog, and Dmitry reached back to grab Chekov.

"Get them moving."

Dmitry began to push forward to what he hoped was the way out. The tunnel he worked toward was narrower and would force them to move in a line, but he hoped at least it wouldn't allow them to be attacked from all sides.

The crush of the attacking monstrous creatures was so tight, that simply firing their guns everywhere struck several at once, and their sticky ichors sprayed every one of them.

Sasha was carrying Katya, and even the scientists were firing off round after round. From behind, more grenades detonated and the squeals became maddening in their crescendo.

In another few seconds, they were all inside the tunnel and Dmitry ran hard, aiming and firing at anything that got in his way.

"Look," Pavel screamed from behind them.

Dmitry turned back and saw there was no pursuit. But what he did see was the tunnel mouth shrinking. As he watched, the creatures squirted a viscous liquid on the tunnel walls, and then used their mouths to fashion it into a curtain. In another moment, they had totally sealed off the hive chamber from the humans.

"Are they sealing us in or out?" Chekov asked.

Dmitry turned away. "Given we probably just took down a few hundred of their hive, I'm thinking sealing us out."

"What about Mila?" Nadia demanded.

Dmitry turned.

"Should we go after her?" She scowled at the soldier.

"No, I am afraid she is gone. She did this to herself. But you are free to go after her." Dmitry gave the other female scientist a hard look until she wilted. He then turned to nod to Chekov. "Take us out of this Hell, Mr. Chekov."

The man saluted and headed off. Dmitry turned back to the group. "And when I say don't touch anything, I mean *don't fucking touch anything*." His eyes burned. "Or I'll kill you myself."

He turned to follow Chekov out of the hive.

CHAPTER 17

The White House, 1600 Pennsylvania Avenue, Washington, D.C

President Dan Redner, Commander in Chief, sat behind the solid English oak desk made from the timbers of the *HMS Resolute*, a gift to the US presidency by Queen Victoria in 1880.

He had his fingers steepled in front of him, and his eyes lifted from the briefing papers on the known details and possible responses to the Russian attack on the Ämari base in Estonia.

Seated before him were his most trusted political lieutenants. The first was Michael Penalto, Secretary of State, and to his left was Mark Jasper, the Secretary of Defense. Both men had stony expressions.

Redner breathed in and out calmly but felt a vein throbbing in his temple. "Two hundred and twelve people." He looked from one to the other.

"Yes, sir; no survivors," Jasper replied.

"Confidence level on perpetrator?" Redner looked back down at the notes.

"One hundred percent, Russia," Penalto said. "But proof? At this time, we have nothing but circumstantial evidence. Our team onsite at deep core is closing in on the Russian team now."

"Until we have something, my hands are tied," Redner said, barely holding his frustration in check.

"Make no mistake, this is a covert act of war, sir. At a minimum, we need to send them a warning," Penalto urged. "It is the deep core team's belief that the Russians are now heading for Camp Bondsteel in Kosovo. That's one of our defensive keystones in the region."

"And has fifteen hundred personnel onsite," Jasper added.

"Jesus Christ."

Jasper sat forward. "We've war-gamed this many times, Mr. President. We can deliver a limited offensive action via our new W76-2 low-yield submarine-launched missiles that are deployed in the Atlantic. We can take out several of their bases outside of Russia."

"Targets?" Redner asked.

"Selected, sir," Jasper replied. "Designated targets would be the 102nd military base in Gyumri in Armenia, the Vileyka naval base in

Belarus, and their major military base in South Oseiita, Georgia, with close to four thousand Russian military personnel."

Redner folded his arms "Escalation scenarios?"

The Secretary of Defense shrugged. "We let them know that we are responding to *their* attack, not first-striking. Chance of escalation is low."

"And if they do strike back?" Redner's brows went up.

"If there was an upscale retaliation, nuclear, then the escalation protocol is to launch higher-yield payloads at all military complexes and several non-major cities within Russia."

Redner sighed. "I've read the scenarios reports. If they retaliate, and they might be insane enough to, then even with our missile shields, high-speed retaliatory delivery systems, and bomber superiority, the American loss of life would also be significant." Redner felt the vein throb faster. "And then there's the chance it gets away on us."

Penalto's mouth was set in a grim line. "Yes, sir; it could move to full escalation: Russia would be obliterated. But we would be weakened and then other world powers could seek to take advantage of the conflict theatre. China might attack us, Taiwan, or Japan. Iran might strike at Israel, North Korea on South Korea and even Pakistan might take a nuclear pot-shot at India. It could mean the entire South Pacific, the Korean Peninsula, Middle East, and Europe would become engaged."

"We're talking world war." Redner sat back.

"We would triumph," Jasper replied confidently.

"Yes, and I've seen the outcome predictions that were understandably depressing. Though we may win any global confrontation, the death toll could be as high as seventy million American lives lost, with ten times that across the globe. That's not a legacy I want to be remembered for," Redner said.

"Unfortunately, sir, the die is cast. They've already thrown the first punch," Penalto replied sombrely. "Whatever happens, we must punch back. And twice as hard."

Redner sat staring at the notes, his mind working furiously.

"We either give them a bloody nose now," Penalto sat forward, "or we'll need to give them a nuclear ass kicking if Bondsteel goes down."

Redner nodded and sat drumming his fingers on the tabletop for several seconds. "What assets do we have in the area?"

Penalto smiled. "Closest is the *USS South Dakota*, a Virginia-class fast-attack submarine with a range of missile payloads with hypersonic glide capability."

"Good. Move it into attack position and put the rest of the fleet on alert." Redner rubbed his chin. "But first, there may be another option."

"What are you thinking, sir?" Jasper asked.

"How long until the Russians reach Bondsteel, or until our team intersects their position?"

"Exact time unknown, but we think within a week," Jasper said.

"Okay. Get our assets into place. Then I'll have a quiet word with the Russian President." He smiled with little humor. "Let's see if we can deliver a bloody nose without throwing a punch."

"Well, I'm intrigued."

"Carry out your orders, then we'll reconvene." Redner stood. "Gentlemen, God bless America."

Penalto and Jasper also got to their feet and saluted their commander in chief. The Secretary of State lifted his chin. "And sir, whatever happens, you will be remembered as the president who stood up for America in its time of need."

The men departed and Redner slowly sat. He called up the image of the last known position of their team at deep core and sat staring at it for several minutes.

"Come on guys, save us all a lot of worry and pain." He continued to stare until the throbbing eased in his temple.

CHAPTER 18

The Monroe Expedition – two days later

"I don't like it," Mike said softly.

Harris snorted. "Oh? And what part of the last few weeks *did* you like?"

Alistair Peterson was talking to Penny and holding some of the resin-like substance. He held it out to Harris. "It's obviously biological; hive excretion. Used for cocoon building, hive building, and sometimes trapping prey."

"Maybe prey like us." Penny looked up at the mesh strung throughout the trees and then in at the tunnels. "It's everywhere; a lot of creatures made this."

Bull pointed to the ground. "Plenty of prints; our Russian buddies went in. They're no more than a day or so in front now."

Harris turned back. "I don't like it either. But whatever is in there, the Russians encountered it first. So, we check it out."

"I think it's a mistake," Jane said. "Mike, what do you think?"

"We should find a way around." Mike walked back a few paces and looked left and right of the web strewn opening. But the trees were like a colossal wall and meshed with angry-looking vines. They were passable with effort, but it meant venturing deeper into the dark jungle and would probably cost them hours or even days. "It's high risk."

"Really?" Harris scoffed. "Every second we're down here is high risk; backtracking or going around is high risk. Fact is everything down here is high risk." He placed his hands on his hips, his muscles straining his shirt, and his voice rose. "And you know what else is high risk? Doing nothing and letting the Russians get closer to Bondsteel so they can kill more Americans. These assholes have decided to hide like assassins and kill us from under the ground; stab us in the back like cowards." He bared his teeth momentarily. "And I am *not* going to allow it."

"HUA," other soldiers voiced their obvious approval of Harris' conviction.

"Ray, we're on the same side here," Mike replied flatly.

Harris stared for a moment more. "Good." He turned away. "Here's the plan. If we encounter trouble, we punch through it." He tilted his head and grinned. "Maybe the Russians have already killed what's in there. Or been killed by it, and in that case our work here is done." Harris nodded forward. "Bull, take us in."

"My pleasure," the huge soldier replied.

Harris organized them again, and Jane and Mike were up front behind Harris. Then came Penny and Alistair, followed by Hitch and Ally.

Even just inside the hive it got darker and the acrid odors more intense. It wasn't long before they encountered the first huge lump glued to a tree trunk.

Alistair approached the mass and held up his flashlight. "*Uh-huh*, as I suspected; the excreted matter is being used to subdue prey."

"What's it doing, storing them for later? Ants do that: store captured bugs in a larder," Jane added.

"So do spiders and wasps." Alistair moved his small light up and down the large package. "But I don't think so." He pointed. "See these rupture holes? Something came out of the carcass. I think what exited here is the larval stage of whatever captured this specimen. My money is on this captured creature having had eggs laid in it."

"Alive?" Mike asked.

"Sure; most probably stunned and therefore fresh meat for whatever hatches on or in the host body," Alistair replied.

"Gross," Ally said.

"Got that right." Harris exhaled. "So eyes out and stay in tight. Hitch, any movement?"

The soldier checked his tracker, panning it around at the numerous tunnels branching off from their passage. "Nothing; like a tomb in here."

"Okay, let's keep moving," Harris replied.

They followed Bull in deeper, and along the way found more of the captured creatures. After edging along a narrowing tunnel of the sticky resin, they entered a larger chamber, and Alistair looked up at the roof.

"Something new."

Mike followed his gaze and saw the large spheres hanging from the ceiling. "More eggs maybe?" he asked.

"There's more," Penny said. She began to frown as she approached it. "Oh no, there's a person in there."

Harris approached and stepped up onto a thick strand of the resin. Mike and Jane followed.

There was an ancient, mummified person, mouth gaping open in an eternal scream, a fist-sized hole punched through the ribs and tattered clothing. Mike stepped up closer.

"One second."

He carefully reached in and slid his hand down along the desiccated body. He grimaced as he carefully dragged something out of a small leather wallet. He opened it and began to read.

"Alexi Domnin." Mike snorted softly. "From the 1972 expedition. Katya told me he was one of their caving party, and their youngest member. She said he was 'taken'." He stepped down. "Looks like this is where he was *taken* to."

"Poor guy. Hope he didn't die in pain," Jane said.

"There's more." Penny crossed to another cocoon that still glistened. She tugged some of the sticky webbing away. "Hey, this one is fresh, and, oh my, *look*!" She stepped away.

It was a woman, youngish, and she only looked asleep.

"Has to be one of the Russian team," Mike said.

"She's alive, but unconscious. Looks like they haven't got to her yet," Jane said.

"Maybe just been stung and paralyzed," Alistair replied.

Mike leaned in even closer and spoke softly to her in Russian. "Can you hear us?"

Her eyelids fluttered and he waited, but after a while of no response he tried again, this time reaching in to touch her cheek with the back of his fingers.

As soon as his hand touched her flesh, the woman's eyes sprung open and she screamed, loud and piercing. The group fell back and Alistair cringed.

"*Be* quiet," Mike hissed to the woman and placed a hand over her mouth.

She did as asked but her eyes rolled. After another moment, her face crumpled into gulping sobs.

"Let's get her out," Mike said and began trying to break away more of the resin.

After several minutes of tearing, cutting and hacking, they managed to open a big enough hole so they could drag the woman out. They eased her down and Mike cradled her as he gave her a sip of water.

"Who are you?" Mike asked in Russian. "Can you understand me?"

The woman coughed and she took another sip of water. She nodded. "Mila Golobev, with the Russian expedition. I am a scientist of biology." Her face crumpled again. "They left me."

"Ask her how many are in her team?" Harris asked.

Mike translated, and the woman looked up at him. "Nine, nine of us." She shook her head. "No, eight now, without me."

"Ask why they're here." Harris' face was grim.

"We already know that," Mike said.

Her eyes darted from Mike to Harris. "I'm just a scientist. Not a soldier. I just do as I'm told."

Mike translated, but wondered how much English the Russian woman actually understood.

She coughed again and sat up. "I feel sick." She held her head and screwed her eyes shut.

"Take it easy," Jane said soothingly.

"Mila, how many days were you trapped?" Mike asked.

Mila shook her head. "I was asleep. I had bad nightmares." She looked around. "We need to get out of here. We were attacked by hundreds of creatures."

Mike turned to Harris. "She said they were attacked by hundreds of creatures, and we should get out of here."

Harris frowned. "From where?"

Mila pointed up to the ceiling and just made little frightened squeaks in her throat.

Jane followed her gaze and saw the bulbous things hanging from the ceiling. "Is that them?"

Mila nodded and put a finger to her lips. "Be quiet. They wake up, then they come. From everywhere," Mila whispered in heavy English. She gripped Mike's arm. "Maybe all my friends are dead. Don't let it happen again. Get us out."

Mike turned. "I agree."

Mila doubled over and held her stomach.

Penny crouched beside her. "Were you stung?"

The Russian woman's face crumpled in pain and her scream was agonizingly loud.

"Shut her up," Harris demanded, looking like he was going to hit her with the butt of his rifle.

"Back off," Jane said and tried to give her some more water.

From behind them, Bull racked his gun. "I got movement, boss. In front and from both sides."

"Multiple signals here as well," Ally replied.

Harris looked at the path ahead for a few seconds, and then decided. "The hell with it, we go back, regroup."

Mila screamed again, this time low and sounding like a wounded animal. All around them came the mad scuttling sounds and the resin mesh began to vibrate like piano wire. A breeze began to waft along the passages.

"We've got incoming, boss. Move it up a level." Bull replaced his rifle's magazine with one carrying explosive rounds.

"Move it, double time." Harris pointed. "Leave the Russian."

"No," Mike replied.

Between them, Mike and Jane carried Mila, who now muttered incoherently. She opened her mouth and let out a long burp that ended wetly. When Mike glanced at her, he saw vomit on her lips that was streaked with blood.

"She's got internal injuries," Mike said.

Penny dropped back and ran beside her. "Harris, we need to stop and lay her down. She's bleeding out."

"The hell we will," Harris shot back. "Not until we've got clean air. Now, move your ass."

They moved as fast and quickly as they could in the confined space, but still probably had several hundred yards of the resin labyrinth to negotiate. Mike and Jane dragged the woman whose head lolled forward and bloody sputum dribbled down onto her chest.

Mike was worried that if she had ruptured organs, then their jiggling would certainly be doing her even more damage. And down here that would prove fatal.

They entered a larger space, and Bull opened up, firing off several explosive rounds and blowing the bulbous spider-like things apart.

Smoke began to fill the sticky amber tunnels and between Jane and Mike, Mila began to first cough up gobbets of thick blood and then what looked like small chunks of meat. The almost-black blood splattered their legs, and when the Russian woman started to convulse, Mike simply stopped and lay her down.

"She's hemorrhaging," Mike yelled.

Penny used the woman's shirt to try and wipe away the blood, but looking at it, she frowned.

"This is stomach lining." She frowned. "What's happening?"

Ally stood over them, legs planted and firing non-stop to give them some cover. Harris swore furiously and pulled his team back as well.

Harris fired in full automatic, drawing squeals of pain from the monstrous things. He yelled over his shoulder, "Goddamn leave her."

"Not a chance," Mike said. He held the woman as she convulsed but noticed that the woman's entire face looked swollen and one of her cheekbones bulged.

Mike and Jane held the Russian woman down as she bucked and jerked, while Penny tried to stem the flow of blood. Alistair knelt by them looking like he wanted to help, but all he managed to do was to look pale and he seemed about to pass out.

Suddenly Mila's scream became a wet gargle, and she grabbed her stomach and chest. Penny also placed her hands there, thinking the woman was having a heart attack.

Penny frowned and leaned forward. She then jerked her hands back from the woman. "There's something in...."

Mila threw her head back, and then with a wet, bone-crunching noise something erupted, first from her stomach, and then to everyone's horror, from her left cheek.

"*Focus*!" Harris roared as some of his team's attention was dragged away from the unfolding horror around them to glance back at the Russian woman.

Jane fell back, teeth clenched in disgust, and Penny held up the bloody shirt she was using as a rag, looking like she wanted to stem the spurting blood and viscera but not wanting to go near the things that were emerging from the wound.

From her cheek, a head emerged. Then from her stomach, and yet another from her thigh. The small creatures forced their way out of her flesh and clothing as Mila shuddered on the ground, her body twitching as her nervous system short-circuited from the trauma.

"They laid eggs in her," Alistair yelled. "I knew it."

In the next few seconds, more larvae began to emerge and Mila's body lay still, looking deflated. The blood stopped flowing as her heart gave out.

One of the long grubs fully emerged and plopped wetly to the ground. Sticky strings of viscera still hung from it, and there were several sharp legs at the front, but the curling tail flicked open and closed like some sort of deep-sea crustacean. They flipped off the body and then used their tiny legs and a peristaltic wave motion to head back into the center of the hive.

Harris swung his barrel around and blew one away with a single shot. "Get back," he said evenly.

The group moved back from the Russian woman's corpse as the other grubs began to leave her body. Harris shot each of them, even one coming from her thigh, where the bullet obliterated it, plus the meat of the woman's leg.

Penny looked horrified, but Harris glared in return. "She's dead."

A noise leaked from Mila's throat and Penny pointed. "No, she's still alive."

Harris swung around and fired point blank at Mila's forehead, punching a hole right through it. "She's dead *now*, so everyone on their goddamn feet and let's get the hell out of here."

Penny still held the woman's bloody shirt, and she tossed it, covering the woman's ruined face. The doctor hovered over the mutilated corpse for a moment more.

Harris fired a round at Penny's feet to get her attention and his voice boomed. "Leave that corpse before you end up just like her."

The group ran, firing as they went, and as the resin thinned, so too did their pursuers. After another moment, they were back where they started, and Mike swung back but to his relief saw that nothing seemed to be following them out.

"That was a bad idea," Mike said as he bent over on his knees and sucked in deep breaths.

"I think we should go around," Jane said.

"Yeah," Harris said as he drew in a breath all the way to the bottom of his lungs. "Why don't we do that?" He turned. "Reload and take a breath everyone."

Harris walked to one side of the burrows into the resin labyrinth and then to the other. In a few minutes he called up Bull and Hitch. "Scout me a path. Be back in ten."

The two men shot off, one to the left and the other to their right, both looking for an opening in through the vines, thorns, and massive, interwoven trunks.

Bull was back within five minutes and Hitch followed a few minutes later.

"No go," Bull said. "Too much of that damn vine growth that's like barbed wire on steroids. Take us hours and a ton of skin to go twenty feet."

"Got a pathway, but steep, and leads down into the jungle valley," Hitch said. "A lot of movement down there, but looks passable."

Harris raised his eyebrows. "I'm guessing once again this is all new ground for you two?"

Mike and Jane nodded.

"Big help." Harris exhaled through his nose and walked a few paces out to where Hitch had just come in. He stood with his hands on his hips staring out at the mad green tangle. "Can't see a goddamn thing."

The jungle was thick, dominated by large trunks of trees with weird bark like popped rice that was strangled by thick vines covered in barbs like fishhooks. There were also fronds of palms that would have covered an entire house. Unseen creatures moved through the dense canopy, and hidden within the foliage was the buzz, squeak, and click of life.

He checked his wristwatch. "Goddamit," Harris barked. The soldier then exhaled and shook his head. "No choice. Hopefully we can intersect with their trail up ahead."

"We need to take some time to rest. We've been traveling now for ten hours," Mike said.

Harris cursed under his breath and checked his watch one more time. "Okay, but first we need to move away from this entrance and find a safe spot." He wiped his brow. "Bull, Ally, find us a defendable campsite."

On a massive, dripping frond in front of them, a creature that looked like a large hand, with sharp legs, no discernable head, but yellow eyes covering its back, edged a little closer to Harris. He spun and fired. The thing was blown apart.

"Fuck off, I ain't in the mood."

*****

It was another hour before they found a suitable tree with limbs that were wide enough for them to climb up into and camp at least fifty feet from the jungle floor. There were a few bugs encountered on their way up but they seemed more frightened of the humans and exited the scene quickly.

Mike and Jane sat together, and Jane shared a half-smile with him. Mike reached out and laid a hand on her forearm.

"How you doing?"

Jane's mouth turned down. "This place takes everything from you. We were lucky last time, and we just gave mother luck the middle finger by coming back."

He scooted a little closer to her. "I know. This place is Hell. But even though I think Harris is a manipulating asshole, I believe him."

"He's not that bad." She turned her face from him. "And I believe him too when he says that the Russians are trying to destroy our military bases and care nothing for the hundreds or thousands of our people's lives that are lost." She used a thumb and forefinger to rub her eyes for a moment. "I couldn't live with myself if I ignored that."

Mike wholeheartedly agreed with her but still didn't like the way she seemed to get behind the military leader.

"Maybe," was all he replied.

She exhaled and leant her head back on her neck. "Just a few years ago I was a biology school teacher and the biggest issue I had to deal with was skinned knees and arguments at recess. Now, every waking moment I have to watch people die, and die horribly. I feel we've landed on an alien plant and are a long way from home. And worse, we're stranded here." She turned to him. "I don't want to die here."

"We won't," Mike said, holding her gaze.

Jane continued to stare back for a moment more before nodding and then lying down and resting her head on her pack.

Mike waited for her to say something else. Anything else. But she shut her eyes.

He sighed and lay back and closed his eyes, but knew just because he was bone tired, the knot in his stomach would never let him fully relax.

It was too late to be worrying about coming here. All that mattered was surviving and getting home. And if that meant finding those Russians and letting Harris and his team do a job on them, then the sooner that happened the better.

Mike closed his eyes. *Yeah, the soon the better*, he thought, and surprisingly, went straight to sleep.

*****

"Goddamn it," Bull yelled. The huge soldier looked about. "My spare ammo-pack is gone."

"You probably dropped it," Hitch said.

"*Nah*, I looked." Bull said. "It's not down there."

"Bullshit," Ally spat.

"Damn well did," Bull shot back.

"No, no, I mean, my handgun is gone, right outta my holster." Ally also looked over the edge.

"You guys better not be losing your kit," Harris warned.

"I'm going down." The female soldier began to clamber down to the ground.

It only took her seconds, and Hitch and Bull covered her as she searched beneath the huge limb they perched on. She looked up and hiked her shoulders. "*Nada.*"

"Just freaking great. Get back up here," Harris said.

As the rest of the group was roused, it became apparent that other items were missing: personal items, food tins, even Alistair's wristwatch was gone from his wrist.

"Anyone want to have a guess as to what the hell is going on?" Harris demanded.

"Could it have been the Russians?" Alistair asked.

"*Pfft*, not even a ninja could have snuck in amongst us and taken our gear." Harris looked about. "Must have been..." He blew air. "I have no freaking idea."

"The items were taken not by someone else, but more like by some *thing* else," Mike said.

"Boss." Hitch was crouched over his open pack. "The tracker..."

Harris stared back at the man for a moment before realization dawned on him. "Oh you gotta be shitting me. It's gone too?"

Hitch nodded.

"*Ah*, so now you can't track the Russians." Alistair raised his eyebrows. "Still think it wasn't the Russians?"

"It's not the goddamned Russians." Harris turned to the young entomologist. "Those guys are down here destroying our bases and killing hundreds of people. If it was them snuck in here, do you really think they'd even blink at the chance to kill us all?"

Alistair looked skyward for a moment. "Well, maybe not," he conceded.

"We should move," Jane said.

"Sure, but not until we find that damned tracker." Harris looked around and then up into the canopy overhead.

"It's gone," Mike said. "Forget it."

Harris' jaws clenched for a moment as his lips pressed together. He looked like he was barely keeping a lid on a volcanic string of curses, but bit it down.

"The last direction the Russians were headed was northeast to Camp Bondsteel. So until we know different, that's the way we'll continue," Harris said.

"For how long?" Mike asked. "I mean, if they decide to go in a different direction, then we're screwed. You read my manuscript, right? This place is an entire world; we'd never just stumble upon them."

"Well, we damn continue until I say stop," Harris replied curtly.

"Hey wait a minute, that wasn't part of the deal," Mike shot back.

"Deal?" Harris turned back. "There is no deal, there's just national security." Harris closed in on Mike and jabbed a finger in his chest. "And guess what? You've just been drafted."

"You sonofa…" Mike grabbed the man's hand and finger still pressed into his chest, not even sure of what he was planning to do.

But three things happened really fast. Harris grabbed his hand and twisted it, just holding him by the twisted arm and forcing Mike down on one knee. Mike felt like his shoulder joint was going to pop out.

The second thing that happened was the soldiers had their hands on their guns and watched the interaction with hawk-like stares. Mike suddenly realized he wasn't just taking on Harris; his challenge meant he was taking them all on.

The final thing was Jane rushing in and slapping Harris' face hard enough to get his attention.

"Stop that," Jane yelled.

Harris looked up at her and grinned. "That was a free one. But don't do that again." He lowered his face close to Mike's. "That goes for you too. This is twice; you're not a tough guy, Mike. Remember that. Next time, you get hurt." He let Mike go.

Mike sprang straight to his feet and rolled his shoulder. He glared and desperately wanted to rub his screaming shoulder but didn't want to show the pain.

Harris just looked calm and only tilted his head and gave them both an understanding smile.

"Ms. Baxter and Mr. Monroe, this is important. We all want to go home, and that means as soon as possible. But we also want to save a hellova lot of lives. Can you please help us do that?"

Mike straightened. "My point still stands. What if you can't find the Russians? How long do you intend looking for them?"

"We'll find them," Harris replied. "You just let me worry about that."

Jane scoffed. "Well, one thing's for sure, we won't die of old age down here; we'll all eventually be eaten, one by one."

"Hey!" Ally yelled.

They turned to Ally in time to see her holding her head and facing up into the canopy.

"My hat. Something just… took it," Ally said.

They all faced the tree branches overhead. At first there was nothing but the crowded green limbs, leaves so thick they blocked light, and an occasional creeper vine adding some different textures.

"There." Jane pointed.

The leaves rustled, and then from within the bunch something raced along a limb to another blush of leaves. Harris and a few of the others pulled binoculars and turned them up.

Harris began to chuckle. "Well, well, you cheeky little bastards."

"What is it?" Alistair asked.

"God damn, they look like… monkeys," Hitch said.

The creature, followed by several others of its kind, broke from cover and raced to another limb to then stop, motionless. It was easy to see why no one had managed to spot them, because they were all a striped, emerald green.

They looked to be only a couple of feet tall, and though their bodies were segmented, they moved fluidly. They had long slender limbs and gripping hands with opposable thumbs on their arms and feet. But the most startling aspect was their face. The visage had a pair of extremely large forward-facing eyes, slit-like air holes for a nose, and a broad mouth.

"Very simian," Alistair said through his wide grin.

"Little creep's got my hat," Ally said and then lifted her gun. "I'll wing it."

"No." Harris held a hand out. "If they're our thieves then odds are they'll have our tracker too. See if you can spot it or where they've taken it."

"This is truly amazing. A simian arthropod species." Alistair turned to Jane. "What was the expression you used? Concurrent evolution?"

Jane nodded.

"Monkey bugs, monkbugs." Bull laughed at his own joke.

Alistair nodded. "That fits, I like it. And the theft of our property shows a high degree of curiosity. I'll bet they're highly intelligent as well." Alistair fumbled in his kit and produced a slim energy bar. "Let me try something." He quickly unwrapped it from its foil case, mimed nibbling at it, and then held it out. He made clicking noises with his tongue. "C'mon guys, come see what Uncle Alistair has got."

The simian creatures saw that they had been detected and began to chatter amongst themselves as if debating their next move. They then eased out from their hiding places; first a handful, then a dozen, and then from multiple places in the canopy.

"Oh shit, there must be dozens," Ally said.

One eased down the opposite tree trunk, using hands and feet exactly like a monkey would. The group saw now that it also used a coiling, tail-like appendage that was perhaps the last two legs fused together.

It sniffed the air, obviously catching the scent of the food bar. It came ever closer, now to within fifty feet. Even from that distance they could see the intelligence in its eyes and they went from Alistair to the food in his hand.

"Come on, little fella, I know you want it. It's real yummy." He crouched down to more the height of the monkbug and started to make kissing noises.

"Hold fire," Harris said softly. "Everyone, look for that damn tracker."

Mike noticed that most of the creatures watched from their perches high above them but several dozen had been dispatched to also come a little closer.

"*Ah*, not to alarm anyone, but I remember seeing a clip from an ancient temple that hosted big groups of monkeys, and they were experts at performing flash raids to steal anything not nailed down from tourists," Mike whispered.

"Got it," Harris replied, not taking his eyes off the creatures. "Guard your gear, people."

Alistair broke off a small piece of the bar and held it out as the creature came even closer.

When it was within a dozen feet of him, he couldn't suppress his grin. "Come on, take it." He stretched out an arm holding the bite-sized piece. The monkbug did the same.

Like Michelangelo's painting of the Creation of Adam on the Sistine Chapel, the two beings' hands reached to one another. The monkbug's eyes darted from Alistair, to the piece of energy bar, and then back to the young man again.

Alistair held the bite-sized morsel in his fingertips and stretched his arm to its limit. Then, suddenly, the small creature darted forward, snatching it from him and scurrying back a few feet. It sniffed, and then immediately jammed it into its mouth.

"Oh my," Alistair whispered.

Colors rippled over its body as some sort of chromatophor display kicked in as it couldn't help the waves of pleasure running throughout its body and then them being expressed as bands of light and color.

The other monkbugs approached it and laid their hands on the food grabber and immediately they also started to express themselves in color waves as though the pleasurable sensation of the food was also passed to them.

After the chunk was swallowed, the tiny creature seemed to immediately overcome any fear and approached again, closer and held out its hand.

"Get my hat back," Ally said.

"Worth a try." Alistair showed the creature the bar, but then held out his own hand, curling the fingers in a 'give it here' gesture. The large orbs of the tiny creature stared for a moment, and if it was confused it was hard to tell as the exoskeleton shell over its face didn't lend itself to many expressions.

But one of the others seemed to get it and crept forward. In its hand it held a small piece of fruit.

Alistair shook his head. "No." He pulled back the food bar.

Another creature tried again, this time with a large bloom. But once again Alistair shook his head and withdrew the treat. He turned to another group and held out the bar and his hand.

Finally a creature approached, bearing Alistair's wristwatch.

Alistair nodded. "Oh yeah, that's it, we trade."

He broke off another piece of bar and held it out in one hand and his open palm for the other to the watch carrier.

The monkbug held out the wristwatch and gradually both hands came closer to their respective prizes.

Alistair saw the watch alight on his palm, and he gradually began to close his fingers. Like lightning, the monkbug snatched the piece of food, and then tried to also snatch back the watch. But Alistair expected it and had managed to grip the band and hold on.

But then just as fast, the creature's other hand went to the full bar, trying to swipe that as well, but Alistair was ready and had already drawn that away.

"Expert little thieves." He laughed softly.

The monkbug scurried off, making a sort of crooning noise, and Alistair turned and held up his watch.

"Trading terms have been negotiated." He grinned.

Harris grunted. "Do it again and see if any of you can trade back our tracker."

Ally and Hitch joined Alistair and the three held out further morsels of food. More of the monkbugs decided there was little danger and scaled down bearing all manner of things, from sticks, fruit, and a few items that were recognizable as being bones. But there were also items of clothing and equipment.

"Hey, check it out." Hitch pointed. "That's a new Russian blade."

"Looks like they came across our Russian friends as well; that's good." Harris cradled his gun.

"There," Ally said. "That's our tracker."

The monkbug held the cigarette-sized device loosely in one hand, and occasionally transferred it to its mouth as it used two hands to swing and climb to the food-bearing human trio.

"Easy, don't scare it away." Harris craned forward. "Just get that damned tracker."

"Come on little fella," Ally said and waggled the portion of food bar.

The monkbug eased forward, but also seemed to drag a lot of other hopeful diners with it. It still held the tracker in its mouth.

"*Nuh uh.*" Ally pulled the food back and curled her fingers, indicating she wanted something in return rather than just play show and tell. The simian-looking creature got the message and took the tracker from its mouth, held it out, and came forward again.

Ally nodded and held out the treat. "That's it, come to mama."

The creature's large eyes were fixed on the treat and it began to ripple with bands of color as if the anticipation of the food was enough to give it pleasure.

Once again the tiny hands came closer, and Ally moved forward and her eyes flicked to the tracker. In the split second she took her eyes off the food and the creature, it shot out its hand, snatched the food, and went to scurry away, now in possession of both the food *and* the tracker.

"Sonofabitch," Ally yelled.

A single shot rang out, and the creature was blown off the tree branch. Harris lowered his handgun.

"What did you do?" Alistair had his hands to his head, his eyes wide.

The now hundreds of gathered simian bugs froze and stared.

"Negotiations concluded," Harris said as he holstered his weapon. "Ally, get down there and retrieve that tracker, *ASAP*."

"On it." Ally started to climb down.

"That was shit," Mike said.

"Yeah, maybe, but unavoidable." Harris continued to watch as Ally scaled down.

Mike shook his head. "Bullshit, you just got impatient."

"Sure did." Harris chuckled softly. "Got what he deserved; little bastard double-crossed us."

Mike and Jane turned to look down at the dead creature. A few of the monkbugs had scaled down closer, and some dropped to the ground to walk, chimpanzee-like, to their fallen kin.

Collectively, they lay their hands on the dead creature, and immediately, their bodies swam with blotches of purple and blue.

"Beautiful, and sad," Penny whispered.

Every one of the simian-looking creatures that had been approaching the humans pulled back and rejoined their fellows. Then from all around them there came an eerie song-like chorus.

"Listen; they're grieving," Alistair said. "They have societal and undoubtedly family grouping links."

"Great, you probably just shot someone's kid," Jane said.

"Got it." Ally checked it. "And A-OK, boss." She held it up.

Beside her, the monkbugs flared a hot red, and then suddenly darted away into the jungle.

From out of nowhere a missile struck Ally's face.

"Ouch." She held her head, and when she took her hand away, it was bloody. "You little bastards."

"Get back here, Bennet," Harris said as he kept his eyes on the now agitated band of creatures.

"These bug chimps are planning something, boss." Bull loaded more shells into his shotgun. "Might be time to move out."

"I heard that," Harris said.

Some of the bigger simian creatures had dropped to the ground, and one cradled the dead animal in its arms for a moment, before the others lifted it and vanished into the jungle.

"I don't like this," Mike said. "They're arming themselves. Looks like you got your war after all."

Many of them now seemed to be brandishing lengths of wood, rocks, or baring long translucent chitin teeth.

"Yeah, well, we're armed as well," Hitch said. "And our sticks spit fire."

Harris took a last look around. "We got everything we need; let's move it out, people."

The group headed back along the branch and climbed down the huge trunk to the ground.

Penny was last to jump down and as soon as her boots struck the leaf litter, they attacked. Stones, branches, and seedpods rained down with unerring accuracy.

"Hold fire. But move it," Harris yelled with his shoulders hiked under the rain of debris as he began to increase his speed.

Above them, hundreds of the monkbugs now followed their escape, and though the flying debris was annoying and sometimes painful, it was far from debilitating.

Up front, Hitch and Bull had their guns up as they jogged along a pathway. Mike watched as one of the creatures dropped from a low tree branch and in one smooth motion landed on Bull's shoulder, darted its head forward to fix a mouth of needlesharp teeth on the top of his ear, and before Bull could react, it pulled back, taking the tip of the big man's ear with it.

The huge man reacted by roaring and spinning, opening up on full automatic. Hitch, just in front of him, did the same, followed by Ally at the rear. The trio roared as they sprayed hundreds of rounds into the canopy above them. Small bodies scrambled for cover, screeching their pain and fear, and some fell from the trees, fist-sized holes blasted through their tiny bodies.

Another tried to drop down on Ally, but the soldiers were now ready for this tactic, and Ally blew it out of the air.

They picked up their pace as the jungle opened up a little. But still the small simian creatures flung debris as well as themselves at the fleeing humans.

The people sprinted, all strung out in a line, Bull leading them and using his big body like a bulldozer. By now his neck and shoulder were red with shining, fresh-flowing blood but he ignored it and made time to fire at the monkbugs overhead, plus anything and everything that got in his path.

Mike and Jane tried to slow them down, but no one listened as Harris urged them on, happy they were increasing their speed and making good time in his quest to run down the Russians.

It was Bull that broke out of the jungle first, and by the time Mike and Jane had done the same, he was approaching a vast plain, perhaps a mile across and totally devoid of any living thing.

Mike frowned. There was something about the lifeless area that just wouldn't come to him. It was Jane who grabbed his arm as she remembered first.

"*Stop. Stop* them," she yelled as she hung onto him. She jerked on his arm, hard. "Crush land."

"Oh shit." Mike suddenly remembered the words of the old woman in her notes and stopped dead. "*Stop, sto-ooop!*" he yelled until he was hoarse.

Alistair, Penny and Ally were behind them and slowed. Out in front, Bull, Hitch and Harris powered on. Only Harris looked back over his shoulder, as his two biggest men approached the edge of the plain of nothingness.

Bull had a dozen feet on Hitch, who had about two dozen on Harris. Bull entered the dead zone first, and simply vanished.

Hitch slowed, his neck craning as he tried to work out what had happened. He slowed but didn't stop and entered still with his head and shoulders leaning forward as he looked for his buddy. Then he too simply vanished.

Harris slowed, lifting his gun as though looking for some sort of assailant. He kept going and turned, his forehead deeply creased.

"Stop, Harris, stop *NOW!*" Mike screamed as he began to sprint at the group leader.

"Where?" He walked forward another few paces. "Where'd they go?" He continued walking to the plain of nothingness.

Mike caught up to Harris, grabbing him at the hips and tackling him sideways. At first Harris fought back, but Mike let go, rolled away and waved him down.

"Crush land," Mike sputtered as the rest of the group caught up.

"I don't understand. Where are my men?" Harris turned to look out over the bleak ground. "Where'd they go?"

Up close, the air seemed to shimmer in something like heatwaves. In the silence, only broken by their gasping breaths, they could hear something: a soft squealing and grinding, like the sound of a millstone's wheel turning, rock on rock, as it ground flour or grains.

Jane stopped behind them, squinting into the vast space. Penny, Alistair and Ally came up behind them.

"Where are the guys?" Ally asked. "Where'd Bull and Hitch go?"

Mike shook his head and stared at the ground in the dead zone. "They didn't go anywhere; in a way, they're still right here."

Jane crouched to pick up a fist-sized rock. "Crush land." She tossed it to the line on the ground that separated where they were to the bleak land where the plants ended as neatly as if it had been cut. The thrown rock vanished.

"Where'd it go?" Harris got to his feet.

"Didn't you hear us? It's still here." Mike also rose. "Or we think at least its atoms are." He turned. "Didn't read all my manuscript, did you?"

Harris shrugged and turned. "Skipped a few bits."

Mike put a hand over his eyes and looked up. "There are places like this throughout this hidden world. The physicists thought the gravity inside the center of the world would be so great it would crush anything down to nothingness. But we thought maybe the gravity wells acted as a pressure valve."

"But not everywhere," Jane added. "There are some areas where the full gravity effects still exert themselves. This is one of them."

"Ah." Ally pointed and grimaced. "Boss."

Harris and the group approached what she had found. Right on the demarcation line was half of a boot. It looked cleanly cut.

Harris reached out.

"Careful," Mike said.

Harris paused for a second, but then inched his hand forward and grabbed the piece of boot. He drew it back, and then lifted it.

"*Jezus,* still got some foot in it." He turned back to where he grabbed it and looked out over the empty plain. "The rest of them is still in there?"

"Yes, the remains are there. Hitch and Bull were just smashed down to atoms by the gravity. Instant death," Mike said. "The crush land only occurs during the few days of a full moon. When it's over it can be passed through. We think."

"Those poor men," Penny whispered.

"There's nothing, not even a mark on the ground," Ally said, crouching down and peering at where the men entered.

Harris bared his teeth. "Sonofabitch." He threw the rest of the boot and Hitch's foot into the crush zone. The piece vanished out of the air as soon as it crossed the line. "I needed those goddamn men."

"Are we go, no-go, boss?" Ally asked.

Harris exhaled and then reached into his pocket for the tracker. He looked at the small screen for a while and then held it up. He cursed under his breath, and then turned to the crush zone. "Well, of course those damn Russians are going to be on the other side of this freaking crush thing."

He turned to Ally. "We go." He smiled flatly and with zero humor. "And you just got promoted to being lead soldier of my entire armed forces."

"Ready and willing. Thank you, sir." Ally grinned.

"Seriously, Harris? You still want to go after the Russians that will undoubtedly outnumber us? And when you find them, take them on? Just with Ally?" Mike asked. "This is ridiculous."

"You don't think she can take 'em?" Harris raised an eyebrow. "Maybe I'll have her kick your ass, then you won't need to ask that question again."

"For God sake, stop competing with us," Jane said.

"Madness," Mike added.

"Well, Mr. Monroe…" Harris turned back to Mike, "…we know the Russians are here, but they don't know we are. So we have the tactical element of surprise and it is a powerful weapon. All we need to do is find them, and then we'll take care of business." He half-turned. "Isn't that right, 1st lieutenant, Allison Bennet?"

"Sir, yes sir. Looking forward to it, sir," Ally shot straight back.

Harris faced Penny and Alistair who just stood wide-eyed. He finally turned away. "Mission profile is unchanged."

"Good grief." Mike sighed.

Harris checked the tracker one last time. "We follow the edge of this damn crush land, and then when we get to its end, we pick up the Russians' trail again." He turned back to the shimmering landscape. "Thank you, Bull, thank you Hitch, you were damned fine soldiers, and even better folk." He saluted.

"We'll miss you, boys," Ally added, then also saluted.

Harris repositioned his kit. "The sooner we stop these bastards, the sooner we all go home. Ally…"

"Yes, sir." Ally led them out.

CHAPTER 19

"What do you think?" Dmitry held field glasses to his eyes as he stared out over the expanse of blood-red water. There was a thin spit of sand running for at least two miles and acting as a land bridge between where they stood and the next landmass.

"Passable." Chekov nodded. "But I think this place has tides."

Dmitry grunted his affirmation. "And is it low or is it high right now?"

Both men faced the water. The pellucid sea before them was mostly like a sheet of glass. But now and then bubbles popped and ripples marked its surface.

"It looks like still blood. But there is life in there." Dmitry nodded over his shoulder. "Just ask the old woman."

Chekov placed a hand over his eyes. "A few miles further down I can just see there is a ridge of mountains that might also cross the water. But it's maybe a good ten to twelve hours march."

"Too much lost time and energy," Dmitry said. "Let's just get across this nightmare sea."

"Will all the water in the ocean wash this blood from my hands? No, instead my hands will stain the seas scarlet, turning the green waters red." Chekov raised his eyebrows.

Dmitry began to grin. "A soldier with a good mind that can quote Shakespeare? Dangerous indeed."

Chekov raised his eyebrows. "And Macbeth as well; a tragic tale." He scoffed softly. "But as to your question, we don't know enough about the cycles down here to know what the tide is doing, how high or low it can get, and even how long between tidal cycles."

Dmitry nodded. "There is no moon for us to be guided by." He squinted into the distance. "There is no other way if we want to cross it quickly. And we will need to carry the woman."

"Two miles, easy. You know the world record runners can do a mile in under four minutes these days?" Chekov grinned.

Dmitry lowered his glasses and turned to his friend. "The last time you ran that fast, it was to the bar when your vodka ran out."

"Yes, I broke records that day." Chekov's laugh was a deep rumble in his chest. He turned back to the sea. "But I think if we double-time, it should only take us a few hours, even with the woman."

"The sooner we start..." Dmitry circled a finger in the air, "...we finish."

Dmitry and his team of Viktor and Chekov would lead them out, the scientists in the middle with Sasha carrying Katya, then lastly, his remaining soldier, Pavel.

For the most part the group had to walk in a single line as the lapping water narrowed the spit down to just a few feet. As they began, Dmitry noticed that the sand created a bank out into the shallow water, and small sprats darted in and then out from the warm sea.

But as they progressed, the depths increased. The water still had clarity even with its red tint from the boiling sky overhead, but the darkness of the water told him that it must have been at least fifty feet: more than enough, he knew, for one of Katya's sea monsters to get in real close.

Dmitry and his team cradled their rifles and shotguns. And after ten minutes, the heat and silence were beginning to lull him into a trance-like plodding. Just the sound of his and his team's boots scrunching on the wet sand was metronomic to the point of hypnotizing.

From time to time they encountered blue, football-sized crabs that waved pincers at them, but scuttled out of the way to let the humans pass as their bulbous eyes twitched as they watched the strange two-legged humans go by.

The red heat continued to beat down on them, and the radiated reflection from the water was burning Dmitry's cheeks. He reached up to touch one, feeling the sting of the burns.

He turned to walk back for a few paces, checking on his team. He was happy to see they were all alert and even the scientists weren't stopping to investigate every interesting oddity they found.

The only thing that concerned him was the old woman clung to Sasha with clawed hands. He stopped and waved the team on to keep going as he waited for the pair. When Sasha and Katya got close, the young man nodded to him, and Dmitry turned to walk by their side for a while.

"Is everything okay? You comfortable, Katya?"

Her head rose and for the first time she also lifted her veil to stare into his eyes. "I don't like being so close to the water; it's too deep."

Dmitry nodded and turned to look out over the red sea. "We're nearly a third of the way now. We should be fine," he said.

She snorted softly. "Your optimism is only matched by your mad looks, Captain."

"And I have a winning smile." He grinned, not being able to help liking her directness. "Like I said, we'll be fine."

"Will we?" Her blue eyes had a hint of cloudiness, but they fixed him like a pinned butterfly. "Have you noticed the tide? The spit is getting smaller every step we take."

Dmitry looked back the way they had come. She was right; the sand spit was definitely narrower than when they had set out. He had been right to wonder what the tide cycles were like here, and whether they would work faster or slower. Now he had his answer: faster.

"We need to hurry, Captain," Katya sighed. "We do not want to be caught here if the tide rises to cover the sand."

Dmitry nodded and looked back to their destination. He reached out to place a hand on the woman's thin shoulder and gently squeezed. "Then, why don't we go faster?" He jogged back to fall into line behind Chekov and Pavel.

Chekov pointed. "The tide."

"I know," Dmitry replied. "Let's pick up the pace."

The men lengthened their stride.

Dmitry turned. "Keep up, people."

In another few minutes, the sand was becoming waterlogged and Dmitry cursed under his breath. They were in a race, and short of running, it looked like the tide was going to win.

He sped up, trying to keep a good pace while not allowing the team to string out too far.

The sudden splash jerked Dmitry from his reverie, and he spun to the water.

"What was that?"

Chekov and Viktor had lifted their guns and aimed out at the water, where a spreading circle of ripples was still fanning out.

"Something came up," Chekov said solemnly.

"There," Sasha said. He pointed with his forehead while still holding the old woman on his back.

"What did you see?" Dmitry yelled back to him.

Viktor stepped to the water line, and then jerked back. "*Putja*," he cursed. "Something there, big." He turned. "Looked right at me."

"*Run, run.*" Katya's voice was dry and croaky like leaves blowing on an old porch. But they carried enough fear for the group to start backing away.

"Double time." Dmitry began to jog. Behind him the others followed, keeping up the accelerated pace.

In the distance the second land mass loomed. But it was still far enough away to be slightly shrouded by the sea vapors rising from the bath-warm water.

Up ahead there was a larger sandbar that lifted their sand spit out of the water by a few extra feet, and seemed like a small island. Dmitry hoped it would mean it would be impossible for anything of size to get close to them. *Would the tide submerge that as well?* he wondered.

He squinted, as there seemed to be something growing on it. *A good sign it stayed above the surface*, he thought.

"Faster now," Dmitry yelled and started to increase his own pace.

"We're being ghosted, sir," Sasha yelled from behind.

Dmitry turned just in time to see a weird sort of spined dorsal fin rise up close to the group at the rear. The rising fin peaked at about six feet, and there was a swirl further back that might have been where the tail ended. It was big, and maybe it knew it only had to wait before the tide would allow it to pick them of without having to beach itself, or even better, its prey would simply float free.

He bared his teeth. "Put a few rounds into it next time, soldier. Send it back to the deep."

Dmitry came up behind Pavel and he remembered the young soldier had been a sprinter in school. "Pavel, run ahead and stake out a defensive position on that sand spit. And put a few explosive rounds into that bastard that's ghosting us."

"Yes, sir." The soldier put his head down and ran hard, immediately leaving the group behind.

Dmitry turned. "Hurry up, people. We do not want to be swimming today."

Pavel closed in on the tiny island with the growths covering it. As he ran, he scanned the water, and finally got to the raised lump of sand that was no more than fifty feet around.

Good, Dmitry thought, *now at least we will have some cover fire.*

Pavel arrived at the sand bank, slowed and walked up through the ring of knee-high stiff growths as he pulled his rifle. He was about to turn to give the group support but instead stopped and looked down. And then strangely, he yelled something and went to run back to them.

But in that single instant the sand exploded around him and Pavel screamed his fear. The sand blew up and closed around him like a trap. The growths became teeth and the fifty foot-wide sandbank was actually the head of some large creature just buried beneath the sand.

With Pavel in its mouth, the buried thing rose about ten feet in the air on a muscular trunk or stalk.

"No, no, no." Dmitry pointed his gun and sprinted forward. He aimed and began to fire into the creature's neck or stem, or whatever it was.

Pavel screamed; he wasn't dead and was only trapped in the soft palate that had used the growths like the bars of a cage to stop him escaping.

The group closed in but stopped several dozen feet back. Dmitry changed his magazine to explosive rounds and fired again. Chekov also fired, and finally a piece of the trunk blew away.

Pavel's screams became strained sobs as the mouth began to compress. But in the next instant, the thing began to draw back into the sandbank.

With a sound like grinding rock, the massive creature withdrew, taking Pavel with it. Their last vision was of the man reaching out from between his prison bars, his face wild and frightened as it was pulled below the wet sand.

Bubbles popped in the sand mass and it swirled like liquid for a moment before it settled. The sand seemed to dry, and then it was as if the creature and Pavel had never existed.

Chekov fell to his knees. "It took him," he said softly. "It was hiding under the sand."

"What the hell was that?" Dmitry spun on his team, demanding answers none of them could possibly give.

"Like some sort of giant Venus fly trap, maybe," Nadia said. "He walked in amongst those growths which must have been like sensory hairs. He triggered its reaction."

Oleg Krupin, the biologist, shook his head. "It bled. It was an animal, not a plant. I think it was more like a giant tubeworm. They live in the ocean and thrive beneath the sand and capture their prey by laying in wait for them, just like that. It's just that they're a hundred times smaller."

"It doesn't matter."

Dmitry turned to the reed-thin voice.

Katya slid down from Sasha's back and held her stomach for a moment. "I warned you about underestimating this place, Captain. You didn't pay attention and now it has taken another of you."

Dmitry pointed at her. "You didn't exactly give us any warnings. If you knew there was danger, you should have spoken up, *Ms Babikov*."

"Fool, I *did* warn you. There is always danger, everywhere, all the time," Katya shot back.

Even with her veil, Dmitry could feel the weight of her glare, and he turned away to stomp out over the empty sandbank. He pulled his gun and fired several rounds into the sand, cursing until his face burned from his surging blood pressure.

Finally he stopped and sucked in a few deep breaths before turning to her. "I don't need people warning me of danger, *after* the danger has struck." Dmitry slid his gun over his back.

She hobbled closer to him. "Then I'll warn you now…"

"What?" Dmitry looked up.

Katya was pointing out at the red water. They all turned. Where she indicated, there was a huge head, twenty feet across, that on seeing it had been noticed slid back below the water.

"It won't be long until it can reach us," Katya said. "Then I think more of us will die."

Dmitry raised his gun, but the thing was gone.

Katya tilted her head. "You're a good man, Dmitry Varanov. But you can't see everywhere all the time. You must assume the worst case down here, because it might just be even worse than the worst case."

Dmitry nodded. "I understand." He slapped Chekov on the shoulder. "We stay in tight, but we move fast. Viktor, you watch the water, load explosive rounds, and anything that moves out there, you shoot it."

He turned back to the land in the distance. "Less than half a mile. We can make it."

Chekov went to lead them out, but Dmitry called him back. "Time for me to lead."

Chekov shook his head. "No, I should lead. If I die it's just another lost soldier. But if you die, we lose our leader."

"Thank you, Leonid. But this is an order." Dmitry half-smiled. "Just watch my back."

Chekov saluted and held his gun tighter. "I'm ready."

Dmitry looked back at his ever-shrinking group. "Move fast and stay in close to each other. Keep watching the water, and yell if you see anything."

He turned and began to run. After a few minutes he turned back to see the tiny sand island had grown its strange projections. Again the beast beneath the sand had obviously digested Pavel and waited now for its next free meal.

Dmitry sucked in a huge breath and let it out through puffed cheeks. He had to believe he was doing the right thing and that he would complete his mission and get his team home.

He wiped his brow with a hand and then glanced at the tattoo on its back, the snarling wolf holding a dagger in its mouth, and underneath, the motto: *Death or Victory.*

Then death or victory it was, he thought. He grit his teeth and continued on.

*****

Slowly but surely they ate up the distance between themselves and the mainland ahead. But equally, the tide was winning the race, and the first thin layer of water washed over the sand, making their feet splash as they traveled.

Dmitry held his gun tight, constantly feeling the prickle of warning his soldier's intuition gave him about hidden danger. He looked to his side and noticed he was passing over another deep spit, and the dark red water here seemed bottomless.

He wondered how high the tide would come up: another few inches, few feet, or so high it would mean swimming? If that was the case, it would also mean they would be dead.

"*Contact.*"

Behind him, Viktor fired off several rounds into the water.

Dmitry half-turned to look over his shoulder and saw the soldier curse and shake his head.

"No hit, no hit." Viktor continued to watch the water.

Dmitry snapped his head back to the front as his footfalls angled a little off the center of the spit and he stepped momentarily into deeper water.

"I'll watch, you lead us." Chekov grinned. "No time for you to go swimming."

Up ahead the land mass drew them on, tantalizingly close, and though the huge towering jungle was as dark and mysterious as it had always been, now it seemed a source of safety and comfort.

The rate of inundation was accelerating, and Dmitry's adrenaline surging through his system made him jumpy and he wanted to sprint, but instead had to slow his pace as the slim sand spit that had been their pathway was totally submerged, and now invisible.

Dmitry knew if he charged on too fast, he might run right into the deeper water and the waiting jaws of whatever thing it was that followed them. He wondered how much water needed to rise before the thing would assail them.

He didn't need to wonder for long.

From his side the attack came fast. The massive head loomed from the depths. Dmitry swung around but instinctively backed away and fell off the narrow strip into the water on the other side.

Chekov went to one knee, aimed, and fired in full automatic mode into the beast. The creature was all shining dark carapace and pitiless eyes like pools of oil. It looked like some sort of mad cross between a lobster and a shark. On each side of its armored head were long grasping arms and the mouth telescoped open to reveal a gullet of inward pointing spikes down a long throat.

The men and women of his team yelled, cursed, and tried to get out of the way of a creature the size of a bus that must have weighed many tons. It split his team; some behind it on the sunken spit of sand, and some on Dmitry's side, closer to the mainland.

The water was still too shallow for it to fully beach itself, but the arms on each side of its head flicked forward and then inward, while the mouth gaped wide, the intention clear, as it hoped to catch some of the humans in the sweeping motion.

The soldiers opened up, but the bullets only scarred the thick carapace and none pierced its many inches thick shell.

"Get down," Dmitry yelled as the arms swept over them again.

On each side of it, huge sets of paddle-like legs thrashed and rowed as it tried to lift itself higher and change its angle so it could make another sweep at water level, where they'd have no hope of evading the feeding arms.

"Explosives," Dmitry yelled, as he and his team loaded more explosive round magazines and fired.

One of the rounds detonated against the massive head with a bloom of orange flame, and the thing hunkered down a little, but once again there was little damage.

It thrashed some more and seemed to be concentrating on Sasha and Katya, who with their combined size, probably seemed the largest morsel of meat to choose from.

Katya buried her head into the back of Sasha's neck and refused to watch as the large man kept his body in front of hers.

The result was looking inevitable as, with the tide coming in and the furious movement of the thing's paddles, it was inching forward and angling itself to be able to scoop them up and drag them into its huge mouth.

Dmitry stood and walked forward as he released round after round. His father, a hunter, had once been attacked by a bear in Siberia and had fought it off with just a hunting knife. His advice: always go for the eyes; it was the softest part.

In a controlled and professional manner, he changed up his ammunition and slapped in an armor-piercing magazine and fired at the closest eye, again and again. And even though the eye itself was covered in hard chitin, this time the tungsten-tipped rounds pierced the hard shell. Unfortunately, whatever damage the projectiles did, they still didn't seem to be worrying the juggernaut as it continued to bore down on Sasha and Katya.

Sasha reached up to his neck and dragged the woman's hands away, and then pushed her back. Dmitry could tell it was the man's last-ditch attempt to save her, for when the next lower sweep of the monster's massive feeder arms occurred, they collected him up.

Katya fell back, as the dispassionate gaze of the creature stayed fixed on the large soldier. Sasha drew its attention and it gave the other scientists time to crawl away as he continued to fire uselessly into its approaching jaws.

Then something struck the huge body of the creature so hard they all felt it, even right through the sand bar. The massive thing was rolled slightly to one side and a high-pitched squeal emanated from its throat.

The thing's arms and legs flayed about, but the churning water behind it was becoming discolored with an inky black ichor and boiling foam erupted around it.

"What...?" Dmitry lowered his weapon. "What's happening?"

In the next instant the creature was tugged backward ten feet. Then tugged some more. It was clear then that something else, something even bigger, had hold of it.

Finally it was dragged into deeper water, where whatever monstrosity was below the surface pulled it down to feast on it.

Dmitry ran to Sasha and Katya and helped them up. He grabbed Sasha's shirt and turned to the group.

"Now we run, *for our lives,*" Dmitry yelled.

Sasha went to help Katya back up onto his back, but she grabbed his forearm and held on.

She leaned close to his face. "Do not try and sacrifice yourself for me again. My life is nearly over, yours is just begun." She patted his cheek.

Sasha tilted his head. "I cannot promise. It is our duty to protect our people."

"Then next time I'll push *you* out of the way." She laughed softly, and then allowed him to help her up onto his back again.

A few more surge waves and splashes from the red water, and the group sprinted. Fear and adrenaline put wings on their feet, with all fatigue forgotten.

Dmitry and Leonid Chekov took the lead, and Dmitry worried that with the water now at their ankles and the sand beneath becoming softer, it was making staying on the backbone of the sandbank near impossible.

Only around two hundred yards separated the leaders from the shoreline, and as they approached, Dmitry for the first time could make out the towering trees, palm fronds as large as rooftops, and vines sprouting purple bulbs that might have been fruits or some sort of weird bloom.

But he also noticed movement. "*Ach,*" Dmitry spat and slowed his pace, forcing the others behind him to do the same. "Something is in there," he said.

"Something worse than that monstrosity that just tried to eat Sasha? Or the thing that *did* eat poor Pavel?" Chekov asked.

"I think it doesn't matter," Dmitry replied. "We're coming ashore whether we like it or not. And that means if we will need to fight."

"Okay with me." Chekov held his gun ready. "Fighting on land is better."

"Then get ready." Dmitry was first off the spit and raced along the shoreline for a dozen feet, then turned to the jungle and lifted his gun.

Sure enough, the people filing off the sandbank created enough movement to draw the predator out. A creature like a spindly-legged spider unfolded itself from the tree line where it was mimicking some of the long slender tree trunks and came after the Russian leader like a stilt walker.

The body was the size of a small car, but the legs were each fifty feet long and like dark tubing.

Dmitry waited, legs planted as the thing bore down on him. He let it get closer and then he fired.

From behind the beast, Chekov also began to fire, and he still had a few explosive rounds loaded. The first one penetrated the shining abdomen, and then detonated. The carapace expanded for a moment, and then the thing became unsteady on its long legs like a circus performer who'd had too much to drink.

The creature's internal organs must have been obliterated, as it simply fell to its side, the body thumping to the sand.

Dmitry watched it shiver in a final death throe and then lay still. Chekov joined him and the pair stared at the corpse for a moment before Chekov turned with raised eyebrows.

"So, how has your day been?" He grinned.

Dmitry laughed softly. "Like a day in paradise. And even better; now we have fresh meat."

He turned about and then waved his group in. "We need to get our bearings, find some shelter and rest. We do our job and then we can go home."

"Now *that* sounds like paradise." Chekov shouldered his rifle. "Dmitry, sir."

Dmitry turned at the sound of his friend's voice.

"One more thing." Chekov's mouth turned down. "Pavel, he was carrying the communication silo."

Dmitry shut his eyes for a moment and groaned. "So, now we have no way to communicate with our base." He sighed.

"Or them with us," Chekov added.

"No matter. Our mission is unchanged." Dmitry turned back to the blood-red sea. Their sand spit was totally gone, as the tide had swallowed all trace of it now. The sea creature that attacked them had been as large as a school bus, but something had preyed on it that must have been even larger. One of Katya's sea monsters, he bet.

"Another day in paradise," he repeated softly. But he knew, they were as far from the light of paradise as they could be. Dmitry sighed and headed back up the sand.

CHAPTER 20

Five miles to the west of the Russian mission team

Mike sat close to Jane, his thigh just touching hers. They'd taken a break at the base of a cliff, and all sat in a line with their backs to the sheer wall.

The group had been moving along a mountain range that seemed to grow ever higher with every mile they traveled.

Mike lifted himself a little to look over Jane's head to Harris. The man had dark circles under his eyes and he stared at the tracker as though divining the meaning of life from its tiny screen.

"He's obsessed," Mike said.

"I guess he has to be," Jane replied softly. "As a soldier, his primary role is to defend and protect. He's going to do that come hell or high water." She clicked her tongue in her cheek. "And now he has to do that with one soldier."

Mike sighed. "You don't have to defend him all the time, you know."

"I'm not defending him." She turned. "Just giving you my opinion."

"Fine." He faced forward. "I'd just feel a little better if I didn't feel we were just pawns to allow him to reach his objective."

"You said yourself; maybe it's our objective too." She lifted her eyebrows and smiled.

He snorted softly. "So we're also fighting Russians now?"

"Sure, but only the bad ones." She shared a crooked smile.

"Hey, do you remember where they said Camp Bondsteel is situated?" Mike asked.

Jane seemed to search her memory for a moment. "Kosovo, wasn't it?"

"Yeah, that's right. And you know what else Kosovo is known for?" He moved closer.

"Their famous bean casserole?" Her grin broadened.

He liked seeing her smile. He'd missed it.

"Yeah, of course there's that. But there's also the Gadime Cave system."

She clicked her fingers. "Oh yeah, I'd forgotten: the Lipljan municipality." She turned. "Do you think...?"

He shrugged. "It's one and a quarter miles deep, and is damned old, at least Mesozoic era. And most importantly, it's still largely unexplored." He nudged her leg. "So, yeah, I do think."

"Best news I've heard all day." She exhaled and nodded. "There could be a gravity well beneath it."

"And a way out." Mike reached across to place a hand on her forearm. "Never give up hope."

"Easier said than done sometimes." She laid a hand over his. "I like your optimism. Sometimes it's a tiny light in a dark room. And I need that."

He took her hand and rubbed it. Her face was more lined even after being here only a few weeks. Her cheeks were streaked with grimy sweat and were also reddened by the constant furnace-like heat from above.

Mike knew he loved her then and wished he could go back in time and ask himself why he had ignored her and then run away from her.

He squeezed her hand. "And I need your friendship. I'm sorry for cutting you off for so long, and sorry you got dragged into this."

She scoffed softly. "Tell me, honestly, if we weren't tricked into this, would you have come anyway?"

"Honestly?" He didn't really have to think about it. "Probably."

"I didn't want to be here." She sighed. "But do you know why I came? Because I thought you were coming, and someone needed to be here to look out for your big, dumb ass."

He laughed softly. "Is that what you've been doing?"

She nodded. "Well, you're not dead yet, so it's working so far."

"Thank you." He lifted his canteen to toast her and then sipped the lukewarm water.

Harris finished speaking to Ally and got to his feet. He held his field glasses to his eyes for several minutes, scanning their surroundings, and then craned his neck to look up at the towering rock face behind them. After a moment he lowered them and turned to face the group. "Okay people, up and at 'em."

Mike helped Jane up, and Penny and Alistair wandered closer, while stuffing canteens, remaining food packs, and equipment back into pouches and pockets.

Harris placed his hands on his hips. "We need to see what's coming. Our direction is known but as you are aware, sometimes a direct path is not the fastest or safest path."

"So, we need a lookout?" Mike also looked up at the sheer cliff.

"Not just a single lookout, Mike, but all of us. Just up ahead there's a ridge we can climb." Harris smiled. "Just as well we're all experienced climbers, right?"

"Experienced but tired," Penny said.

"Well, we gotta do it," Harris replied. "And I'd like to promise you we'll get a cool breeze up higher, but I'm thinking it'll more than likely be even hotter."

"Oh boy," Mike said.

"Ms. Bennet." Harris turned to her.

"Yo," Ally replied.

"Plot us a route and then we'll head up." Harris replaced his binoculars in their pouch. "I'll bring up the rear."

"On it." Ally headed out.

They set off, sticking close to the cliff wall, and after another thirty minutes of trekking, they came to a fold in the rock that followed the edifice all the way to the top.

Ally and Harris both used their field glasses to check on the slope before he slapped her on the shoulder, and like a mountain goat, she headed up. The group followed.

The going was hard, steep, and lots of loose, heat-pummeled granite rolled under their feet. Most of the climb was on a natural jutting pathway, but a few areas required them scaling up and over jutting boulders.

Though all of them had been chosen for their caving abilities, the complexity added to the mix was the heat. Harris had been right about not getting any breeze at altitude as for every hundred feet they ascended, it seemed to add an extra few degrees.

The heat lifted off the dry stone in waves and was even hot to touch. By the time they neared the top it must have been a hundred and ten and there would be no shade or respite from the blasting red heat hammering down on them.

It took them another twenty minutes of straining, sweating, and exhausting effort to reach the top. It was a narrow ridge of stone, like the backbone of a huge slumbering animal beneath the ground.

The ridge wasn't all that high as far as mountains go, but it did give them a panoramic view over the blood-red inner world.

Harris and Ally immediately took to their field glasses, scanning the distance, while Penny tended to Alistair's back for chafing from his backpack.

Mike took a single sip from his canister. He tugged the brim of his hat lower and felt fresh rivulets of perspiration run down the side of his face. He knew the precious mineral and water loss he and the team were experiencing was exceeding his intake, and that meant soon they'd all start to suffer from the effects of dehydration: headaches, dizziness, and cloudy thinking, potentially deadly during a taxing climb.

He and Jane turned slowly, looking out over the immense primordial inner world; in every direction there was mostly an immense jungle of leviathan proportions. A flock of flying creatures, stiff membranous wings spread wide floated over one area, and though from the distance it was impossible to verify their size, by using the colossal trees they floated over for comparison he bet the things must have been the size of airplanes.

In amongst the green canopy huge heads lifted, hundreds of feet from the ground to graze on the new leaf shoots. Enormous mouths opened at the front of bus-sized heads to take in thousand-pound clumps of food, and when the things moved to a new area, the entire portion of forest shook in their path.

To their west a sea sparkled in the red light, and far back the way they had come, their ridge of rock joined up with the massive column mountain that was beginning to disappear over the horizon's curve of their inner world.

Harris joined them and pointed. "That way."

Mike and Jane followed his finger. Mike squinted as he could just make out something in the distance. "Is that what I think it is?"

Harris nodded. "Smoke. Has to be the Russians." He handed Mike the glasses.

Mike put them to his eyes and could see the ribbon of smoke rising from the dense jungle, only a few miles from where they were now.

"Yep. Looks like a campfire." He handed the glasses back.

"We've got two options," Harris said. "We can cross the water, or we can stay up on this ridge which will get us there a little slower."

"Stay on the ridge," Jane replied quickly. "If at all possible, we stay out of the water where we can. Far too dangerous."

"Everywhere is dangerous." Harris turned. "Right?"

"Right," Mike replied. "But some options are dangerous, and some are basically suicidal."

"I have to see this world's ocean up close. Just once." Alistair had come up behind them. "If only to take some samples for analysis when we return." He looked to the water. "In our world all life started in the oceans. It will be the same here. Is it a different ocean?" He turned with a finger raised. "Or is this the same ocean? Perhaps a portion of the surface water world that was hived off, many hundreds of millions or even billions of years ago. And therefore contained the same seed of life." He nodded. "I have so many questions."

"This world, and this ocean, is what happens when climate change doesn't tame it." Jane turned to the young man. "In our benign world on the surface, great and terrible beasts rose to prominence, but mass extinctions removed them from the planet. Whether it was ice ages, mega droughts, or asteroid impacts, the monsters of the past were removed." She turned back to the distant water. "But not here. Here they just kept getting bigger and badder."

Alistair nodded, and then looked from Jane to Mike. "Those monsters of the past were magnificent: the dinosaurs, the mega fauna, the geology. Hey, did you know that after the dinosaurs' reign had ended, the time of giants hadn't? As an example, when the great mammals ruled there was a creature called a *Paraceratherium* that was twenty-five feet tall and weighed in at twenty tons; a relative of the rhino. Looked like a giant horse, but three times bigger than the biggest elephant."

Mike whistled.

Alistair pressed his hands together. "Would you not give anything to see them or one of the largest saurians again?" He smiled. "I've studied arthropods all my life, but have been captivated by the thought they were once the rulers of the planet during the Permian period nearly 300million years ago."

Alistair waved an arm out at the vast jungle. "I want to see them as I doubt I'll ever get back here."

Jane snorted derivatively. "Yeah, Mike said the same thing."

"And you too." Alistair smiled.

"Let's not go there right now." Jane folded her arms. "Take it from someone who traveled on that sea: it's more deadly than anything you can imagine. We lost good people to what lives in it." She smiled ruefully. "I don't want to see anyone else, or you, die, Alistair."

He looked back at the sea. "No one actually plans on dying, ever."

"Group discussion over, the ridge it is then," Harris proclaimed. "Let's get moving."

"I will see it before I leave." Alistair turned away. "Of that I am sure."

The pathways they moved along were seared by the red radioactive heat from above that had beaten down unchanged for hundreds of millions of years.

Mars, Mike thought. This was how he imagined the surface of the red planet must look if you trekked along its surface. Except the Mars temperature was about eighty degrees below zero and its surface was subject to continual blasting windstorms. But down here, though there was a form of weather in the inner world, there was no tectonic plate movement, no real severe climatic shifts that created glaciations or drought, and so the atmosphere and environment remained largely frozen in place.

Most of the group had thrown shawls over their hats to act as long veils to keep the reflected glare off their faces, and their march in the one hundred and ten degrees was arduous and energy sapping.

Many times during their climb they encountered weird objects attached to the rocks that could have been some sort of unique geological formation, or maybe even an ancient limpet species that had long since petrified to stone. The major difference being that these things were three feet across.

The rocks to the peak were harsh, sharp and dangerous, and any slip meant damage that penetrated their thick clothing. But the uneven nature of the rocks wasn't everywhere; now and then there were places that were glass-smooth that could have been polished.

Alistair crouched by one and rubbed it with his fingers. "Sort of looks like it's been finely sanded." He snorted softly, and then looked up. "I wonder if the heat and radiation did this somehow?"

He then stood and walked to one of the limpet things. He kicked at one and then stamped at it, but the thing was either bedded down tight or part of the actual stone. Penny barked at him to stay in line like a mother scolding their child.

"Fossilized I think," Alistair said. "But possibly once was some form of oversized *Patellogastropoda* a polyphyletic limpet." He looked about. "But what are they doing away from the water?"

"Maybe they dried out; hence why they're all just fossils now," Jane replied.

Alistair pinched his lower lip as he walked up and over the top of another. "Maybe."

In another fifteen minutes they came to a flatter area just before the mountain ridge started to decrease in size. The water now lapped at the rocks below, and looking down they could occasionally make out things swimming languidly in its depths. Alistair stared as if hypnotized.

"Good a place as any," Harris announced. "Take five... and only five."

The group sat, letting packs slide from soaked backs, and then used their veils to firstly wipe their faces and then pull them further over their heads. They nibbled on remaining protein bars that were hard to swallow in dry mouths. The upside was that the jungle ahead was lush and thick, and promised water somewhere hidden within its mad green tangle. Even Mike forgot about the dangers lurking inside, as fresh water was all that mattered.

He turned to Jane. "Hey, remember showers?"

"*Pfft.*" She leaned closer. "And baths filled to the brim." She flipped her veil up. "And swimming pools with a wet bar at one end."

Mike groaned. "I'm homesick for my cabin by the lake. The cool, blue lake."

She dropped her veil. "You mean your fortress of solitude?"

"If I asked you, would you come and stay there with me?" He rested his chin on his hand.

"You'd have to ask re-*eeeally* nicely." She lifted one edge of her veil, revealing one eye. "And even then I might say no."

"*Ooh*, a challenge." He smiled. "I can be charming and persuasive when I want to be."

Alistair sat on one of the large shield-like objects stuck to the rocks and splashed a little of his precious water on it, then quickly pulled a magnifying glass out and examined its structure.

"Definitely biomineralization. Sclerotin I think," he said to no one in particular. He looked up and caught Jane watching him. "Sclerotin is a component of the cuticles of various Arthropoda, most familiarly insects."

"So, not a limpet?" she asked.

"Hybrid, maybe?" He went back to rubbing the rapidly drying wet patch on the fossil with his thumb and then held the spyglass over it again.

"Sclerotin is formed by meshing together of different sorts of protein molecules. It increases the rigidity of an insect's chitinous exoskeleton that gives them their armorplating." He moved so close his nose was now almost touching the thing. "It's especially strong in the plating over the head, back, and the biting mouthparts of arthropods."

"So, an insect." Mike smiled. "Or was once."

Alistair chuckled. "Yeah." He lay the magnifying glass down, reached into his pack for a sample bag, and unsheathed his knife.

"Going to try and collect some." He began to chip away at the thing with little success, and then moved to the side. The young scientist then tried to dig the blade in where the limpet thing was fused to the rock.

The toughened steel was hard and sharp and he managed to wedge it in a fraction. "Hey…" he frowned as he got down to give himself more leverage as he worked the blade in.

With a tearing, sticky sound the oval thing rose up on multiple pointed legs. Two quivering feelers erupted from the end closest to Alistair as he fell back and just stared.

Penny rushed toward the young man, and as she did, two tiny, black eyes fixed on her movement. A jet of orange liquid shot out, directed at the woman doctor. Most of the sticky fluid missed her, but about half a cup full splashed her arm.

Penny looked at it, and then in the next second grabbed her elbow.

Holding the arm out she began to scream, steam rising from her limb.

Mike jumped to his feet and sprinted to her. Alistair scuttled back as the forgotten bug thing now looked like it was positioning itself to spit more venom or bile or whatever the corrosive fluid was.

Harris ran forward and pumped a dozen rounds into the thing. Every shot struck its outer shell and ricocheted away, so he dived flat and put just as many more into where it had risen from the ground, and what he hoped was its unprotected belly.

This time the bullets penetrated but instead of trying to flee, or keeling over from its wounds, the creature simply hunkered down and hugged the rock again.

Penny continued to scream as her hand and arm turned a blistering red. The liquid that now dropped from her limb was also foaming with blood as the caustic substance dissolved her flesh.

Mike emptied the last of his canteen water on it and held her tight. "Grit your teeth, this is going to hurt like hell."

Penny did as asked as Mike began to use a towel to wipe her arm down. Penny looked away and courageously only let a groan of pain slip between her bared teeth.

In another second she slumped as she slipped into unconsciousness. Ally went through the female doctor's bag as she searched for antibiotics, painkillers, and gauze.

She held up a small bottle. "Got some water here." She handed it to Jane and she splashed the woman's scarred arm again.

Jane looked at the damaged flesh as Mike waited to bind it. "Skin's gone, and some of the epidermal fat layer." She patted it dry.

"Ready for this?" Ally held up a small shaker of antiseptic powder.

"Yeah, while she's out cold." Jane held Penny's arm out.

Ally shook some of the powder onto the arm which immediately soaked up the weeping fluid from the acid burns.

Mike then began to bind the arm. "Will it heal?"

"Down here? Not a chance." Jane grimaced. "More than likely she'll need a skin graft."

Harris pointed his gun at the now motionless bug that had attacked them, and then swung the muzzle to Alistair. "Hey asshole, can we damn well stop pissing the bugs off?"

"*I didn't know. I didn't know.* I thought it was dead, a fossil." Alistair hovered over Penny. He looked up, his features wrecked. "Please tell me she'll be alright."

Jane waited until Mike finished. She checked the binding wasn't too tight. "I'm not going to sugarcoat it but she needs to be in a hospital. The longer we're down here, the more chance of infection."

Alistair held his head and groaned.

Mike looked around. They were in the center of about half a dozen of the limpet-like bug things and they had been walking between them for an hour. But for now, they had all gone back to pretending they were part of the geology.

"What was it?' Mike asked the young man.

Alistair just rocked back and forth holding his head.

"*Alistair*!" Mike roared.

"*Huh*?" Alistair looked up. "I don't know. There's nothing like that, well, not exactly. It's like a cross between a limpet and a slater bug."

"They don't spit acid," Ally said. "No bug I know topside does that."

Penny started to come around and Alistair slowly got to his feet. "*Musgraveia sulciventris*." He kept his eyes on the woman, his forehead deeply creased. "Or more commonly known as the bronze stink bug, they live on citrus plants. They concentrate the citric acid in their guts and can shoot it out of their abdomens in a jet. It can kill predators, or even blind inquisitive pets."

"Thank god it didn't get her in the face," Jane said softly.

"We should move soon," Mike added.

"Agreed; can she walk?" Harris asked.

"Walk, yes. Climb, no." Jane bobbed her head. "But she'll be in pain, and if it gets infected then…"

"Good enough. Get the hell out of here." Harris cut across her and then glared at the young scientist. "Alistair, you get to carry our doctor. And you better hope she improves, as I'm thinking we damn well need her more than we need you right now."

CHAPTER 21

"Is that a person down there?" Doctor Nadia Zima squinted into the distance.

Dmitry followed her gaze and after a few moments turned to her. "Where? There's nothing."

Nadia frowned. "In that clearing, there was a large man, I think a man. Looking up at us."

The Russian team stood on a slight hill that was sparsely populated with clumps of trees with huge paddle-like leaves. Orange pendulous bulbs hung from their branches that might have been fruits, but not a single one was being eaten by any local creature, so they left them be.

"Was it a human?" Chekov asked. He handed the scientist his field glasses.

Nadia took them to scan the foliage of the clearing again. "I think human-shaped, but they looked extraordinarily large." She lowered the glasses. "Gone now."

"Well, that's where we're heading. So either he, it, didn't see us, or did see us, and didn't want to be scrutinized. Either way, we may find out soon enough." Dmitry turned to Chekov. "A moment, Leonid."

He walked a few paces away and his friend followed.

"You think there may be trouble? An ambush?" Chekov asked.

"I think we need to be ready. Our little babushka, Ms Babikov, never mentioned any people down here. Maybe they are from the surface as well, yes?" Dmitry looked back at the group. "We leave in two minutes." He then moved closer to Chekov. "I don't want to panic the scientists, but tell the military team to be ready for an assault."

"Understood." Chekov headed to where Sasha and Viktor stood talking softly as they loaded up their packs.

Dmitry checked his weapons, making sure they were functional and fully loaded then waved the team on.

The strange paddle-like trees became sparser as they traveled down into a small valley and there came bursts of strange color growing in clumps that had waving tendrils and gave off a citrus-sweet odor. The scientist, Oleg, sniffed and approached one of them.

From about six-feet back he peered in. "It's attracting animals to it and trapping them in some sort of sticky extrusion."

Dmitry paused to watch for a while and saw some of the stout tendrils had fist-sized creatures stuck to them.

Oleg turned. "I bet those tips are loaded with stingers." He grinned. "You know what it reminds me of?" His eyebrows went up.

"A sea anemone," Nadia quickly finished for him.

"Yes, thank you." Oleg's face dropped at the intrusion. He turned back to the thing. "A land anemone?" He slowly lifted a hand and held it closer.

"Don't," Dmitry said. "If you get stung and cannot walk, no one will carry you."

"I just wanted to…" He shook his head as if to clear it. "I'm okay." He then reached into his pack for his camera and took several pictures of the strange plant or creature. "For our records."

"Hurry up." Dmitry turned and then led them down the slope.

As they traveled, they trampled down a spreading clover-like ground cover that squished and bled a green sap beneath their feet. Once exposed to the air, it oxidized and changed to a brilliant red, and when looking back, it clearly showed their path in a trail of bloody footprints.

It was only when they reached the bottom of the slope that Dmitry saw the benefit of this: there were other fading footprints at the ground level.

"Oleg," Dmitry called up to his scientist. "What do you make of these?" He pointed at the line of faint tracks.

The biologist knelt beside several series of prints. "By the look of the depths of our tracks compared to the shape and size of these, then this thing must have been of considerable size; twenty feet and a maybe a ton in weight."

Oleg moved aside a little to a different set of tracks. "But these here are strange. Sometimes this particular creature walks in a bipedal fashion and other times it seems to move more on legs. And it doesn't seem to be much bigger than we are."

"The person I saw?" Nadia suggested.

Oleg turned to her. "Maybe you are right. The footprints of the biped seem to be the most recent; they're still bleeding sap."

Dmitry held up a hand. "Quiet… listen."

The group stopped moving or talking and concentrated.

"You hear that?" Dmitry asked.

Chekov nodded. "It sounds like horns blowing."

EPISODE 09

"It seems wisest to assume the worst from the beginning...and let anything better come as a surprise"

— Jules Verne

CHAPTER 22

Ray Harris raised a hand to stop the group. He held his position for a half-minute with his head tilted.

Mike looked from the man to the jungle and then whispered close to Jane's ear, "What's happening?"

She shook her head. "I think he's listening for something."

Ally finally approached him. "What is it?"

"Did you hear that?" Harris asked with a furrowed brow.

Ally turned back to the water, and then the thick jungle ahead and looked along the distant wall of towering trees. After a moment she shook her head.

"I got nothing."

Harris finally shook his head. "Forget it." He chuckled softly. "Sounded like Gabriel's trumpet."

They continued, and though they had now crossed over most of the water, their mountain range had reduced to little more than a raised rocky shelf and they would soon re-enter the jungle.

Harris stopped again when they were just a quarter-mile from coming off their rocky path and waved them all down.

"We'll take five here. The jungle is always a little more... stressful." He sat down against a slab of raw granite.

Mike noticed he looked ill or was reaching the limit of his endurance. Perhaps the man hadn't slept well, or was finally showing the effects of the arduous mission. Mike would have loved to have Penny look him over.

But when he turned to the doctor he saw she was sat hunched over and cradling her arm. Jane was with her and had already taken to unwrapping her bandages in preparation for a change of dressing.

There were a few more bandages in her kit, but their supply was near exhausted now. That meant that when she got the bandages free, she handed the blood-dampened material to Alistair.

"Rinse these out well in the salt water; in this heat they'll be dry and when needed we can reuse them. The salt residue won't do the wounds any harm either."

The young scientist took them, sullenly, and glanced at the water down from the rocks. He looked about to object, but a glare from Jane made him change his mind.

Jane peeled away the last bandage and it came away stickily, taking with it much of the remnants of her ruined flesh. Mike sat close to Jane and also examined the female doctor's arm. It was swollen and wet-looking as if it had been skinned. In effect that's exactly what the acid had done to her.

"Grit your teeth," Jane said as she applied more of the antiseptic powder.

Penny gave her a half-smile as the powder alighted on her damaged arm and was immediately soaked through with red and yellow fluid.

"Does it hurt?" Mike asked.

Penny turned to him. "No, and that's the problem. The nerve endings have probably all been damaged as well."

Jane pulled Penny's sleeve up past her elbow. There were red streaks moving up her arm. Penny nodded when she saw. "I knew it, but hoped…"

"It'll be fine," Jane said as she began to wrap the new bandage around it.

Penny gave her a dreamy smile. "Those red veins were moving up my arm; I know you know what they are, Jane, and what they mean."

Jane kept her head down for a moment but then began to nod. "Possible blood poisoning."

"Yes, septicemia. And not just possibly, but definitely," Penny said softly. She rested her head back against the rock. "If, *when*, the red lines get past my shoulder, the infected blood cells will begin to lodge in my organs. I'll go into toxic shock, coma, and then die." She sighed. "Whatever that stuff was that damn thing spat at me it must have had some sort of digestive toxin in it, similar to the Komodo dragon whose saliva contains deadly bacteria."

"Jesus, what can we do?" Mike asked. "Don't you have antibiotics?"

"I do, but for this I'd need penicillin or something a little stronger than the field antibiotics I brought along," Penny replied wearily.

She had turned to face them and Jane noticed that she was perspiring heavily, and losing even more water through fever.

Penny's smile dropped. "But there is something you can do…"

"Remove the infection." Harris' voice from behind them made Mike jump.

"What? How?" Mike asked. "Penny just told us we don't have the drugs down here."

Harris kept his eyes on Penny as if waiting on her. After another moment, the female scientist's face screwed, and she nodded. When she opened her eyes they glistened, and she gave him a smile that was fragile at the corners.

"Field amputation," Penny said bleakly.

"What the...?" Jane shot to her feet. *"No."* She swung to Harris, scowling. "We need to leave, now."

Harris shrugged. "Two options. One, the hard option, we remove her arm at the elbow. Perhaps stop the infection and buy her some time. No guarantee she won't pick up further infections, but it gives her a fighting chance." He kept his eyes on Penny's. "Option two, the easy option, for us anyway: we leave her as is. Then she'll be delirious in twelve hours, unconscious in twenty-four, and dead soon after."

"Nope." Mike shook his head. "Nope." He also got to his feet. "Got to be another way."

"Let's hear it, Mike. And remember, the clock is ticking, and the infection will be at her shoulder in another few hours. Once it gets into her organs, she's had it."

"We bind it, cut off the blood flow," Mike pleaded. "That'll work."

"Binding is short term and only designed to buy you time. Any more than an hour, and the limb will die. The infection is slowed but not stopped. What else you got?"

"Well, we're not damn well cutting off her arm in the middle of a primordial jungle at the center of the world," Mike yelled back.

"So, easy option, *huh*? Let her die?" Harris' voice was deadpan.

Mike's eyes bulged. "We just can't..."

"Mike, it's my decision," Penny said and looked up at Harris. "Take it off."

*****

Alistair crouched on the rocks down at the water level. He held the soiled bandages in one hand and looked out over the red-tinged water to his left side. The huge jungle loomed behind him, the mountain ridge and the bizarre limpet-like creatures extended until it curved down with the horizon and before him was the seeming endless sea.

Its placid lake-like surface calmed him and took his mind away from the horrors of their travels, and of Penny's injuries. *It wasn't his fault*, he told himself again. *How was he to know?*

Alistair blinked it away and let his eyes travel over the water's misted surface. He knew he'd get to see the ocean, and he smiled abstractedly as he stared. In those warm, sultry depths all manner of weird and wonderful creatures swam. He sniffed, smelling the brine, and looking down he saw small shellfish stuck to weed-covered rocks. Though red from the sky's reflection, the water was clear, and a small part of him wanted to pull on a dive mask and slip into those red depths to see for himself what was below.

That was the thinking of both the curious scientist and excited kid in him, but as the rational adult he remembered what Mike Monroe had written, and coupled with what he'd seen for himself, he knew in deeper water he'd be a small morsel of food for the monsters hiding there.

He leaned forward and let the bandage unfold and soak for a moment. The blood made the water a little cloudy but didn't change its color. Small things like miniature brine shrimp came out from the weeds to zoom through the cloud, perhaps looking for fragments of food, and he lifted the bandages and squeezed them out. He replaced them in a different section of the rock pool and did the same again several times until the traces of Penny began to dissolve.

When the bandages were as clean as he could manage, he wrung them out and looked once again at the tiny animals speeding back and forth through the blood cloud. He scooped his free hand through the feeding frenzy, catching several of them in his cupped hand and lifted them to his face for a better look.

They were pale, almost transparent, multi-legged, and zoomed about like little motorized machines. "Maybe, *Artemia*, of the family *Artemiidae*," Alistair whispered. "And you little guys are unchanged since the Triassic."

Alistair looked up at the red, boiling ceiling. *What if*, he wondered, *a gravity well appeared at the bottom of one of our oceans?* There were undoubtedly deep caves in the ocean depths, but what if the animals, these center Earth dwellers and our surface creatures, could somehow mix?

"What would arrive here?" Alistair asked himself. "And what of this inner world would be released to ours?"

Alistair let the tiny crustaceans drop back into the pool and stood, hung the bandage over his arm, and climbed the rocky hillside to rejoin his group.

*****

"You're gonna do what?" Alistair's mouth dropped open.

Penny reached out a hand and Alistair took it and sunk to his knees beside her.

"It's okay, I'll be fine." She smiled. "Just keep holding my hand."

He nodded, his eyes swimming. "I'm so sorry. I wish…"

"Not your fault. Don't think like that." She turned away to Harris. "Let's do this while I still have my courage and wits. In my bag there's a

147

medical kit with scalpel, wire saw to use on the bone, and a strong local anesthetic."

Harris nodded. "Anyone else feel they would be able to perform the surgery?" He looked along their faces and stopped at Jane. She was the only one who had any sort of science degree above being a bug expert.

She shook her head and wouldn't meet his eyes.

"Okay then." Harris went to Penny's kit and searched for the equipment. As he searched, he spoke in deadpan tones. "I want a fire, I want knives sterilized, and I want bandages and antibiotics ready."

"On it," Mike said.

Harris turned back to Penny. "This ain't gonna be pretty."

She nodded, her face already draining of color. "I don't think I'll watch." Her lower lip trembled.

"Jane, I'll need you to assist," Harris said.

Jane sucked in a deep breath and let it out with a *whoosh*. "What do you need me to do?"

Mike brought back the tools, and Harris told him which ones he'd need to put in the fire, laid out the scalpels and wire saw and splashed them with a small bottle of alcohol.

"Wrap a belt around Penny's wrist and then when I say, I'll need you to hold her arm up and out tight, and don't let it go." Harris filled a hypodermic needle and without another word jabbed it into Penny's arm and depressed the plunger.

After a few seconds, Penny nodded. "I'm ready." She sniffed wetly, turned away and shut her eyes, and pressed her lips together so hard they went white.

Harris tied off some rubber tubing as a tourniquet at her upper arm, real tight, and then looked from Jane, to Mike, and then back to the arm. He held up the scalpel and without another word, moved in.

Mike had seen injuries before. He'd seen compound fractures where bones poked up through the skin, he'd seen crushing injuries, and bodies that had fallen hundreds of feet to rock; all of them were bloody and all of them ugly.

But there was almost artistry in the way Harris moved; he was swift, using the laser-sharpened scalpel to ring the flesh just above her elbow. He dropped the blade and picked up the wire saw, wrapped it around the exposed, pink bone and turned to Jane and then Penny.

"Brace yourself, both of you."

Mike and Jane held on tight and kept the arm out straight. Mike grit his teeth unable to turn away, but Jane shut her eyes tight.

Harris exerted force and jerked the toothed steel saw back and forward quickly. Penny sobbed through her bared teeth and even though the flesh was deadened from the anesthetic, the vibrations right up her bone must have felt revolting.

Harris grunted, and then Jane and Mike fell back, holding Penny's freed arm still held by the strap.

"Knife one," Harris yelled.

Mike handed him the blade from the fire, and Harris sealed the stump of the arm. He let the knife drop.

He quickly checked his work then held out his bloodsoaked hand. "Knife two."

Mike handed him the last, and Harris finished searing the flesh. Mike held his breath, not wanting to smell the cooking meat.

Harris then quickly splashed the stump once again with alcohol and bandaged it. Harris finished by releasing the rubber tubing and quickly rolled her sleeve down and tied it off.

Harris knelt in front of Penny who sobbed quietly.

"Thank you for being so brave." He leaned forward and whispered, "When the painkillers wear off, that's gonna hurt like a bitch; be ready." Harris kissed her sweaty brow and then stood. He wiped his forehead with the back of his hand, leaving a red smear.

Mike noticed that he was also speckled with blood. The ex-soldier moved his dead eyes to Mike. "Sometimes this job is shit." He turned to Alistair who looked like he was about to throw up. "Clean up those instruments and knives; we may need them again."

"What about..." Jane indicated Penny's arm.

"Toss it far away." Harris then walked off to stand with Ally. She put a hand on his shoulder and talked quietly to him. *Maybe using words of encouragement*, Mike wondered.

Jane came into his arms and he hugged her. "There is no good in this place," she said into his chest.

Mike stared down at Penny's severed arm that now looked tiny and pale under the red light. He couldn't disagree with her.

*****

Eight hours later they finally entered the jungle. Jane walked with Penny, but for the most part the woman walked unaided. Though she kept her head down, Jane could see she was pale, and given her blood loss, combined with the little water they had, she must have been seriously dehydrated.

Harris had dropped back to check on her about thirty minutes ago and had promised them they'd stop for a rest soon. But for now, he powered ahead.

Through a veil of hanging vines they came to a tumble of boulders set into the side of a hill with several of them creating a natural opening at the front. Harris stopped them and sent Ally in. In minutes she had ejected the existing resident, which looked something like a ten-foot millipede, but without any pincers. A few curses and nudges and it vacated with little trouble.

Inside the cave, it was dry, defendable and roomy. Further in it proved an even bigger find; there was a pool of water that filled from the ceiling and drained into the back of the cave and then fell away somewhere below ground. It meant the water wasn't stagnant.

They all had purifier kits, but Mike still also had his water testing kit which he took from its sleeve and dipped it into the pool while they all waited with dry mouths, muscle cramps, and headaches.

The tiny device checked for heavy metals, nitrates and nitrites, and biological containments from bacteria and fungal spores. The only thing it couldn't detect was a virus; but in water they were rarely an issue.

After a moment he nodded and hiked his shoulders. "Normal pond water. Not the best, but at least we can drink it without getting sick."

That was enough confirmation. Everyone filled canteens, drunk their fill and also took cupped hand-fulls and rubbed it on grimy faces.

Jane filled Penny's canteen, changed her bandages and checked the stump while the female doctor drank. Jane noticed that water ran from her lips as though they were partially numb.

"How's it look?" Penny asked.

"Not bad." Jane bobbed her head. "Well, as good as it can look. But there's no sign of further infection. How's it feel?"

Penny scoffed. "It feels like my arm is still there but only numb. When I look down I'm still shocked to find it missing." She smiled weakly. "At least I'll have some cool stories to tell, right?"

"You sure will." She rubbed the woman's shoulder. "I'm gonna go check on Mike."

Alistair was sitting by himself and gazing into the small pond, and Mike was sitting with Harris and Ally. Jane came and squatted between them.

"Penny's doing okay. For now," Jane said.

"Good," Harris said. "I was just giving an update on our position. We're only a few miles from the Russian team. For some reason they seem to have slowed down. Normally, I'd send out a scout, but we're a little resource-poor right now."

He meshed his hands. "Here's the deal; our priority is to stop the Russians from attacking our bases. But I'm under no illusion about the difficulty of our task with them probably having the force advantage. But on the upside, we have the tactical advantage of surprise."

"We get close, we can take 'em," Ally said.

"That we can." Harris nodded. "Our fallback objective is to destroy whatever technology it is they are using. Without that it means they'll just be another group of assholes wandering around six thousand miles below the Earth's surface."

"So what now?" Mike asked.

"Now? Now we get some rest, and then we should be able to catch up to them well before they're underneath Camp Bondsteel."

"One question?" Jane asked. "What do you expect us to do when we find them?"

Harris smiled understandingly. "I can't compel a civilian to actually fight. But if Ally and I are repelled or killed, then I can guarantee they won't be taking any hostages." He shrugged. "Might be in your interest to pitch in on this one."

Jane looked briefly at Mike and then exhaled.

Harris looked about in their small cave. "Everyone get some rest; just a few hours. I'll take first watch." His smile faded. "Going to be a big day tomorrow."

CHAPTER 23

Senate Building, the Moscow Kremlin Complex, Russia

President Volkov slowly lowered the phone and sat staring straight ahead. As General Yevgeni Voinovich watched, the President's face began to turn the color of a ripe plum.

The general remained standing at strict attention; he was the chief architect of the DEM, the Deep Earth Mission, and he suspected it was in trouble.

Volkov's eyes slid to the general. "They know."

Voinovich frowned. "They…?"

"*They know*." Volkov pounded his fist down so hard everything on the twelve-hundred pound desk jumped an inch.

"How? How is that possible?" Voinovich asked.

"Maybe they have a spy, maybe they are there, maybe they use ESP. Doesn't matter." Volkov waved the question away and his eyes took on a far away look. "I have just been told by the American president that if we do not cease and desist…" His glare intensified, "… and *also* destroy one of our military bases within the next twelve hours, the Americans will obliterate three of them, as payback."

The general sucked in a breath suddenly realizing that as the sponsor of the mission, his neck was suddenly at risk.

The president rose from his chair. "And if there *are* any further attacks from Deep Earth, it will be regarded as a declaration of war. And they will respond devastatingly." He bared his teeth for a moment. "We are not ready for a war with the Americans."

We haven't been ready for a war with the Americans for forty years, Voinovich thought. *That's why we attempted to weaken them from below*.

Voinovich stood even straighter. "What are your orders, sir?"

"Cancel the mission immediately." Volkov rested his knuckles on the table. "And bring me a list of our military bases outside of Russia."

*****

Rossiyskaya Gazeta (Russian Gazette) – Breaking News: Tragedy in Armenia

Early this morning the Russian 102nd Military Base of the Group Russian Forces in Gyumri, Armenia, part of the Transcaucasian Group, and home to three thousand military personnel was destroyed in an earthquake.

A team of rescue and medical professionals have been dispatched but first reports indicate there were no survivors.

At this point in time all access is prohibited until investigations have been completed.

CHAPTER 24

"What are they?" Dmitry gripped his gun tighter.

On the hill above them was what looked like crosses planted sporadically on the slope. But there also seemed to be things stuck to them.

Chekov audibly swallowed. "I know what I think they look like." He glanced at his leader. "My cousin uses them in his wheat fields."

"Scarecrows." Dmitry nodded. "We have no choice; there's no other way around." He drew in a deep breath, let it out slowly, and then turned to his group. "In tight, and everyone stay alert."

They closed in on the effigies, moving slowly. He and Chekov took the lead, with Sasha and Viktor at the rear, keeping the scientists and Katya in the middle.

Dmitry held up a hand and the group halted. He and Chekov then approached one of the closest cross structures.

"I think maybe you are right." Dmitry stared up at the creature lashed to the x-shaped poles.

It was now like an empty suit of armor; the exoskeleton shell was hollowed out, and the plating was scorched and flaking from the continual bombardment of the red heat and radiation from above.

The creature seemed to be some sort of huge grasshopper thing standing seven feet tall with a bovine face, but on the end of each of its six limbs were grasping digits like fingers, but now more like empty armored gloves.

"They're not all the same," Chekov observed.

Sure enough, just fifty feet away at the next effigy, the lashed animal was a body: a human body. Chekov approached it and craned his neck to look up into its open mouth. He turned.

"It's got fillings in its teeth."

Dmitry approached and examined it. He turned. "Katya."

The old woman hobbled closer. "Is this one of your team?"

She shook her head. "Those fillings are ceramic. In the seventies Russia only did metal fillings." She turned to Dmitry. "And even accounting for the weathering and decay those remains are not fifty years old."

"She's right." Chekov turned. "Not Russian... but definitely human."

Nadia joined them. "Male, probably around mid-thirties, I think." She squinted up at the lashed skeleton. "There's something wrong with his skull."

Sure enough they could see several holes in the bone, perfectly round as if drilled.

"Torture?" Dmitry asked.

"Or examination." Nadia reached out and tugged some of the desiccated flesh from the arm. "This body hasn't been here all that long; maybe only a year or two."

"Who was he?" Chekov asked. "I assume he didn't come down by himself, so where are his friends?"

They turned about, each looking for any sign of other people. Nadia turned around to scan the other bodies lashed down. From where they were at the near crest of the hill, they could see there were a long line of them, perhaps fifty or more, and many different species.

"Do you think he was kidnapped from the surface, and brought down here?" Oleg suggested.

"What a terrible thought," Dmitry's mouth turned down, "that people could be snatched from our world to end up like this."

"Not snatched, I think more like he came down with others." Katya nodded slowly. "Others came to see me a little more than a year ago. I know they were following Arkady Saknussov's trail." She stared again at the skeleton. "I warned them not to."

"Well, we have never heard about it. So I think they all met their fate in this inner world." Dmitry sighed. "I wish we could talk to him."

"He ended up a scarecrow. So he *is* talking to us." Chekov snorted. "What do you usually put a scarecrow up for?"

"To scare away the crows," Dmitry replied.

"Not sure if we are the crows," Chekov asked. "But it is certainly working on us chickens."

"Well, at least we're chickens with guns." Dmitry chuckled. "Our GPS is telling us that we are not far from our destination, so why don't we see what's over this hill?"

They began to move off and only Katya remained staring up at the lashed skeleton. After another moment she shook her head and turned away.

The group came in tighter and moved cautiously up to the crest of the hill. Chekov and Dmitry still took the lead and in another few hundred yards reached the top. They gathered under the canopy of a medium-sized tree and stared out over the landscape far below.

"Amazing; it's in the water. I wondered about this," Doctor Oleg

Krupin said softly. "What effect would that have on the gravity well? Will it still allow the transfer of matter?"

Dmitry stared into the distance. There was a band of jungle that ended at what could be an inlet that fed out into an ocean. But just a few miles off its shore there was another of the column mountains except this one went from the boiling red ceiling above, and then disappeared back down into deep water.

There was also a smooth island close to the column that was totally devoid of vegetation and more a greyish-looking lump. He looked back to the massive many-miles-wide column reaching the ceiling.

"Maybe that gravity well is full of water," Dmitry replied. He turned to Sasha. "Take a position check." When he turned back, the island was gone. "What the...?"

"What is it?" Chekov asked.

"I thought..." *I must be getting tired*, Dmitry thought. "Nothing."

The soldier set to checking their coordinates, and in a few minutes looked up from the device. "We're under the Mediterranean Sea. Close to Crete."

"The Mediterranean. Deep water and..." Nadia turned to Oleg. "Are you thinking what I'm thinking?"

"The Calypso?" Oleg grinned. "Imagine if..."

"Would our scientists like to share their little observation please?" Dmitry raised an eyebrow.

Oleg grinned and formed his hands and fingers into a ball. "The Earth's Crust is a skin like the skin covering an apple. It is thinner in some areas than others. Under the continents it can be up to twenty-five miles thick. And under the oceans it can be as little as only five miles thick. But if there were a deep trench..." He shrugged. "Then maybe it is only three miles."

Nadia nodded. "And guess what is at the bottom of the Mediterranean, near Crete?"

"A trench... called the Calypso, maybe?" Chekov's voice was deadpan.

"Yes." She pointed at his chest. "The Calypso trench, located in the Matapan–Vavilov Deep, and it is over seventeen thousand feet deep."

"Just over three miles," Dmitry added. He turned back to the well. "So maybe we have a gravity well that feeds into the bottom of the ocean." He turned back to the pair of scientists. "How does that help us?"

The pair looked at each other and then turned back. Oleg shrugged. "Maybe it doesn't. But it is possible that as we terrestrial land-based creatures found our way down, then maybe some of the denizens of the ocean's surface or the oceans at the center of the Earth, are able to find their way back and forth as well via a water highway."

Oleg turned to Nadia. "What if creatures have been passing through these water wells for millions of years? There are dozens of super deep-sea trenches all around the globe."

Nadia's eyes glowed. "All the legends of inexplicable giant sea beasts that have been spotted over the centuries, they may all have come from down here. Just imagine if you had a deep-sea submersible and could locate the entrance and travel along it."

"And what about all the massive sea beasts of our prehistory that vanished, some for no reason?" Oleg clasped his hands together. "So many questions."

"Are you two finished?" Dmitry's patience had expired.

"For now." Nadia grinned. She looked back at the huge column mountain just visible in the distance. "You could spend a lifetime researching down here."

Chekov laughed. "I think then it would be a very short lifetime."

Dmitry used the GPS points to plot his course. They still had many miles to go until they were underneath the Kosovo base, and the course they'd travel would take them away from the water. For some reason that made him feel better. That missing island still bothered him.

Chekov came and stood at his shoulder, and his friend lifted field glasses to scan their surroundings. At the base of the hill was a line of dense bushes that was so thick it seemed solid. But there seemed to be a path at its center.

After another moment he lowered the glasses. It was the only way through, but as a military man, he saw it as a perfect place for an ambush.

He spoke without turning. "Do you feel it?"

"Yes." Dmitry looked up from his positioning plotter and folded it away. "Ever since we got to the top of the hill. We are being watched."

"And I think not just by the scarecrows," Chekov replied softly. "We should keep moving. But we must be onguard."

"Agreed." Dmitry turned to his group. "Okay, people, we're going on. Everyone check their weapons and stay alert. Whoever made these scarecrows didn't do it as an invitation."

Dmitry took one last look back down the steep hill at the human skeleton. "So long comrade; may you rest in peace." He waved them on. "Let's go."

He led them down and over the hill. The feeling of being watched only grew stronger.

*****

Within the line of bushes huge, hard-shelled bodies stayed motionless except for their eyestalks quivering with excitement as the small soft creatures headed to them.

Clawed hands slowly lifted nets, waiting.

CHAPTER 25

Senate Building, the Moscow Kremlin Complex, Russia

President Volkov's pale and unblinking eyes were like chips of ice and seemed to see right into his soul.

General Voinovich swallowed. "There has been no response to our messages for twenty-four hours." He felt the perspiration run down under his arms as he remained at attention. "There could simply be a technical malfunction, or they are passing through an area that will not allow transmission."

"Or they could all be dead. Which might be a good thing." Volkov leaned forward. "Or, they might have lost the transmitter or permanently damaged their equipment and are proceeding to their designated target."

After a moment, Voinovich nodded slowly.

"And if they are successful, it would trigger an all-out American military response." The president's eyes narrowed. "General Voinovich, this was your project. And now your mess." He rose to his feet. "Clean it up, or it is your head."

Voinovich snapped to attention. "Yes, sir."

"Get out," Volkov said from between clenched teeth.

Voinovich turned on his heel and headed for the door.

"One more thing, General."

Voinovich paused and turned. "Yes, sir."

"Bring me the heads of our armed forces." The president came around his desk. "We may have no choice but to strike before being struck."

Voinovich exited and strode down the long, tiled corridor, his heels clicking ever faster on their polished surfaces. He knew without communication there was absolutely nothing he could do.

He suddenly wondered whether now was a good time to take that holiday he always dreamed of in Spain.

CHAPTER 26

The jungle began to change, moving from its usual cacophony of millions of living things to a growing pall of silence.

Ever since Harris had roused them from their rest break, he had pushed them hard trying to run down the Russian group. After several hours they had entered yet another jungle thicket, and this one nearly devoid of any creature over a foot tall. It was if they had all be pushed out, or maybe eaten.

The thought filled Jane with trepidation, but then again, everything about this place filled her with that dread sensation.

"*Get down,*" Harris hissed.

Mike and the rest of the group flattened themselves to the ground or took cover.

Up ahead, the man and woman broke from the jungle and sprinted hard along the track to the group's places of concealment. They both wore a form of jungle fatigues that had glistening mud to the waist. The woman was in the lead and she was young, average height and looked terrified. The man was big, bristling with weapons, and looked formidable. They were going to pass right by them.

Harris made hand signals to Ally and she nodded in return. She pulled back into the foliage and vanished.

The woman went past first, and then when the man came close to them, Harris stood up, and used the butt of his gun against the side of the man's head. The big guy went down with a grunt.

The woman in the lead half-turned and stopped to stare. From out of the foliage Ally appeared and silently put a knife to the woman's throat. The woman said something in Russian and held up her hands. Ally then turned her around and shoved her back to the group.

"English?" Harris said to her, as the man was still on the ground, dazed and holding his head.

"Yes," the woman said in a heavy accent. "Who are you?" she asked.

"We'll get to that." Harris smiled. "Your name and rank."

She shook her head. "Nadia Zima. No rank, I am a scientist working for the Russian Institute of Science and Technology. I work in evolutionary biology."

160

"So do I," Alistair offered. "Specializing in entomology."

"Shut up," Harris barked at him, and then turned back to Nadia. "How many more of you are there?"

She seemed to think. "Seven, now, if all still alive. There were nine, then we lost…"

Harris cut across her. "Are they coming this way?"

She shook her head. "We got separated after we were attacked."

"By who, what?" Harris asked.

"Things like people, but not people. After we passed through the scarecrows."

"Scarecrows?" Jane asked.

"Yes, things erected to frighten us or warn us. We didn't listen." She snorted softly. "Creatures tied out on stakes. There was also a man, human, not dead more than a few years." She looked up. "We think he was a westerner."

Jane looked to Mike, who nodded.

"*Ne govori im nichego,*" the man said groggily from the ground.

Harris went to hit him again, but Nadia held out a hand to stop him.

"*Mozhet byt', oni mogut pomoch,*" she said. "I tell Sasha, maybe you can help us."

"Just tell us where your group is, and we'll go see," Harris said.

"Your turn. Who are you?" Nadia asked.

"Americans," Jane offered. "On an exploratory expedition. We found your colleague, Mila. But she died, infected by something." She glanced at Harris. "We decided to follow your trail to see who you were." She tilted her head. "This man looks like Russian military. What are you doing here?"

"His name is Sasha, a good person." Nadia glanced down at the man, who glared back up at her. He gave an almost imperceptible shake of his head. Harris saw it and cracked him again with the gun barrel, splitting his eyebrow.

"Stop." Nadia held her hands out. "Please."

"No secrets now, children," Harris said with little sympathy.

"It's a scientific mission…" she began.

Harris hit Sasha again, harder, making a crunching sound and this time making his ear bleed.

"Easy," Mike said.

Harris looked up at Nadia and grinned. "My bullshit detector just went off. Try harder."

Her eyes went to Sasha again, and Jane could see the woman was clearly panicked about what to say. Sasha's eyes darted for a moment, and then he went for Harris' gun.

Harris was not just ready for him, but seemed to expect it. He took a step back allowing room for Sasha to leap at him. He then turned his gun sideways and shot the big Russian twice in the ribs. The soldier was blown back to lie on the ground gasping like a fish. Already bubbles of blood popped on his lips.

"You didn't need to do that," Mike yelled.

Nadia went to run, but Ally grabbed her by the scruff and kicked the legs out from under her, making her sprawl at their group's center.

Harris crouched to grab Nadia's hand and slowly stood bringing her with him. His face was grim. "Madam Nadia, believe me when I tell you this, we're the good guys here. We have the angels on our side when we simply try and stop you from killing our people." He stepped closer to her. "We know you destroyed our base in Estonia, killed over two hundred good men and women."

Nadia's mouth drew into a tight line for a moment. "I, I don't know anything about that. I'm just…"

Harris turned and fired a third round into Sasha, this time into his head. The man bucked and lay still. Alistair shrieked, and Harris spun back to Nadia.

"Chasing you and your team has cost us some good people. And caused us no end of pain." He indicated Penny who sat apart from them cradling her arm stump. "So if you think I now have any patience or mercy for Russian agents or their science team, then think again." His expression was deadpan. "Start talking."

Nadia brought her hands together. "I am a scientist, not a soldier or agent. There are three of us on the science team, and we had no idea what the soldiers were doing, until…"

"Until they goddamn destroyed our base." Harris bared his teeth as he shouted the words into her face. "How? How did they do it?"

"I don't…" She wilted under Harris' glare. "I think, I think it was by using some sort of resonance pulser."

"Go on," Harris asked.

"I don't know everything," Nadia pleaded.

"Then goddamn guess," Harris demanded.

"I think that it directs a high-energy resonance beam up, like a laser, but instead of focused light, it would deliver focused vibrations. The pulse remains compressed until it reaches its destination." She grimaced.

"Pretty good guess, Nadia," Ally scoffed.

Nadia shook her head. "I didn't even know it existed. And if I did, would doubt it could even work," Nadia pleaded.

"We have electromagnetic weapons, sonic weapons, pressure pulsers, and a range of other energy armaments in use. But we have never heard of that type of technology at this range." Harris frowned. "What else?"

Nadia seemed to search her memory. "They have somehow improved the strength and compression capabilities. Consider it like the technology used to shatter kidney stones through the flesh without touching any of the healthy flesh around the hard matter. This works on a similar concept, with more power and more precision. This is not my field."

Harris turned to Jane. "Is this possible?"

She shrugged. "Sure, anything is possible. But I have no idea how they can keep the vibrations compressed until they're delivered to, *at*, a target."

Nadia folded he arms. "That's all I know, and if you don't believe me, then you might as well just shoot me now."

"Okay." Harris lifted the gun to her forehead.

Ally grinned, and Mike yelled. Nadia squeaked and covered her face.

"Wait." Ally still grinned. "She can lead us to her team and the weapon, can't you, comrade?"

She took her hands away from her face. Harris still looked furiously at the Russian woman and kept the gun pointed between her eyes. Nadia let her eyes slide to Ally and gave her an almost imperceptible nod.

Ally shrugged. "Then she's still useful."

Harris slowly lowered the gun. "I guess."

"Show us," Ally said.

Nadia took a last look at Sasha and shut her eyes for a moment.

Ally gave her a push. "Move it."

Nadia finally turned away. "This way."

Harris winked at Ally, and she jiggled her eyebrows in return. Mike saw then that it was all a setup to get Nadia to lead them back in. He looked at the dead Russian soldier; *or perhaps not all game playing*, he thought.

Nadia walked beside Ally, with Alistair talking to the Russian scientist in their own particular language of science and enthusiasm. Jane and Mike steered Penny forward who seemed to be lost in some sort of semi-fugue state or maybe a dark depression was settling over her.

Harris was at the rear, but seemed to have been invigorated now that he had a goal, and on hearing that the Russian team had been attacked, he perhaps hoped that the odds had swung in his favor.

Mike saw that Jane's mouth was turned down as she walked, and he gently nudged her. "Hey, look on the bright side."

"*Huh?*" His voice broke her from her reverie. "There's a bright side?"

"Yeah, our mission here looks like it might be just about over. If the Russian team has been scattered, or their machine has been destroyed, then we're all done." He smiled. "The biggest decision we need to make will be whether we backtrack, or head on to the Kosovo Gadime cave system. Maybe find another gravity well there."

She turned to him and smiled. "I love an optimist." Her smiled broadened. "But yeah, that's a nice thought and I like it."

Ally held up a hand and the group bunched up. Harris joined her at the front and she looked from Nadia to her boss.

"Ms. Comrade says there's a swamp from here. They went through it, but something attacked the other science nerd that was with them."

Nadia turned. "It was Oleg. We were moving quickly through the swamp when something came out of the mud and took him. Sasha couldn't rescue him."

Mike sniffed. "I can smell it already, the methane and rot." He turned to Nadia. "Was there a way around it?"

"Maybe, I don't know," she replied. "We didn't have time to decide on choices."

"Nope, we press on. Nadia will lead us and hopefully keep us out of danger, right?" Harris said.

Nadia released a string of curses under her breath and Mike smiled as he understood every one of them. She suggested Harris was some sort of stupid offspring of his mother and a pig. For the most part Mike didn't disagree.

The group paused, looking in through the twisted boughs at a steamy, twilight landscape.

"This is a bad idea," Jane whispered.

"No, this is a shit idea," Mike replied. "Stay close."

They headed in.

*****

The ground quickly went from stable to soft, and then to squelching under their feet. With that came the miasmic odors as the heat and humidity combined to rot everything down to slime.

The first pools of water had a skin on them that was sticky and dark like thick oil, and when they came to the first large pond. Nadia stopped.

"It gets bad from here," Nadia said.

"It's bad already," Alistair replied.

"For how long?" Harris asked.

"We were moving quick, running at the end, after Oleg was taken."

She bobbed her head. "Maybe an hour."

"That's around a mile; freaking great," Ally replied. She turned to Nadia. "Now would be a good time to tell us what happened to your buddy in here."

"He was at the back, so we didn't really see. We were moving through deep water, and he screamed. When we turned, Oleg was gone." Nadia's voice trembled.

"We avoided swamps, because we assumed there'd be some sort of arthropod version of the crocodilian species." Jane joined them at the edge of the water.

The heavy canopy overhead cut down on the light, meaning there was no chance of any depth perception in the water. Everything would be invisible. And there was no way to judge whether the water was an inch deep, a foot, or ten.

"Sooner we enter, sooner we're out," Harris announced. "Ally, take us in."

Ally blinked a few times, and Mike could tell she thought it was a shit idea as well. She half-turned. "Everyone stay in tight and cover each other's asses. And arm themselves." She faced Nadia. "You're excluded." Ally drew her gun in tight to her shoulder, flicked on the powerful flashlight beam on the muzzle and waded in.

Alistair helped Penny, but instead of his gun he held his camera. He hurried to be just in behind Jane. "Did you see any? The arthropod crocodilian species?" he asked.

"No." Jane half-turned. "But given they're one of the most global species of ancient creatures it makes sense there'd be some sort of concurrent evolutionary match-up."

"Right, right." Alistair's head bobbed. "But a perfect theory. Hope we see one... from a distance I mean." He gave Jane an apologetic grin when she turned to frown at him.

Mike held his handgun in one hand and flashlight in the other. He panned it across the water's surface that popped with bubbles of fetid gases. Slime-covered branches rose from its depths, and now and then an eddy from a current swirled on top, indicating something had moved out of their way beneath the inky surface.

It didn't take long for the ponds to join up and soon there were no islands to rest on. Shawls of dripping weeds or moss hung from branches and tree trunks rose from the brackish water, but they did so on stilt-like legs to perhaps try and lift themselves from the corrupt waters beneath them.

After wading for nearly thirty minutes, Harris' voice was filled with impatience. "How much further?" he demanded.

Nadia called back over her shoulder. "Halfway, I think."

"I'm assuming we're going the right way?" Mike asked. "Might help."

Harris snorted. "Don't even ask it."

Mike laughed, but his mirth fell away when he felt the pressure wave against his thighs. "Movement," he said. "Everyone hold it."

Harris didn't even question him. "Get in tight, everyone. Ally, hold up."

They bunched up, all facing out, and guns and lights pointed out at the swamp.

"What did you see?" Harris asked.

"Not see, feel; something moved past us, big enough to create a surge wave under the water." Mike looked about slowly. "Last time I felt something like that I was diving in Australia and a nine-foot hammerhead passed within a few feet of me."

"Shark, *huh*? That's just great, and if it's below the surface we're not going to see it. And standing here we're just a big bunch of delicious sitting ducks." Harris moved his light across the water's surface.

Harris was about to move his light beam on when something jerked back below the putrid water's surface. He flicked his light back in time to only catch the ripples.

"O-*oookay*, why don't we keep moving?" Harris kept his light and gun focused on where he had seen the ripples. "Kinda get the feeling something is trying to get in a little closer without us seeing it."

Ally began to move, and Nadia was right at her shoulder.

Jane and Mike were next, followed by Penny and Alistair, and Harris a few paces behind, guarding their rear.

From out to their right side, something big and dark rose and fell momentarily, making the slimy weed on the surface create eddies as the water was pulled after it.

"A whale?" Ally asked.

In the same area something like a rounded fist rose in the water. Then another. On the front of each was a black dot no bigger than a thumbnail.

"Eye stalks," Alistair whispered and took some pictures.

As Harris swung to them, they were pulled below the surface with a double *plop* sound.

"We're being circled," Harris hissed. "Let's get the hell out of here." He gave Alistair a shove in the back. "Move it, mister."

As soon as Alistair took a step back a shadow fell over him as something lifted from the water. The eyes on stalks rose again, and this time following them came a broad, greyish body, six feet across and glistening with slime.

Alistair stared up at it, mouth hanging open. *"Gastrapoda,"* he breathed.

The thing seemed to flatten slightly as it lifted from the dank water. Frill-like growths down its side flared wide, and then a foot-long, vertical mouth opened like a wound showing rows of comb-like teeth inside.

Harris opened up, putting a dozen rounds into it in rapid fire. But it was like striking a pillow as the bullets went in and might even have passed right through the seemingly boneless thing.

"All muscle, all foot and head." Alistair backed up, pushing Penny to the side.

Further eyes rose from the swampy water as more of the creatures approached, and Mike and Jane fired into where they believed the things hid just below the surface.

Ally screamed, more in surprise than anger or fear. "Below the freaking water; they're right under us."

"Can't fight 'em here, soldier," Harris yelled back. He pulled a grenade from his belt, pulled the pin and threw it out about twenty feet. It splashed into the murky depths. *"Fire in the hole!"*

The dark water exploded in a geyser covering the group, and Mike felt the percussive wave against his legs as it nearly knocked him over. He held onto Jane to keep them both upright.

Whether it was the explosion or the creatures simply made a decision to attack, the murky water around them suddenly revealed what they were up against as monstrous slug-like creatures rose from the murky waters.

Half a dozen of them, some as tall as the people, and others towering ten feet over their heads. They flared open like slimy cobras and the vertical mouths gaped wide. They looked like giant glistening bags that had unzipped at the front.

Behind them were rows of downed trees. To the right of them was more open water, and the depths must have been crowded with the things as more crept and slid in the ooze along the swamp bottom to the stranded humans.

Alistair's scream was so high pitched it sounded like a siren and Mike sensed the huge shadow loom over them. He spun in time to see the massive head bending forward, pod-like eyes fixed on Alistair as the vertical mouth flared open as it dropped to him.

Mike turned to fire, but Alistair had frozen to the spot and had thrown his hands up in front of himself, giving no clear shot.

Penny used her good arm to grab his collar and yank him back into the water. Whether she expected it or not, the force of her action pulled him back but propelled her forward, just a few inches, but it was into Alistair's position.

The flattened head fell on her, and the flared gastropod enfolded the entire top half of her body like a slimy blanket. It immediately sunk below the water, taking Penny with it.

"Ally, get 'em moving. Anywhere but here," Harris yelled as he swept the swamp with bullets. His rifle clicked on empty and he ejected the magazine and slapped in another in a well-practiced motion.

Ally started to run, fire, and scream her fury as she barged through the waist-deep water. Jane and Mike used their handguns to shoot anything that wasn't human. Mike had to drag Alistair with him who wailed about Penny, and at the rear Harris shoved Nadia before him.

The water lumped and swirled and out to their right where Penny had been taken, they saw that it boiled and then flushed a muddy red. The creatures seemed to be forming a knot as they wrestled together, and Mike had a pretty good idea what they were fighting over below the surface.

As they surged forward, it now became clear what had taken Nadia's friend. Ally kept them moving and just a few hundred yards further on, they passed underneath a network of vines that housed a flock or school of creatures like segmented stingrays that tried to drop down on top of them. Fortunately, they were slow, easy to discourage, and even easier to hit. The few of them they hit fell into the water and were instantly set upon by the slugs, giving the people a few extra yards grace.

"Getting shallower," Jane said.

Sure enough the water only came to their thighs, then knees, and then their calves, ankles, and finally it was only splashing beneath their boots.

"Keep going." Harris forced them on, wanting to be as far from the stinking bog as he could manage.

It was only when they found some dry ground, grass, and beams of red light that Harris allowed them to slow.

"Ease up," he said.

There were a few patches of open ground, still the red boiling heat, and shadows that could be hiding a dozen deadly denizens of this underworld, but after what they'd been through, it seemed like an oasis.

"Smell that?" Ally sucked in a deep breath. "Air without freaking methane." She let her breath out with pleasure. She grinned, showing teeth streaked with the mud from the bog.

"Take five. Ally, do a quick scout." Harris stopped below a tree, first checking up into its branches above for hidden ambushes, and then lowering his pack. Ally shot off into the jungle as the others crashed to the ground.

Alistair buried his face in his hands. "She saved me."

"She did; she was a hero," Jane said softly.

"Why? After what I did, it was stupid." Alistair sobbed and looked up.

"No, not stupid. She was a doctor, and her first instinct was to save lives," Mike said. "Her arm was becoming infected again, and I guess she knew you had a better chance of surviving this place than she did. She gave you her chance at life." Mike placed a hand on his shoulder.

"Thank you, Penny," Alistair said softly. He rubbed his eyes, hard, and then turned to Jane. "I should have known."

"Known what?" Jane's brows knitted.

"When you said, you said..." he sniffed, "...that you expected to see in the swamp some sort of arthropod crocodilian species, as they'd been so successful and first appeared during the Late Triassic Epoch." He started to giggle and put a fist over his mouth. "But you know what's been around even longer, and is even more successful?"

"You okay, Alistair?" Mike asked.

Alistair nodded vigorously and turned back to Jane. "Gastropoda Mollusca; they've been with us since the Cambrian period, half a billion years." He started to rap against his head with his knuckles. "And we blockheads just wandered into the home of the granddaddies of them all."

"That's enough, son." Harris sat forward. "I know you're a little busted up right now. Penny was a good doctor, and good soul. But you start coming apart, especially down here, and you're as good as dead. Then you'll have thrown her life away for nothing."

"How do you know we're not already dead?" Alistair's eyes blazed and his voice rose. "Yeah, that's right, we're already dead and in Hell."

Ally came back in. "All clear."

Harris got to his feet. "Good. I'll keep watch and try and get our bearings. You take some rest," he said to Ally. He thumbed over his shoulder at Alistair. "And shut him the hell up."

Ally sat on the ground a few feet from Alistair, knees up and rested her forearms on them. "You okay there, little buddy?"

Alistair kept his head down and shook his head. "No, I just want to go home."

"Yep, I hear that." Ally nodded slowly. "We've come through a lot. But keep in mind we're in the end zone now, final quarter. We finish our job and the next thing you know you'll be back in your dusty old library, or wherever you get your kicks, eating hot pockets and reading comic books."

Alistair looked up at her, his eyes red-rimmed and glistening. After a moment he sniffed and then nodded. "Trivia nights," he said softly.

"*Huh?*" Ally turned.

"I like trivia nights." He gave her a broken smile.

"And who doesn't?" She grinned. "Bet you kick ass on those bug questions."

"I do." He brightened.

"Well, Penny gave you a second chance. Use it wisely." Ally lay back and pulled her cap down over her face. "Now while you guys keep watch, I'm shutting my eyes for a few minutes." She momentarily lifted one corner of her hat to stare at them. "And don't do anything dumb."

Mike grinned as in thirty seconds time, there was soft snoring coming from under her mud-spattered cap.

*****

Harris came in fast and crouched. "Got a signal up on the rise; they're close by, less than a mile, and stationary."

Nadia jerked forward. "Did you see them? Are they alive?"

"No idea," Harris replied. "But the tracker is still giving off a signal. That's good enough for me."

Then they heard it: the horn.

Ally froze and Nadia's eyes went wide. "This is the sound we heard before the attack."

Jane turned to Mike and grabbed his arm. "Like back at the cave city, just before…"

Ally sprang to her feet and went through a quick weapon's check. Jane stood, held out a hand to Mike and pulled him up. Alistair also got to his feet, slowly, now looking like he'd aged ten years.

Harris turned slowly. "Whatever it was, it was a long way away. Might have been some sort of animal."

"That was no animal," Mike replied.

"Doesn't matter. Let's finish this." Harris gave them one last look over, and then waved them on. This time he took the lead and Ally dropped back to rear.

They moved fast, but tried to stay alert. Though the jungle here was still thick, there seemed to be no animals to bother them or even take an interest in them.

After about thirty minutes of moving fast and staying low, they came to a small clearing with something piled at its center.

"What the..?" Harris frowned as he stared at the small tracking device. "Signal receiver says that's our target," he whispered. "Stay here."

He crept to the mound, and when he was just a few feet away he stopped to slowly scan the jungle surrounding him. Satisfied, he waved the group in closer.

"What happened here, comrade?" Harris asked Nadia.

They stared down at the mound which consisted of clothing, weapons and ammunition, climbing equipment, water cans, and even food packs. But thankfully, no blood.

"I, I have no idea." Nadia lowered herself to lift some of the clothing and examine it. "My team."

"They stripped?" Alistair asked. "Why?"

"I doubt they did it by choice," Jane said.

Ally pulled clothing and equipment aside. "Bingo... boss." She dragged out the suitcase-sized box. "Nadia, is this what we're looking for?"

She nodded. "That is their pulse weapon."

They heard it again, the long mournful blare of the horn.

Jane's jaw clenched and she glared at Harris. "That was closer."

"Nearly done here." Harris quickly went to the machine, flipped it open, and looked along the dials and switches. All were in Russian. "It's undamaged. Quick translation here, Mike."

Mike came and crouched beside him and translated the settings and naming conventions, from direction, distance, strength, and duration, while Jane looked over his shoulder. It seemed that basically all that was required for calibration was to tell it where, how far, and what power level, and then you aimed and fired it.

Harris nodded and grinned. "Ladies and gentlemen, our job here is done."

"What about my friends?" Nadia asked.

"You mean those guys who came down here to kill my people?" Harris looked up at her. "Fuck 'em.

"Bring the pulser," Harris said. "Also grab anything else we can use for the return trip." He began to take suitable rifle magazines, grenades, and also began to shake water bottles and sort through foil packs of dehydrated rations. He tossed a grenade to Mike who caught it and examined the Russian device. And Ally set to putting all the food and water she could find into a single pack.

Nadia squeaked and cringed as the horn blared from even closer.

"They're here," Nadia whispered, her eyes like saucers.

"Let's get the hell out of here." Mike began to pull Jane with him.

A small flock of flying creatures took to the air like an iridescent cloud, and the group momentarily cringed at the sound of their screeching fright.

Mike spun to Jane: it was too late.

The nets seemed to fly over the jungle top to land with expert precision amongst them. They were heavy mesh, made of some sort of woven hemp-like material, and must have weighed fifty pounds with rocks tied to the edges to ensure they flared wide as they flew.

The first pinned Ally and she quickly began to move to its edge.

"Run," Harris yelled.

The next nets fell over him and Alistair. Mike and Jane ran to the forest line and when they were just a dozen paces from the shadows of the canopy, out stepped the nightmarish creatures they remembered from the city cave of crystals over a year before.

Twitching eyes on stalks, mouths hanging with tendrils that quivered with anticipation on top of seven-foot high, powerful bodies of chitin. And all with extra sets of arms at their waists.

They carried spears and things like crossbows. Squeaks and pops emanated from their alien mouths, and Jane and Mike had to split, forced to flee in opposite directions.

As Mike sprinted away, he turned back briefly to see the group more interested in following Jane.

"No." He stopped. "*Hey!*" Mike yelled back at them.

They ignored him and continued to pursue her, so he quickly fumbled in his pouch pocket for the Russian grenade Harris had given him. He pulled the pin and tossed it after them.

The effect was devastating; several of the creatures were blown to pieces and showered the clearing in fishy-smelling shell fragments and translucent meat.

It also worked in distracting them from Jane as the remaining creatures now came for him. He turned, put his head down and began to sprint again.

As he went to exit the clearing, he saw that Harris, Nadia and Alistair were being collected up and ropes looped around their necks. His plan was to enter the jungle and loop around to try and meet up with Jane and then form a plan to rescue the rest.

He grew more confident as the weird squeaking language of the arthropod people began to fall behind. And then something smashed into the back of his head so hard everything immediately went black.

*****

Jane stayed down, gun pointed as she watched. Mike was dragged from the jungle by the ankles and thrown roughly to the center of the clearing where he was stripped down. He started to come around, and the shelled monstrosities spent a few moments looping him to the others in the rope capture line.

Jane held up her gun, teeth grinding but her hand shaking. She wanted to charge in, put holes in some of those horrors, or at least try and get her friends free. But the sensible side of her mind warned her against it. The things had just subdued two trained soldiers so she'd have zero chance.

She lowered her weapon and watched as the arthropod people began to pull the clothing from the rest of them, stripping them down to their nakedness. Harris and Ally seemed calm but their expression held a barely restrained fury. Alistair helped by quickly taking his own clothing off and only Nadia began to sob.

Mike was droopy-eyed when he came around and he spoke softly to Alistair. The young man just shook his head and looked white as a sheet and about to fall over, his slim, pale nakedness looking vulnerable in the harsh red light.

One of the creatures came close to him and leaned forward, examining him in detail. It reached up and dragged a clawed hand down his belly, leaving a red scratch line. It turned and made some sort of pops and squeaks to the others of its kind who responded with a similar sound: *joking, laughing?* He wondered.

In seconds more the people were marched out of the clearing, their clothing and possessions now joining the mound of Russian gear.

Jane waited a few minutes and then followed.

CHAPTER 27

Mike winced as he was tugged by the neck when their procession started up. His head still throbbed and he felt a trickle of blood run down the back of his head.

As they moved through the jungle he felt his vulnerability without his clothing. There are some pieces of the human anatomy that do not take to being brushed by stiff branches, especially by anything with sharp edges.

Harris was in a worse position being lashed at the front of their line, and it was him that had to endure making a hole in the foliage. He was followed by Ally, then himself, and then Alistair.

The huge creatures walked on either side of them with their twitching and darting movements reminiscent of crabs on a shoreline that were darting back and forth to avoid waves lapping on the sand.

Their clicks, pops and squeaks were constant, and after a while, Alistair sped up a little so he was close behind Mike.

"These are the things from the wall image at the cave city," Alistair whispered over Mike's shoulder. "*Y'ha-nthlei,* the deep old ones."

Mike nodded, and Alistair continued.

"It's definitely a language," he said. "There are certain repetitions, nuances, and cadences that repeat which bear all the hallmarks of conversation."

Mike looked over his shoulder. "I don't suppose they're saying they want to make us their leaders."

"Why, would they do that?" Alistair said hopefully.

"Forget it." Mike sighed.

They hadn't traveled far before they came to stone paving and then they encountered pits that contained tons of more discarded clothing. They saw that some had rotted down to nothing, and even had plants growing through it.

Was this the fate of the race that lived down here in the crystal cave and was unlucky enough to be captured? Mike wondered.

But then as they passed closer to one of the pits, Mike was sure there was more modern apparel, and he thought he even saw an old naval uniform, plus a rifle with a wooden stock. There were also swords, shields and items from their history, perhaps from some ancient race that existed down here or maybe even from the Earth's surface history. *And if that was true, how did they get here?* Mike wondered.

Then they broke through the last of the trees and beheld the city.

"Oh wow," Alistair breathed.

"It looks like a Mayan city," Mike said softly. "But there's something wrong with it."

The stone city was built on the edge of a vast sea, with the huge sea-borne mountain column a few miles offshore.

"Maybe that's the Y'ha-nthlei's developmental level," Alistair replied from over his shoulder. "They're indigenous primitives."

The buildings were mostly squat and crafted from stone blocks. Few were over two stories, but that was where architectural normality ended.

Mike blinked, trying to make sense of what he beheld. In his time he had worked with people on building construction and design. But the cityscape before him defied the rules of physics.

There were weird shapes of non-Euclidean construction. Towers that were larger at the top than the bottom, and a few that looked like they were made from dripping wax. There were also some smaller structures that seemed more biological as if they were grown not built. And still growing.

Also, oddly, where the city extended to the shoreline and then into the water, he could see that there were houses or buildings that were totally submerged. But there was still activity in and around them.

"I think they're being inundated," Alistair whispered. "The city is sinking."

"No, I don't think they've sunken," Mike said. "I can see movement below the water. I think it's a semi-aquatic race."

"Oh my," Alistair replied, spellbound.

Mike remembered now their previous time down in this hot, red world, and when they sailed across the vast sea. He had dived down to what he thought was a sunken and long-abandoned city. But maybe what he had visited had always been like that. That it had been constructed on the sea bottom to begin with.

Mike felt a sharp tug on the rope at his neck and he staggered for a moment as one of the shelled creatures wanted to slow them down as their procession was reaching its destination.

On the outskirts of the main city, they were untied and herded into stalls. There were dozens of the cells each separated by a few feet, and each contained a different sort of creature.

"This is unbelievable," Alistair whispered and walked to the bars of their cage. "I wonder if they know we're intelligent."

"Or if they care," Mike replied.

In the next few stalls there were some animals the size of elephants, and others only waist high. Most, but not all, were some sort of insect form. But some looked like upright lizards or tiny dinosaurs. There were also a few creatures that might have been a form of furred pig, but squinting, Mike could see more than four legs underneath them.

Some of the other animal captives turned to scrutinize the new prisoners, while others ignored them to continue to work at the bars of their confines or huddled together as if plotting. And there were still more that just stood silently in a vegetative state.

"You asked about intelligence. Well, here's a good test." Harris pointed. "Those that accept their fate, those that use activity to try and escape, and those that use their minds to plan."

The ones working on the bars of the cage would sometimes elicit a jab from the butt of a spear of one of their arthropod captors.

"I see," Harris said as he watched the response.

Their cage was about fifty feet square and obviously built for a bigger group of prisoners. But they didn't have it all to themselves.

In the corner, small and huddled, was a wizened old human female, with her hands held over her head. Mike could see her stick-like arms were covered in sores, and maybe that was why she had been left alone.

"Oh shit." Mike walked closer and crouched before her. "Katya," he said softly. "Katya Babikov."

The woman slowly took her hands away from her face. Mike wished he had some sort of cloak or garment to cover her nakedness, but he had nothing.

Though she was streaked with dirt, heavily lined and spotted with crusted sores, he knew her, and he knew, she him.

Her face creased in a rueful smile. "I told you, you were a fool to come. And a double fool to come twice, Mr. Monroe," she said. Her eyebrows went up. "But then what does that make me? The biggest fool of all I think."

Mike held out his hands to take hers in his. "Tell me what happened here. Where are your friends?"

"They were not all my friends. They were my chaperones, and bodyguards, and my captors." She snorted softly. "And the captors got captured. These thinking lobsters stripped us and brought us here. Then they came back to take everyone out just a little while ago, but I think they didn't like the look of me, too skinny, too sick, so they left me behind." She shook her head. "I haven't seen them again."

"How many of you were there?" Mike asked.

She bobbed her head. "Six were captured." Katya leaned around

Mike to gaze at Nadia. "But three got away. You, Oleg and Sasha."

Nadia nodded.

"Where is my only friend, Sasha? He was my helper," Katya asked.

Nadia's eyes went to Harris momentarily. "He's dead now."

Katya's mouth turned down. "Of course he is. Down here, everyone dies." She lowered her head. "I hope it wasn't painful."

"So only three left." Harris snorted and turned to Ally. "No problem."

"Heads up," Mike said.

A small group of the arthropod beings slowly approached their cage and stopped to stare in at them. Alistair held up his hand and approached them, eliciting another round of their chirping, squeaks and pops.

"The Y'ha-nthlei are clearly intelligent," Alistair said over his shoulder. "I'm going to try something." He cleared his throat and began to attempt to mimic their noises.

"What are you doing?" Ally asked.

"These are the sounds they made when they first appeared. Maybe it was some sort of formal greeting." He turned back just as a pair of the creatures came even closer to the bars of their cage; their bulb-like eyes shivered as they lowered themselves toward Alistair. At the end of each bulb were three black dots like pupils that fixed on the young scientist.

"Phew," Harris said. "They stink."

"Like low tide," Mike added.

Alistair waved to them. "Yes, that's it," he said and began to make more of their noises.

"Be careful, Alistair, you have no idea what you're doing. Or saying," Mike warned.

"Yeah, for all you know you might be asking them for a date," Ally jeered.

One of the things reached in carefully and gently touched Alistair's chin. It levered open his mouth and lowered its head to look inside as though checking to see if he had anything hidden in there.

Alistair reached up to pat the hard claw. "It's just me, trying to talk to you. We are friendly. We come in peace," he said, and then turned to wiggle his eyebrows at Mike.

"Ask them to take us to their leader," Harris said. "So we can kill it."

The creatures talked excitedly again and then they called more of their kin over. One of them went to the pole holding the keys and then to their stall's gate, while others stood guard. The thing stood in the open doorway and motioned Alistair to come closer.

"Don't." Mike went and grabbed hold of the young scientist.

Alistair smiled, kept his eyes on the creature and carefully extracted Mike's hand. "I'll be fine, I'll be fine. Like I said, they're intelligent, and when they find out we are, we may be okay." He turned to give them a fast smile. "I've waited my whole life for this moment."

They gently led Alistair out, locked the cage door and hung the keys again.

"Goodbye, young man," Katya said.

Mike watched him go for a moment more and then sat cross-legged in front of the old Russian woman, but not facing her directly, as he guessed she was already uncomfortable with her nudity in front of the strangers.

"So this is where Arkady Saknussov has led us both," Katya observed.

Mike smiled. "We're not finished yet."

"I'm not going home this time," Katya said softly. "This I know."

"Don't give up hope." Mike reached out and laid a hand on her bony forearm.

"Hope." She looked up at him. "Did you see the big one?"

He shook his head. "We came through the jungle… from the east."

"Then you have yet to behold a terrifying wonder. They brought us in along the waterfront. There, in the ocean, was a monster so big it was like a living mountain. It even froze the blood of our captain: a strong and experienced soldier."

"I think I saw it. I thought it was an island," Harris said.

"An island?" She laughed darkly. "I think it was their god."

Mike frowned, remembering back to the hidden vault in the cave city and the depiction in the artwork of the colossal creature rising over the landscape. Was this great creature the thing that they imagined? This Dagon, and its minions?

"I have a bad feeling," Katya whispered. "That it is to their god, have gone my friends."

Harris held onto the bars of the cage but turned to Mike. "What did she say?"

Mike sat back. "She said that thing you thought was an island, is a living creature. And their god." He turned and smiled with little humor. "And that she thinks her friends were given to it."

"Well then, guess what we've got to look forward to," Ally spat.

Harris began to chuckle. "This day ain't getting any better is it?" He tested the bars but once again they held firm. "I'll tell you one thing, I'll fight to the death before I'll allow these big shrimp to feed me to any damn god of theirs."

CHAPTER 28

Dmitry grunted in pain as the rope around his neck was yanked down when Viktor, lashed in front, stumbled. In turn, Chekov, tied behind him, was also tugged forward, bumping into him.

"Sorry, friend," Chekov said.

Dmitry just shook his head, too frightened to trust himself to speak. They were in a procession of all manner of creatures that made him feel was a parade of the damned. Beside, in front, and behind them, were madness-inducing creatures like long-legged spiders with intelligent eyes that rolled in fear. Mustard-yellow scuttling things with dozens of sharp legs, lizard-like creatures reminiscent of man-sized snapping dinosaurs, and even a few furred animals that might have been giant rodents that walked on their back legs and all trembled and held hands.

They had been herded along a cobbled street in the nightmare city where everything was of an aberrant design, with some of the dwellings looking like they were excreted rather than built.

The city's denizens gathered to watch them pass, some throwing leaves on the ground before their procession as if in worship or exultation.

"I think I see where we are going," Chekov said from behind him.

Dmitry nodded. "Yes, up there."

Their procession was exiting the city and moving up a long ramp that was constructed up high and also several hundred feet out over the water. Down below them the red water quickly went from shallows to mysterious depths, and in the sea, just a few hundred yards to their east, was a large grey lump of an island, totally devoid of vegetation.

As they arrived at the top of the platform all the creatures' tethers were tied to a central stake, with the animals radiating out like spokes. Some of them fought with their fellow captives, some whispered in strange tongues amongst each other, and some stood mute with heads down.

Their crustacean captors began to depart, save for one, who went to the farthest edge of the platform and lifted a horn to its nightmarish mouth. It then blew a long, mournful note that drifted out across the water.

The creature waited for a moment until an answering bellow was returned. It then quickly turned to scuttle back down the ramp, looking like a crab fleeing an oncoming wave.

"What is happening?" Viktor asked in a hushed tone as he worked at the rope collar around his neck.

"I think…" Dmitry felt the blood drain from his face as he stared. Chekov sunk to his knees behind him and began to pray and Viktor slowly began to back up, but there was nowhere to go and no slack in the rope at his neck.

In front of them the island began to rise up.

Dmitry felt his knees tremble. "I think… we are about to meet their god."

CHAPTER 29

Jane belly-crawled to the top of the slope and slid under a shrub. She peered out the other side of the branches and then lifted her field glasses to her eyes.

Her mouth dropped open and she lowered the glasses. "Holy shit."

It looked like an ancient city but she had to blink several times to try and make sense of its bizarre design. There were structures that reminded her more of intestines coiled, looped, and dripped onto the ground, rather than buildings.

The structures also continued on into the water, and she saw some of the arthropod people simply walk the dry streets in their twitchy, scuttling manner, then enter the water, and continue on as if the changing environment and atmosphere was nothing to them.

But the thing that drew her eyes was the enormous ramp, running from the end of the city, rising to a platform many stories high and leaning several hundred yards out above the water.

Groups of beings that were lashed together like slaves were being herded up the ramp in a procession. It was a mind-bending sight as there were all manner of nightmarish creatures collected together of varying shape, size, and color.

Jane stared and then quickly reached for her binoculars, and focused on one of the lead groups.

"Oh, please no." There were people there, humans, naked, and also roped together. She prayed it wasn't Mike and the others.

She fiddled with the focus and could just make out that there was no Ally or Nadia, and just three men, all large, and looked fit. It could have been her friends, except the men of her own group were Harris, Mike, and Alistair. And there was no way one of those big guys was Alistair.

"The Russians," she whispered. "Has to be." For some reason she felt enormously relieved.

All the captive beings and the people continued to be herded up the long ramp to a rounded platform at the top that hung out over the water. The arthropod people pushed the creatures up, forcing them in ever tighter. She guessed there must have been about fifty animals and people overall.

Jane looked along the waterfront and her brows snapped together. Was that a boat? And a little further along a submarine?

"What the hell?" She moved her glasses further along the shoreline and saw there was also a myriad of other craft. Some were wooden wrecks with masts still carrying the sagging remnants of ancient sails. But others looked new and had been carefully beached.

She focused again, concentrating her focus, and saw there was an older style ship of iron. It was huge at probably five hundred feet long that still had its name visible on the side.

"*USS Cyclops*. How, *what*, are you doing here?"

Her vision of the ships was then blotted out. Something immense was rising from the water: huge, bigger than huge. The creature lifted hundreds of feet in the air. On its body, there clung many of the arthropod creatures, perhaps cleaning it, and servicing it. *Its minions*, she thought.

The face was a monstrous combination of baleful red eyes and tentacles dangling below them like a beard that was constantly moving in a sinuous curling of anticipation. It used huge scaled arms to lift itself closer and then turned its vile gaze on the platform of bound creatures.

Panic set in, and even from her distance she imagined the howls, screams and squeaks from all those alien mouths, plus in amongst it she imagined the shouts of fear from the men.

Some of the captives became furious in their movements, but all were securely lashed in place with nowhere to go.

But then the biological mountain shifted, and before any more of them could escape, the huge monstrosity lurched forward. The tentacled mass hiding its mouth flared open and flowed over the entire platform, enfolding the creatures, large, small, and human, and then drawing back to the head.

She knew what was happening; she'd seen cephalopod feed before. That tentacle mass was some sort of maw or beak, and those poor, damned creatures, and the Russians, had been pulled into it.

She looked away, feeling her gorge rise.

A part of her wanted to run then, far away, forget everything and just flee madly into the jungle. But she knew she never could. Not while Mike was down there somewhere.

When she turned back the monster was beginning to sink below the sea's surface again, perhaps to digest its meal, and the platform was scraped clean of anything living.

Jane swallowed dryly and shifted her focus back to the city, carefully scanning its outer edges until she was rewarded by spotting what might be cages.

Though she couldn't make out Mike or her team, she bet that's where they were. *At least until next feeding time*, she thought.

She needed to get Mike out. But right now that was impossible with a knife and a handgun. She gritted her teeth and cursed. *How often did they feed that monstrosity?* she wondered. For something that size, she guessed it might be daily or every few hours.

"*Shit, shit, shit.*" She needed a plan. She needed a diversion. And it would need to be a big one against something the size of a mountain. Then it came to her.

Jane slid back out from under the bush, got to her feet and ran.

*****

In thirty minutes she was back with the Russian pulser device, plus had several guns strapped to her waist. She opened the device and looked at the switches: all in Russian.

"I should have paid more attention."

She tried to remember Mike's brief translations. "*Uh*, maybe, this one was direction, and these were strength and distance." She moved the dials estimating the distance to the platform, calibrated it to only half-strength, and then aimed the device.

Here goes nothing, she thought. She lifted the covered switch and pressed the button.

Nothing happened.

"Oh come on." She aimed and pressed it again.

Still nothing.

"Maybe this one was distance and this was strength…" She recalibrated, aimed the device, and pressed the switch again.

There was a hum and a tingling in her hands as she held the box with the barrel structure pointed. She watched open-mouthed, her eyes fixed on the ramp and platform, and then sure enough the structure began to become distorted and shimmer in the air.

In the next second, it exploded into fragments.

"*Yeah.*" She fist-pumped through clamped teeth.

And the effect was everything she hoped as just like army ants that had their nest poked, the things boiled out of their houses and other structures, both on land and from under the red sea. They swarmed to the platform, everything else seemingly forgotten.

"*Now.*" Jane left the pulser, got to her feet and sprinted for the cages.

*****

"What was that?" Mike sprang to his feet.

The animals in the other cages were going berserk, and all the Y'ha-nthlei arthropod people scurried away, making an excited or nervous clicking-chittering sound.

"An explosion maybe," Ally said and turned to Nadia. "Could it be your Russian friends fighting back?"

Nadia's brows shot up and she clasped her hands together. "Maybe they got free."

Harris straightened. "Alistair didn't have any grenades, so for now, all it is, is an opportunity." He charged the gate door and kicked out at it. It held. He tried again.

"Damn it," he yelled and hopped away.

Mike knew that even though Harris was a fit and formidable guy, without boots, a bare foot wasn't a great battering ram.

Harris then ran a hand around the edge of the gate, looking at the weakest point. "Little help here guys." He backed up and lowered his shoulder. "Give me a little extra force and mass."

"Don't bust something important, or you'll be useless to us and as good as dead down here," Mike said.

Mike and Ally got behind him, and he counted down. When he got to one, the three of them ran at the locking side of the gate, Harris first.

They piled into the gate, and Mike and Ally piled into Harris, without the door flinging open.

It creaked, but held and they bounced back. Harris rubbed his shoulder, cursing even more.

"Plan B?" Mike asked.

"You got one?" Harris straightened and touched a hand to rub a red dent on his forehead.

"I do now." Mike grinned and rushed to the bars.

Jane reached through to grab his hand. "Thank god you're safe," she gasped, still out of breath.

"Was that you?" Harris asked. "The explosion?"

She nodded. "Yeah, the Russian box. Works on short range as well."

"Brilliant." Harris grinned.

Ally pointed. "Jane, quick, there's the keys; ours is the one closest to us."

Jane ran to the pole, took the huge key and placed it in the lock. It opened easily and Harris pushed the door wide open.

"Where's Alistair?" Jane asked.

"They took him," Mike replied.

"Where?" Jane frowned. "Can we get him?"

"Not now," Harris replied. "We get outside the city and then plan our next move. Otherwise, they come back and we'll all be back inside, you included."

"Shit," Jane spat.

"Hurry," Ally said.

Mike went back to the far corner of the cage and helped the old woman to her feet.

Jane's brows went up. "*Katya.*"

The old woman smiled. "Another fool; that makes three of us."

"Indeed it does," Jane said and turned. "Let's go."

Mike lifted Katya in his arms, the old woman weighing next to nothing. They ran, all following Jane as she threaded her way back out of the city, up the slope and into the forest.

Nadia caught up to her "Did you see my friends? The other Russians?" she asked.

Jane didn't look at the woman. "They're dead."

"What?" Nadia grabbed at her. "You saw?"

Jane faced her. "Yes, I'm sorry."

"How?" Nadia persisted.

"Later." Jane shrugged her off.

It took them another twenty minutes to reach the bush that Jane had sheltered beneath.

"What are we doing?" Ally asked. "Be a good idea to get some freaking clothes on for a start. Maybe a gun or two as well."

"Where was Alistair taken?" Jane asked.

"We don't know." Harris grabbed the field glasses Jane had used before and trained them on the city. His eyes narrowed. "But given how those crab things are back at the cages, I'm betting they'll be after us in a few minutes."

Mike placed a hand over his eyes. "The platform is gone. Is that your doing?"

Jane nodded.

"Well done." Mike turned back. "That's odd; the island has moved."

"That's no island," Jane said. "It's some sort of giant creature. The arthropod people tend to it, feed it."

"Alistair called it Dagon," Mike said and turned to Katya. "That's their god, isn't it?"

"And my team went to meet it," Katya said softly.

"You said they fed it." Nadia shut her eyes. "What did they feed it?"

Jane sighed. "Sorry, Nadia."

"Oh no." She sat down in the dirt, her pale body already reddening from the heat and radiation blasted down from the boiling ceiling.

"That's their god, *huh*?" Harris repeated. "The head of the snake."

"There's something else," Jane said. "Look… beyond the creature to the far shoreline."

Harris put the glasses back to his eyes. "Holy shit, there are ships there. And damn submarines." He lowered the glasses for a moment. "Some of them are old, damn old. And some…"

His mouth gaped open and he handed the glasses to Ally. "Ms Bennet, the big iron hulk, at two-o'clock."

Ally took the glasses and adjusted the focus wheel. "Does that say the *USS Cyclops*?"

"Yes, I saw that as well," Jane replied. "It's one of ours, but I don't recognize the name or shape."

Harris took the glasses back from Ally. "You would if you were alive about a hundred years ago. That's the *USS Cyclops*, at the time the biggest ship in the US Navy. It vanished without a trace somewhere between the West Indies and Baltimore. Lost at sea, or rather vanished at sea to the end of World War One."

He shook his head and lowered the glasses. "She was, *is*, nearly 550 feet long, and when she disappeared she had a crew of 306 people. Her job was to assist in saving refugees."

Ally snorted softly. "Lost and now found. How the hell did it get here?" Ally asked. "How did they all get here?"

"Want to hear a mad theory?" Jane asked.

They turned to her and she nodded to the lump of the thing they thought was an island, and then the huge mountain column a few miles offshore. "Like we thought, that gravity well is a water well. And it's a doorway between here and the surface world. But not dry land; instead, the world's oceans."

"They were sucked into it?" Ally frowned. "Like in a vortex?"

"That's one theory," Jane replied. "The other is that the massive creature we see there is passing back and forth between the surface world and then here at the world's core. Maybe it has a taste for human flesh, and sometimes it decides to go and get it itself."

"That sonofabitch," Harris spat from between his gritted teeth. "About two dozen large ships vanish from the world's oceans every year. We don't even find wreckage."

"How long has that thing been doing it? Some of those ships are old, centuries old," Ally added.

"Maybe even longer than we humans have been around," Jane said. "It looked like the thing depicted on the wall in the hidden room at the crystal cave. And we thought that might have been abandoned for around twelve thousand years. For all we know that monster doesn't have a lifespan as we know it."

"Remember what Alistair told us in the cave?" Mike turned from the water. "That he thought it was an ancient god, or elder being called Dagon, the Great Old One. He said it was supposed to slumber in the depths, and maybe those depths weren't the depths of the ocean at all, but the depths of the planet."

"It has always been here," Jane said. "He also said that there was a billion years of lost Earth time that something could have evolved that bore no resemblance to what exists today on the surface. Maybe this thing is from a race that evolved at that time. It could be one of many or maybe it's the last of its kind. And maybe it has been traveling back and forth forever, wreaking havoc on the surface creatures, eating its fill, and then diving back down to slumber. For all we know there is no Bermuda Triangle, or lost seas, but instead there's only this thing."

"Things can't really be immortal, can they?" Ally asked.

"To a mouse, who only lives a few years, we would seem immortal," Jane answered. "And there are cetaceans called bowhead whales who can live to be 200, or how about jellyfish, who get old and then simply revert back to their juvenile stage to reset the clock and grow up all over again, and again, and again: *that* is almost immortality."

Mike looked back out at the huge mass in the water. "It's a thing of whispered legend, and not from our time or place."

In the distance a horn blared, and they all turned to look back at the city.

"They'll be coming soon," Katya croaked. "And they move very quickly."

"They'll run us down and overwhelm us," Mike said. "And I don't think we're in a state to run all that far. I've near had it already."

"Then we need to buy time," Harris said. "And nothing will buy time like putting a great big fucking hole in their boat-stealing god-monster."

He pulled the pulser toward himself and called Jane closer to give him a thumbnail overview of what she had done.

"Got it," Harris said and turned to Ally. "Take 'em back to collect our gear and anything else we can use. Everyone suit up, and when I join you, we're bugging out ASAP."

"What about Alistair?" Jane asked.

Harris sighed. "I'm sorry, he's not recoverable."

She turned back to the city, where she could now see a large group of things assembling.

"I'll stay to show you the way," Jane said.

"*Aw* Jane." Mike scowled.

She turned. "Get Katya back and find something for her to put on.

You're going to need to carry her and need a head start."

"Yeah, okay," Mike replied sullenly.

Ally got her bearings and then clicked her fingers. "Let's move it, Mike, Nadia."

She turned away and began to jog.

Jane turned briefly to watch the naked Ally, Mike, Katya, and Nadia depart and for the first time noticed a large wolf's head tattoo on the military woman's buttock. She shook her head and grinned. *I'm sure there's a story there*, she thought.

Harris pointed the pulser weapon. "Payback time." He fired at the large greyish lump in the water.

Nothing happened at first, other than the air in front of them became slightly oily and distorted. And then a large rip opened in the top of the smooth, greyish mound. Immediately the ocean erupted as the colossal thing reared up. Jane covered her ears, as the furious bellow was so loud it created a physical wave that battered their nerves.

"Take that you big bastard," Harris yelled.

The creature rose higher, up and up, filling the sky. It was insanely huge and kept rising on two large arms that were heavily muscled and dangling with tendrils that were oak tree-sized frills like seaweed.

Once again the grotesque face was revealed, and the red eyes contained eon's-old intelligence and an unbound fury. The dangling tentacles furiously coiled with agitation and for the first time she saw on its back were two vestigial wings.

Misted air blew out from the sides of its neck, indicating there must have been gills there. It glared, looking for its attacker, perhaps not even understanding how anything could dare attack it.

"Shit," Harris said. "I only winged it." He looked at the dial. "Hey, you only had it on half strength." He pushed the dial up to maximum. "Time to send it to Hell..." He grinned. "...from Hell."

He fired again, and this time the earth-shattering scream filled the air. But whether it took the hit or not was unclear as it dived away.

Its immense size meant the titanic creature's sudden submergence created a wave fifty feet high that surged in every direction.

Jane and Harris were well above the tsunami, but the city wasn't. The wave passed over it, washing everything not made of stone down streets, including the hundreds of creatures who were gathering in preparation to pursue them.

"That's our cue." Harris got to his feet, still carrying the machine. "We're outta here."

Jane led him back to where they had been stripped of their gear. By then the others were dressed and with guns. Katya had been clothed in some of Alistair's gear. However, it still sagged on her tiny, emaciated frame.

Harris was dressed in seconds, and he quickly found the pack where he had collected all the Russians' spare weapons he could carry. He used a belt to lash the device to his back.

Jane checked a GPS. "Options are we make our way back to the crystal cave, which is around a month and a half trek. Or we go around the lobster people city and head to the Gadime cave system in Albania." She lowered the tracker. "Upside, it's a lot closer, maybe under a week to get there. Downside, we have no idea if there is a gravity well there."

"Jezuz." Harris scoffed. "That's some damn big downside."

"You choose," Jane said.

Harris turned to Ally. "Are we feeling lucky?"

She grinned. "We're still alive aren't we?"

"Good enough for me." He turned to Jane. "The Gadime it is. If we're wrong, we can always double back to the crystal cave." He shrugged. "What's another month in the garden of Eden, right?"

"Then think lucky and let's go home," Jane said and turned to lead them out.

*****

Jane pushed them hard, and they traveled as fast as they could move, but not so fast that it forced Mike to drop behind while he carried Katya.

At first Jane had suggested Harris share the burden in taking turns carrying the small Russian woman. But she had been overruled, first by Katya, who didn't like the look of him, and second by Mike who agreed with Harris that it was best to have the soldier running for them, rather than some caver with dubious shooting abilities.

After six hours she felt they were finally moving out of the horrifying race's territory as they began to see more wildlife. It was a good sign but it also meant that they could run into larger predators so caution slowed them even more.

According to Harris' estimation their surface position put them under the Ionian Sea. Then they would need to make their way under Greece and Albania, a distance of hundreds of miles. But down here it was only dozens.

Even though they hadn't run into any problems, the going was hard. It was torturous on the limbs and lungs that were already fatigued, and they were all being worn down by the hour.

Jane was conscious of the fact that even though they had collected the Russian's food packs, they'd need a lot more before they attempted to scale up through the labyrinthine caves of the Gadime. In fact, they might be scaling in the pitch-black underworld for days before they even found the known zones of the Albanian cave system.

A dark thought intruded on her: she knew that they might expend all that energy and time and never find an exit to the surface at all. And then what would happen? She shook away the dismal thoughts, trying to focus instead on one set of problems at a time.

They climbed to the top of a hill, and looking down Jane beheld an unexpected sight. "What the hell are they?"

"Boss, check it out." Ally pointed.

"Take a break." Harris stopped them beneath a large tree and took out his field glasses.

Jane put a hand over her eyes. They were structures that formed a long line down the slope and into the valley. They seemed to be crossbeams and were spaced about fifty feet apart.

"The scarecrows again," Nadia whispered. "But different ones."

"What?" Mike asked and then turned back to stare.

"I've seen something like them before; the crucified animals. Maybe this marks the outer edge of the creature's territory." Nadia turned to them. "We think they were placed there as a warning." She turned back. "There were animals staked out, and a person."

Jane could see that one of the crosses had things swooping down upon it. They'd alight, dart their heads forward to pull free a piece of the thing and then flap away again.

"One's still a fresh kill by the look of those scavengers," Harris said. He half-turned. "Ally, cover my ass while I take a quick look."

"On it," Ally replied and lifted her rifle.

"I'll come with you," Mike said and carefully sat Katya down in the shade.

Mike and Harris approached cautiously in a crouch. Even though there didn't seem to be anything living other than the few scavengers in the vicinity, Mike felt a sense of tension and foreboding, and he guessed Harris did too.

Harris held up his hand and Mike froze. The soldier panned his rifle around slowly, and then lowered it. He then ducked down to snatch up a small rock and threw it at the scarecrow, scattering the things working at it. They flew away making a pissed off skittering hiss.

"Come on," Harris said.

The men walked forward and then around to the front of the x-shaped structure and the pair stared up at the scarecrow.

"*Ah*, shit." Mike felt his gorge rise.

*****

Jane went and sat with Katya, and made sure the woman took some water. She saw that her face was pitted with dry, fingernail-sized sores with black edges as the skin cancers ate away at her. Before she was clothed, she remembered her tiny emaciated frame was covered with them. Whatever treatment she had previously been getting had stopped and so the disease was now free to ravage her.

Katya obviously noticed Jane looking at her sores. "They will win the race." She smiled. "I don't think I'll see the sun again. Perhaps it is fitting that I stay here and continue my search for the ghost of my sister." She leaned forward and her voice dropped to a conspiratorial level. "Do you know I had this silly idea that I might find her?"

Katya scoffed and sat back. "But maybe if my ghost keeps her ghost company, she will be able to rest." The tiny woman smiled ruefully. "I hear her; she still cries out for me in my sleep."

Jane suddenly remembered something and dug into the small pocket at her waist. In beside the two gold coins they had recovered in the crystal cave, she found what she sought. She carefully lifted it free and held it out.

"Lena's."

Katya stared for a moment with her lip trembling. Then she took the small trinket and held it in her open palm. The tiny locket had her sister's name in stylized writing on one side.

She traced the writing with one bony finger for a moment before she laid her other hand over the top and pressed them together.

Katya closed her eyes. "Where?"

"In the caves on the way down. I think she had been caught in a rock fall," Jane lied.

Katya's eyes opened a crack and slid to her. Jane didn't think she believed that for a second, but the old woman nodded anyway.

"Thank you." She held it out. "Help me."

Jane took it and hung it around the woman's neck. Katya's eyes welled up and she touched the small gold heart with her fingertips.

"Rest in peace, little sister. I think I will see you soon."

CHAPTER 30

Moscow Kremlin Complex, sub-level-6 – War Room

President Volkov was dead-eyed as he watched again and again as computer software predictive attack simulations played out on the screen before him and his assembled military leaders.

Even with overwhelming first strike scenarios on all American weapon's facilities, military bases, and command structures, they still ended with only sixty-two percent destruction to the US war capabilities. The following retaliation resulted in ninety-seven percent to their own: it was devastatingly unacceptable.

China had refused all requests to join in any attack, and suddenly his calls to the Middle East and North Korea went unanswered. The message was clear in this, Russia was on its own.

Several hours ago their advanced hydroaccoustics had picked up significant movement of US attack class submarines in the East Siberian Sea, the Bering Sea, plus Kara and Barent Seas. Russia was slowly being ringed.

Volkov's back teeth ground in his cheeks. The USA had developed advanced stealth surfaces to their submarines known as anechoic coatings that worked by absorbing sound waves from sonar. However, Russia's hydroaccoustics had still detected them.

They were confident they could track them.

Until they vanished.

Volkov felt dead inside. He had heard in a previous briefing his adversaries were working on some sort of glide capabilities, meaning their craft could travel for many miles from their last known position without sound. So, now those nuclear-armed killer fish could be anywhere.

"Stop." He exhaled in a long, exasperated breath. "No more simulations." Volkov's eyes slid to General Yevgeni Voinovich. "Anything?"

Voinovich swallowed a lump as the eyes of the other generals swung to him. "Nothing, sir. But we will know in eight hours if they survived."

"And we will know that only if they contact us, or carry out their attack, yes?" Volkov's eyes were like ice as he stared. "And then in eight hours and one minute we will know just how much of Russia is to be destroyed." He slowly rose to his feet. "Because of your incompetent planning."

Voinovich stood at attention, waiting.

"You did this." Volkov's voice was like death itself.

General Yevgeni Voinovich didn't flinch when President Volkov took the revolver from his desk drawer and aimed it at him. And he didn't flinch and kept his eyes open when the man fired at near pointblank into his forehead.

*****

United States President, Dan Redner, slowly rose to his feet, his eyes blazing. The phone in his hand creaked as he squeezed the frame as he listened to the Russian leader.

He then replied through gritted teeth. "President Volkov, you may just have avoided total obliteration. But be advised, our military assets will stay in place, and one way or another, you will pay a little, or you will pay a lot depending on what happens in the next few hours. We will speak again when this is over."

Redner hung up and immediately turned to Michael Penalto and Mark Jasper. "Mark, we need to evacuate Camp Bondsteel in Kosovo, ASAP. It was their next target and they're nearly there."

"Sir." Jasper immediately lifted the phone on the desk, dialed and began to speak urgently as he barked orders.

Redner began to pace. "Volkov is blaming a rogue general, Yevgeni Voinovich." He stopped and turned. "The man has already been executed. He says they've lost contact with their deep Earth team, and they expect the attack on Camp Bondsteel will or won't happen within, now, seven hours."

Jasper hung up. "It's begun sir. They'll pull back ten miles, and all the birds will be in the air and away within an hour." He shrugged. "Still gonna lose a lot of hardware and real estate if it goes down."

"If that base is destroyed, they'll pay for its rebuild, bigger and more formidable than ever." His eyes burned. "And then Volkov will pay in more ways than he can imagine."

"Do you believe him that it was all done by a rogue general?" Penalto asked.

"Not a chance in hell." Redner seethed as he stopped his pacing. "They, *he*, tried to cut our throats while we slept."

"It needs a response, sir, but something surgical," Penalto replied.

Redner looked up slowly and began to nod. "Agreed. Get me Colonel Jack Hammerson. I've got a job for his HAWCs."

CHAPTER 31

Mike coughed and then spat out some bile as he looked back at the body lashed to the cross.

"Poor bastard," Harris said. "They damned tortured him."

Mike wiped his mouth, imagining the horror the young man endured. Alistair's jaw was hanging open, obviously broken, and his tongue was cut or torn out. But even though his eyes had been removed, probably by the scavengers, the expression on his face was one of agony.

"I don't know," Mike observed. "Maybe they were intrigued by how he, a human, could make the same sounds they did, and wanted to investigate."

Harris scoffed. "So they cut his damn tongue out; I'm suddenly thinking I should have spent a few more minutes taking out more of those bastards."

"Should we take him down?" Mike asked.

"And then what?" Harris looked around. "We don't have the time to bury him or even find stones to cover him. Plus it'll alert whoever, or whatever, comes by that we took him down."

Harris looked up at the young man on the cross. "Sorry Alistair, but best we just leave you be, and make sure no one else ends up like you."

Mike didn't like it, but understood the logic. Fact was, they were being run down right now, and even basic honoring of the young scientist would erode any head start they had given themselves.

They moved quickly back to the group, who all rose to their feet.

"What was it?" Jane asked.

Mike looked to Harris who simply shrugged. Mike turned back and sighed. "It was Alistair staked out. It's not pretty."

"Why didn't you cut him down?" Nadia asked.

From far behind them a mournful horn blared again.

"Because that's why," Harris replied. "We better start moving, or we'll all be nailed to damn crosses soon."

They gathered their packs and set off again, into the valley that had a stream at its base that ran with clear and burbling water. There were flat areas like grassy meadows and several large trees like willows hanging over the brook, trailing long thin branches into the languid water. For some insane reason, Mike thought it would have made a nice place for a picnic.

They decided to follow the streambed as it provided cover of their movement, but had to be traded against the chance they would encounter some creature that decided to come down to drink, or worse, lay in ambush waiting for some dumb or oblivious animal who itself had come down for the water.

Mike was once again carrying Katya in his arms and noticed the gold locket around the woman's neck. She had a bony arm looped around his shoulder and she squeezed his neck. Mike looked down at her.

"If I get too heavy, you can just leave me. Maybe I can slow them down."

He grinned. "You'll fight them?"

"To the death." She grinned back. "But I know there are more hardships to come, and I will not countenance my slowing you down."

He shook his head. "Not a chance."

"Long is the way and hard, that out of Hell leads up to light." She raised her eyebrows.

He nodded. Mike recognized the quote from Milton's *Paradise Lost* as Virgil started his escape from Hell. Right now, it could not be more apt.

"But the caves above us will be the real test of our metal," Katya said softly.

"That they will," Mike replied, trying not to think about them.

They broke free of the tree cover as the brook vanished below ground as swiftly as if it fell into a drain. In only another half mile the trees too became sparser, and when topping the next rise, the group saw the featureless plain laid out before them.

"There," Jane said.

In the far distance, rising through the shimmering heat haze, they beheld the column mountain, and potentially their way home.

"About five miles, give or take," Ally said.

"Yep." Harris turned and narrowed his eyes back along the way they'd just come. "But you hear that?" he asked.

Concentrating, Mike could just make out a constant background noise like grinding that was reminiscent of a locust swarm feeding on dry husks in an old cane field.

"What is it?" Jane asked.

"That's the sound of feet, lots of them. Seems our pursuers are a little faster than we expected." He turned back to the plain. His mouth turned down and he shook his head. "Not good, no cover, not for miles."

The plain was a rocky desert and extended to the horizon. Mike didn't know how much head start they had on the approaching horde, but they had no choice but to try and stay ahead of it.

"Any other options?" Jane asked.

"Hide, or run, or fight," Harris replied. "But, we don't have the firepower to hold off an army. And there's no real cover to stay hidden for very long. So that leaves one option."

"Run," Jane said and sucked in a deep breath.

"Like jackrabbits." Harris repositioned the pack on his back, and Ally also tightened the straps on the Russian weapon pack she had slung over one shoulder.

"Reach deep, people. Let's do this." Harris set off at a fast jog.

The five people ran out onto the stony plain. There was little to no cover, and without any vegetation, and with the red heat beating down, Jane was reminded of some sort of alien landscape, and they were astronauts running to find their spaceship before it left without them.

The red heat beat down from above and was radiated back off the dry, rocky surface under their feet, creating an oven effect. Jane already felt the start of a dehydration headache and knew the others would be feeling the same. She looked across to Mike carrying the small woman. He ran with his mouth open, and his face ran with precious perspiration.

"Smell that?" Ally shouted over her shoulder.

"Oil," Mike yelled back.

As they jogged, they had to leap over streams of black liquid that were spaced several dozen feet apart like bands. Jane was no geologist, but had no idea how it could have formed, and wondered about it simply being a natural phenomenon down here, where raw oil ran in rivers after it had somehow bubbled to the surface.

Harris turned to look over his shoulder to check on the group, and then began to run sideways for a while.

"We got company, people. Time to lift it up a notch."

"They're coming now," Katya said as she looked over Mike's shoulder.

Mike also looked back and saw that breaking from the tree line were hundreds upon hundreds of the Y'ha-nthleian creatures. They were far enough back that any projectiles they slung wouldn't reach them yet, but even in the few seconds he watched, he saw them begin to scuttle forward, kicking up dust as they ate up the distance between them far too fast.

"We'll beat them," Mike said to her.

Katya nodded, and her disbelieving eyes went from his to once again look back at the horde.

Mike's back and neck screamed at him as, even though Katya must have only weighed about the same as an eight-year-old kid, she was now starting to drag on his arms, back and shoulders. He knew he had no more sprint bursts left in him. For now, he simply put his head down and ran on like an automaton.

He glanced at Jane and saw her face was beet-red and her cheeks were puffed as she sucked in and blew out breaths.

She saw him watching. "How're you doin?" she gasped.

"Walk in the park." He tried to grin back but stumbled and nearly fell flat, on top of Katya. He managed to catch himself and continued on. He bet if he fell on her he'd actually feel her bones break like dry twigs snapping.

"Yeah, some park," Jane said. She turned to yell over one shoulder. "Nadia, okay back there?"

Ally and Harris were in the lead, then Mike, Katya, and Jane, followed by Nadia who had fallen back a dozen paces from the main group. The woman nodded and waved, but her running style was ragged and she seemed to have developed a limp.

As Mike watched her, he started to see arrows fall to hit and stick in the dirt not more than a hundred feet behind them. It wouldn't be long until they were in range.

He turned back to the front. There was no wall of jungle, rocky outcrops, or anything for miles. It was starting to look like their last stand was going to be one where they were simply run down or speared by oversized arrows.

One thing he knew: there was no way he was going to end up lashed to a cross frame, or being fed to some behemoth from the underworld.

He knew Harris would fight to the death. And he kinda had a feeling Jane would be thinking the same; to surrender was to be handing themselves over to torture or being a plate of food.

Mike's foot struck something that sounded hollow, and he glanced down and back but saw nothing other than rocks and dirt.

It was only minutes more before an arrow sailed past him to nick his ear. "Shit," Mike yelled. "We're in range."

Harris turned and fired about twenty rounds back at the approaching creatures. Mike shot a glance back just in time to see shell fragments fly in the air, and even some of their limbs be shattered and blasted away after the soldier's volley. But he guessed creatures with a totally different nervous system had little to fear. For all he knew they'd simply grow the limbs back in a few days.

"Harris, can you give them a blast from the pulser?" Mike asked.

"I think they're too spread out," Harris yelled back. "But I don't think we have a choice."

He started to veer to the largest thing around: a mound of rock only about three-feet high.

"We get run down and speared in the back. Or we make our stand," Harris said. "I know what I vote for."

"Let's give 'em hell," Ally said and was first to the rocks. In seconds Mike, Jane and Katya had joined them. Harris put Jane onto working the pulser, and he and Ally took to aiming and firing at the approaching horde. They also laid out their grenades in easy-to-reach rows and emptied the Russian weapon and ammunitions sack.

Nadia came in last, gasping like a fish, and Harris immediately handed her a gun.

The Russian woman looked at it for a moment, and then pointed it at Harris. "For Sasha."

Harris simply stared back, waiting. He didn't look afraid or even surprised. He laughed darkly. "Save it; bigger issues right now, comrade." He reached out to push the weapon's muzzle to the advancing horde.

Katya sat with her back to the rock and seemed to simply close down. Jane and Mike readied the machine and aimed at the throng of hard-shelled bodies bearing down on them. The things were jammed together so tightly and there were so many, that even if one of the vibration blasts took out a hundred, there were thousands more.

"I got a funny feeling that blowing a hole in their god meant we've declared war on their entire nation," Mike said.

"Can't understand why." Jane grinned as she pressed the button. "Fire in the hole."

In front of them, a column of distortion flowed forward. It struck the group leading the charge, and they exploded into wet fragments no bigger than a quarter.

It cleared a path twenty feet wide, and hundreds of feet long, and the beam continued on before the power waned.

"*Hell yeah,* that's what I'm talking about," Ally whooped.

"Well the rest of them don't seem to give a shit, so fire that sucker back up and blast 'em again." Harris picked off the lead attackers, but they all found that unless you achieved a perfect headshot, just winging them didn't do much damage, even if you punctured their exoskeleton.

"Hurry up there. This piece of real estate is gonna get real crowded soon." Harris pushed his gun over his shoulder and took a grenade in each hand. He pulled both pins and threw them a good hundred feet into the horde.

The orange bloom of the explosion and the percussion destroyed around a dozen more. But still on they came.

"Damn thing won't...." Jane began.

"It needs to recharge," Nadia said. "I think maybe takes ten minutes."

"Ten minutes?" Jane's mouth dropped open.

"*Ah*, for crying out loud," Harris yelled. "We won't be here in ten minutes."

The first arrows began to land around them, and both Mike and Jane took to picking off individual targets. Though they weren't crack shots, the things crowded the field making it impossible to miss them.

By now they could hear the excited squeaks, pops, and chittering of the things that bore down on them.

Jane reached out and took Mike's hand. She looked from his gun and then back up into his eyes.

He shook his head. "Don't worry, we're not there yet."

"Keep firing," Harris yelled.

There was a grunt of pain from their side and Nadia went down, with an arrow embedded in her shoulder.

"Shit," Harris roared. He grabbed the woman and dragged her behind the rock. As he did, more arrows struck his back with a deep thumping, and he coughed in pain but kept dragging the woman to safety.

Once Nadia was out of the firing line, the tough soldier let her go and lifted his rifle again. He ignored the two arrows that stuck out from his body.

But dishearteningly, Mike saw there were arrows now sticking from the pulser.

Harris and Ally fired in full auto mode, spraying bullets over the field, and when empty, snapping in another magazine and commencing firing again. Mike and Jane now picked their targets. But it was hopeless, and he knew their ammunition would soon run out.

Mike paused momentarily, suddenly wondering whether to wait until the bitter end and hope to die in the fight, or if they should turn the guns on each other to ensure they weren't taken alive.

The thought of Jane being held captive to be tormented and tortured made him feel shaky all over. But he also knew if he took the easy way out, then he would be taking with him some of the group's firepower and would leave Harris, Ally, and Nadia to be quickly overwhelmed.

Mike gritted his teeth, pointing and firing as the monstrous shelled creatures came ever closer and he tried to ignore the giddiness-from-fear sensation threatening to make him panic and lose it completely.

The huge crustacean people towered over them and up close he could see their mottled green color, the thick bristles on their multiple legs, the twitching feelers around their mouths and the buzz saw-like pieces working behind them, and even the tiny dots in their bulb-like eyes that were fixed on them, now with triumph.

Jane's gun clicked empty, and she reached for her belt and found no spare magazines. She just sat holding the gun in her hand and then looked up at him. They both knew she didn't even have time to try and make a grab for the Russian's spare ammunition bag to try and thread more bullets into the empty magazine. All she had left was her knife. Useless against things that were naturally armor-plated and more than three times as strong as they were.

Mike kept firing, and Jane came to him to put an arm around his waist. She buried her face into his side, not watching anymore.

The ground shook beneath their feet from the approaching monstrosities, and Mike swallowed down his fear. He put an arm around her and fired until his gun also clicked on empty.

I hope it doesn't hurt, he wished.

CHAPTER 32

The chance that now seems lost may present itself at the last moment
— Jules Verne

From beside and in front of them the ground exploded open as dozens of trapdoors were thrown back.

A roar went up and a cacophony of human-sounding voices rose in a war cry. Hundreds of people poured from their hiding places, launching fire-lit arrows and swinging what looked like balls of flaming material on rope around their heads and then releasing them to sail into the massed crustacean people.

"What the hell?" Ally spun between one group to the other, not knowing yet if the new arrivals were friend or foe.

"Insane," Harris shouted back at her. He knew those primitive weapons had little chance when the advanced firepower he and his team had used caused little damage.

But then it became obvious what they were doing; they weren't aiming for the creatures, of course, but instead for the rivers of oil they had obviously laid down themselves.

Several arrows hit their target and curtains of fire reared up fifty feet into the air. It became clear now that the way the oil rivers had been positioned wasn't just to create a barrier, but the staggered design was to actually trap hundreds of the creatures within the fire zone and roast them alive.

"Of course," Jane said. "All creatures fear fire."

From within the barriers of fire, squeals of pain and fear erupted. The mottled green of the arthropod people began to turn a brilliant fire engine red as they cooked in the blasting heat.

"*Yeah,*" Ally yelled.

"Who are these guys?" Harris kept watch on them and his gun up even with two large arrows protruding from his back.

A group of the people approached Mike and Jane. They were around four and a half feet tall, had brilliant red skin that seemed natural and not dyed or stained, and also shoulder-length, coal-black hair with a sheen like shimmering insect wings.

They gently took Jane's hand and began to lead her to one of the trapdoors. They did the same to Ally, Katya, and Mike, and when they got to Nadia and Harris, they chatted in their burbling language and began to take greater care when they saw the arrows stuck in their bodies.

Now they knew what the hollow-sounding noise they heard was when they were running across the plain; it was probably one of the trapdoors that were dotted along their perimeter. Perhaps they had been preparing for war, or been at war with these creatures for decades or centuries, or even forever.

The small race of people finished by collecting up the human's goods and then the trapdoors were shut and sealed behind them. Jane saw they were no mere gates but heavily vaulted closures. When locked, massive bolts were slid into the rock walls. It would take explosives or significant force to open one.

The smell below ground was of oil, sweat, and cooking. But the first thing they noticed was that the cave they were taken into was lit in a magnificent blue.

"The crystals," Jane said and approached an alcove containing a foot-high rod crystal. She noticed this one was set in an iron base like a form of candlestick, except the wax was the glowing mineral. And it looked old, ancient old.

"Down here these things might keep glowing forever," Mike said.

Harris groaned, finally giving in to the pain, and the small race hurried them on. One of the red warriors who seemed to have more adornment than the others shouted commands in a tongue that was incomprehensible, but on hearing it the group were split; Mike, Jane, Katya, and Ally were ushered down one corridor, and the wounded Harris and Nadia down another.

They even came in closer to check on Katya and once seeing the ulcers on her face and body, cried out in their pleasant-sounding tongue and then she too was taken with Harris and Nadia.

"No freaking way." Ally went to go after Harris. But a wall of the small people stopped her. One made motion to his back, and then took one of his own arrows from a quiver, mimed pulling it out of his back.

Ally stopped. "You're going to remove those?" She touched her back and also made the tugging movement. "You make them better?"

The small warriors nodded and then hurried on their way.

Mike, Jane, and Ally were taken to a larger vestibule and inside there was a long and wide room blessedly cool after the oppressive, arid heat of the rocky plain. The walls looked like raw stone but magnificently carved and polished to a mirror sheen, and everywhere there were objects of artistic design or perhaps religious iconography. In addition, there were small statues of men and women in vain, glorious poses.

The room was lit a bright blue and as they waited, members of the small, red race soon followed them with bowls of food, water, and flowers. The smell coming from the cooked food was delicious, and Mike only then remembered how little they'd eaten over the last few days.

Mike took a moment to examine the walls; as well as the artworks and images of people and cityscapes, there were also some familiar pictoglyphs, whose purpose he guessed was to tell a story.

Jane pointed. "That looks like the cave kingdom we arrived at."

"It does indeed," Mike agreed.

Ally looked over the food. "Hey, all this for us?"

"Maybe not just for us; we have company." Mike nodded to the end of the long stone table in the center of the room.

A woman sat silently watching them. She was mature but not old, and at least the oldest person they had seen down here. It was hard to judge, but Jane estimated she was anywhere from thirty to fifty. Around her neck were magnificent stones of red, green and blue, with a giant raw stone of gleaming white at the center. Around her forehead was a band studded with what looked like teeth.

She smiled and motioned to the food, and then waved them closer.

"I really hope this isn't another group fattening us up for tonight's feast," Ally said.

"Right now, I'm nothing but gristle and bone." Jane looked over the food. There were plates and bowls of fruit, some cut, and most in bunches. Some of the fruit almost looked recognizable but were odd-shaped or the texture or odor was different. A fruit smelling like a strawberry hung in bunches like long beans. And a melon when broken open had a pungent, earthy aroma and was filled with gelatine-like balls that smelled of cane sugar.

There were also plates of steaming meats, and Jane took some and sniffed at it.

"Smells like crab," she said.

"You don't think it's those lobster people, do you?" Mike raised his eyebrows.

She took a bite. "Delicious. And I damn well hope so."

"*Inglut.*" The old woman pointed at them.

"Anyone speak tomato people?" Ally asked.

The old woman pointed at her chest. "*Ulmina.*" She tapped her chest again.

Jane pointed at her "You name is Ulmina?" then pointed at her own chest. "Jane." She pointed at Mike. "Mike." And then Ally. "Ally."

The old woman nodded and smiled to each. "Jane. Mike. Ally."

Ulmina then pointed a finger at the ground, and then waved an arm around. "*Grunda. Omada, Ulmina.*" She opened her arms wide. "*Ulla Grunda.*"

"This place is called *Grunda*?" Mike asked.

"*Grunda.*" Ulmina pointed at the ground and nodded again. She pointed at the three people and then hiked her shoulders. "Jane, Mike, Ally, *Omada*?"

"Where are we from?" Jane smiled. She pointed at the ceiling. "The Earth's surface."

Ulmina frowned, not getting it. Jane sighed and turned to Mike. "I have no idea how to explain it."

Mike looked around. "*Um.*" He mimicked writing. Ulmina shrugged again. He then mimicked drawing on the table. Her eyes narrowed in confusion. "Come on, woman. I know you've got language and writing."

"Maybe it's all carved," Jane said.

"Then, when in Rome." Ally pulled out one of her blades and handed it to Mike. "Do as the Romans do."

Mike cleared a space on the table. With a clear space and the knife poised, he paused to look up at Jane. "Hope this isn't their best table." He began to carve out his picture. Ulmina stood and came closer to watch.

Jane noticed that the small woman barely came to her chest. It was hard to judge her age as her eyes looked old and there were lines at the corner of her mouth, but her hair was still raven-wing black with just a strand or two of grey at the temples. She was still well-muscled and physically in good shape.

Mike drew several rings all inside each other. Jane got it immediately and she hoped the old woman would too. He finished by drawing a line between the outer and inner rings, and then he began.

"The core; *Grunda – Ulmina*." He tapped the center pellet that represented the solid core that had cooled and was now their world. Around it he had drawn the still-molten core which was a ring now as the center pulled away from it. Then came the vast thickness, which was the mantle.

Mike finished it with several slim rings, representing the crust, and then the surface. Mike tapped the surface, and the pointed to each of them. "That is our home; our Grunda," he said.

He then made his fingers walk to the line leading down to the core and mimed them sliding all the way down. "And we traveled down this pipe to reach you, here." He tapped the inner core.

"Here," Ulmina repeated and tapped where the pipe ended at the core. Her eyes widened and she looked a little fearful for a moment.

"I think she knows about the gravity wells," Jane said.

"Wait a minute." Jane reached into a pocket and pulled out just one of the gold coins she had found in the cave city. "We came to this place." She handed over the coin.

Ulmina took it and her eyes widened momentarily. She turned the coin over, looking from the regal-looking human head, to the creature on the back. She squeezed her eyes shut, gripped the coin in her fist and held it tight to her chest.

The small, red woman opened her eyes that now glistened in the blue light. "*Grunda Asanta lun.*"

"Means something to her," Ally said. "Maybe that's where they came from: *Asante lun.* Maybe these are the descendents of that city that fled to the land."

Ulmina pointed to the coin, the image of the great beast, and then to the wall. The group followed where she indicated and saw there was a mural there that had a similar depiction of the hulking colossus.

The carved image showed the monstrous creature towering over the sea and land, a head of coiling tentacles, and massive arms crushing the land and beasts, and feeding it all into its cavernous maw.

And there was a city, teeming with the shelled people. "*Y'ha-nthlei*spat." Then she pointed up at the monster and her face hardened even more. "*Dagon.*"

Jane slowly turned to Mike. "What Alistair said."

He nodded. "The ancient dreamer from the deep: Dagon."

The heavy door of their room was pushed open and a bandaged Harris, Nadia, and Katya entered, escorted by a group of the small, red warriors. Ulmina spoke to them and they departed. One returned a few minutes later with a handful of things that looked like quills and some parchment.

Jane turned to Mike. "Guess who just vandalized the chief's table for no reason."

"*Oops.*" Mike chuckled softly. "Damn out-of-towners."

The small warriors used one of the quills to expertly copy Mike's drawing. Jane also noticed that Katya was now covered in some sort of ointment. Amazingly, even after just a few minutes, the crusted sores looked a little less angry.

Harris pointed at the food. "Don't start without us, will you." He grinned.

"How are you, boss?" Ally asked.

"Nothing a few shots of bourbon won't cure." He rolled his

shoulders, and then grimaced. "Okay, maybe a full bottle."

Nadia also nodded. "They packed the wounds with some sort of herb. I hope it will be okay."

A few moments later a group returned with their clothing they had removed and also some of their gear. Harris saw that the pulser had several arrow holes in the case and he quickly flipped the lid open to check on it. Pieces fell out and to the floor.

The soldier sighed. "Well, that's that." He roughly flipped the device closed. "Maybe the eggheads can put it back together." He turned to the small, red woman. "And who have we got here?"

"This is Ulmina. We think she is their leader," Jane said. "We were just working out some form of communication."

Harris turned to her and bowed his head momentarily. "Thank you." He touched his chest. "For saving our asses, and for patching us up."

"We need to go home," Mike said. He reached forward to the newly drawn diagram. He pointed at himself and the others, "Need to go to our *Grunda*." He motioned traveling up the pipe to the outer circle representing the surface world.

Ulmina moved to another of the room's walls and pointed. There were images of small figures floating up into darkness. There were also images of pale things that were crouched on all fours in the dark.

Jane joined her. She nodded and pointed to the floating figures. "Yes, we need to do this. We need to float."

Ulmina shook her head and tapped the wall where the crouching white things were. She shook her head and made a guttural sound in her throat. But then she placed her hands together as if praying and bowed to them.

"Do they worship them?" Jane asked.

"Maybe, or maybe they think they're cousins or ancestors, as they all descended from the same source," Mike replied. "Bottom line, we need to get past them."

Mike went and tapped the cave creature's image, and then went back to his diagram and indicated where the things lived on his drawing. Then he tapped his own chest, pointed at the other humans and motioned to the circle above the cave creatures that were above it. "That's where we are from. Our *Grunda*." He waited.

She seemed to think on it for a while, her expression troubled. After another moment she sighed and then shrugged. She held her arms wide and motioned with her fingers, making them walk. She then held her arms even wider.

"Yes, *a long way*," Jane agreed.

Jane went to the wall and pointed at one of the rod crystals. Then

207

she went back to the table and pointed at the food. She mimed putting them in her pack. "We need supplies for *long way.*"

Ulmina looked at each of their faces, and her eyebrows slid in sadness. She looked to the cave beasts again that perhaps were her people's ancestors and motioned her teeth snapping together.

But then she pointed at herself and made a sleeping motion by tilting her head and shutting her eyes. She then clasped her hands together as if in prayer again, pointed at her chest, and then up.

Ulmina noticed that they were still confused and moved to one of the walls with artwork. It showed the tiny red people, but these ones had white hair. All had halos of light around them and were flying upward. Ulmina tugged at her hair where there were just a few grey strands showing. She mimed it covering all of her head.

"They're all old? Just for the old people? What does that mean? Is she inferring it is their heaven? That they ascend there, perhaps when they die?" Mike asked.

She pointed at Jane and Mike and then shook her head.

"I know, but we have to." Jane shrugged. "We have no choice."

Ulmina turned and called out. A warrior quickly entered the room and she spoke rapidly to him in their burbling language. He bowed and retreated.

"What now?" Mike asked.

In a few moments he was back and handed her a small box. She called them all closer and carefully opened the lid. Inside was something that looked like a bulbous beetle as long as Jane's thumb with open ribbing on its back. Ulmina reached a finger in to prod it and it immediately made a high-pitched screaming noise that hurt their ears.

"Jesus, lady." Ally covered her ears.

Ulmina snapped the box shut and the noise was cut off immediately. She put the box on the table, put her hands over her ears and nodded.

"Yes, we get it, very painful," Jane said and nodded along with the woman.

She then went to the wall image and pointed to the pale creatures in the dark cave. She placed her hand over her ears and then made a fluttering motion with her hands as though something was running away.

Mike snorted. "Of course, it hurts *their* sensitive ears even more." He turned. "Things that are nocturnal or troglodytic, *ah*, cave-dwelling, and never see any light at all, navigate by senses other than sight, smell and hearing. A blast of this, to something with ultra-sensitive hearing, will be agony. It should send them running."

Mike and Jane looked at more of the images while Harris and Ally spoke together and checked their remaining weapons. Nadia picked at the food.

Mike turned to see the small red woman speak softly to Katya. She placed a hand on her forehead, and then gently touched some of the cancers. She pulled the fringe of her hair back and showed Katya a similar sore. It seemed, even after all the time the people had been down here, there was no escaping the radiation's poison.

But then again, Mike thought, *people on the surface were still getting sun cancer, so maybe down here like up there, it was all a matter of time and exposure.*

As Mike watched, Ulmina reached into a small woven bag she had at her waist and produced a small container. She opened it and dipped a finger inside, producing a nail-sized blob of some ointment. She then lifted it to Katya's face and began to gently rub it on Katya's cancers.

When Ulmina had finished, she pointed at Katya's chest. "Katya."

Katya smiled and nodded. "Yes. And you are Ulmina."

Ulmina nodded, pleased. And then held up her hand. "*Droma.*" She then splayed her tiny, red fingers. "*Indrema.*"

Katya did the same. "*Hand.*" She splayed her fingers. "*Fingers.*"

Ulmina made some markings on a page of parchment. "Droma." She then made some more notations next to it. "Hand." She obviously wrote her own language for the word 'hand' and then passed the quill to Katya, and nodded to the page. "*Hand.*"

Katya took the quill and looked at it for a moment.

"I think she wants you to write your word for 'hand' next to hers," Jane said.

Katya turned. "Russian or English?"

"Well, there are one and half billion English speakers in the world, against one hundred and seventy million Russian speakers, so, please, do English," Mike urged.

Katya nodded and wrote the word 'hand' next to Ulmina's scratchings.

Ulmina repeated the process for their word for fingers.

"She wants a teacher, and also to teach," Jane asked. "She wants to know more about us." She nodded. "This small woman is a wise leader."

*****

The group had rested, eaten and drunk their fill, and been supplied with significant dried fruit and meat, plus had their water bottles filled to the brim. Ulmina had given them all crystals, and Jane thought that if they used the crystals first, and only when they began to expire used their flashlights, they might just have enough supplies and light to make it out.

Harris and Ally had reloaded all the weapons and Harris strapped the broken pulser to his back. Jane was given control of the *sonic beetle* as she referred to it, and the last thing they were given was a long metal key. Ulmina said something in the red race's lilting language, and though none of them understood her, Ally took the key and bowed.

"Thank you." She bowed again. "Guess we'll know what it's for when we get there." Ally tucked the key into one of her thigh pockets.

"Wait." Mike rummaged in his bedraggled pack and pulled out the diamond key. He held it out. "This is from the crystal cave, uh, *Grunda Asanta lun.*"

Ulmina's mouth dropped open and she took it in both her hands, turning it around.

"The children." Jane lifted a hand to about her knee height.

"*Indrini.*" Ulmina's eyes closed and her mouth set in a line. She nodded. "*Alla Indrini.*"

Ulmina laid a hand on Mike's forearm and looked earnestly into his face.

"*Awana demornee Bowarn.*" She gripped him tighter. "*Demornee Bowarn,*" she repeated, and then pointed at her eyes and crouched. She mimed looking fearful and turning about.

"That has got to be a warning," Jane said.

Mike nodded and patted her hand. "Okay, we'll be careful." He straightened when she returned the nod and released him. "Just wish we knew what it was you're warning us about."

"We'll know soon enough," Harris said over his shoulder.

Katya and Ulmina were talking softly, and even though the old Russian woman couldn't understand, she stood spellbound before the small red woman. Ulmina stroked the old woman's hands, and when she went to go, Ulmina shook her head and hung on.

When it came time to leave, Harris called them to get ready. But Katya stayed where she was.

"I'm not going." She smiled, looking content for the first time. "There is nothing for me but hospitals and death on the surface. Even if I could make it." She smiled ruefully. "Besides, all my youth, my friends, my past and my future are now here."

Jane frowned. "Are you sure, Katya? We can make it out again."

"Maybe you can. Maybe. But I know I cannot. I can't climb to the surface, and then having one of you carry me again creates a deadly risk to you." Katya came and stood before Mike and Jane. "A lifetime ago I asked you not to come, and you didn't listen. Now I want you to listen." She grasped Jane's hand. "Make it home. And *stay* home." She looked from Jane to Mike.

Mike smiled. "You have my word." He turned to Jane. "You have my word," he repeated.

Jane gave Ulmina a small salute, and then turned to Katya. "Do you know what you two are working on? The equivalent of the Rosetta Stone. When you're finished, you will know each other's language and secrets."

Mike sighed. "I'd love to know them."

Jane gave him a hard look and he grinned sheepishly. "I mean, mail me a copy, okay?"

Harris had one last look around. "We're out of here."

Mike waved to Ulmina and Katya one last time. The small red woman held Katya's bony hand and spoke to her warriors. At first they seemed strangely fearful and shook their heads, but Ulmina was insistent.

"Are we that scary?" Jane asked.

"Remember Ulmina's warning? Maybe it isn't us they're scared of," Mike replied.

The group was first led out along large and ornately carved corridors, and Mike saw in through an open archway: a huge hall with hundreds of the cave dwellers gathered within. The vast cavern was filled with carved buildings, stoned paved streets, and even tinkling fountains, all lit a luminous blue from massive rod crystals.

It was obviously their main underground city, and for some reason, they weren't yet ready to share knowledge of it with the surface dwellers. But in that few seconds glimpse, Mike saw the same architectural design and structure that they saw back at the cave ruins. Except in the ancient cave ruins where there was broken, moss-covered stone, in this place there was color and movement, shining architecture, and the sounds of life.

It was proof for Mike that some of the race down here had survived the attack of the Y'ha-nthlei.

Finally the warriors relented and turned to begin leading the group down along a magnificently carved tunnel and along their own underground highways to what they hoped was the gravity well.

Harris and Ally talked softly to each other just behind the lead warriors, and Nadia dropped back to Jane and Mike.

"How's the shoulder?" Mike asked.

Nadia rolled it. "The wound is already closing up. And no pain." She held up a small wooden container with a lid. She handed it to Mike. "They gave me more of the salve. Enough for all of us."

Mike took the lid off and sniffed. "*Hmm*, a little like eucalyptus oil. We'll have to get this analyzed." He handed it back. "Though any plant species it's from might be a little hard to come by up top."

The tunnel they moved along was paved with a smooth interlocking stone, and interspaced every twenty or so feet there were alcoves, and in each of them statues stared blankly back at the passing surface people. There were figurines of men and women, some in standard leader pose, but others depicted as fighting warriors, and even children holding baskets of food.

"Their heroes," Mike observed.

"Do you think they have a religion, a god, or many gods?" Jane asked.

Mike shrugged. "If they do, one thing's for sure; it won't be that Dagon abomination."

Jane laughed softly and gazed at more of the statues. "I wonder if this was the only band of people down here? I remember from the original murals in the cave city that another group set out over the water. Maybe they survived somewhere as well." Jane slowed next to one depiction of a family.

"And if they do survive somewhere, if these people are in contact with them?" Mike said. He followed where she was looking and there was a depiction of a warrior with a long spear skewering one of the monstrous Y'ha-nthlei. "I get the feeling these two races have been at each other's throats forever."

"Well, if we have to take sides, I know who I'm rooting for." She turned and gave him a half-smile.

After a while they pulled up behind a huge door set into the end of the tunnel. The warriors slowed them, while one produced a key, exactly like the one that they had recovered from the cave city secret room.

The warrior unlocked the door and pushed the heavy frame in. The men braced themselves and held their spears ready. A draft of hot air blasted into them, and Mike could smell fish, and something else unidentifiable, but nonetheless unpleasant.

They also noticed that the fine carvings of their tunnel ended, and the passageway from here on looked more rough-hewn.

"Might be the limits of their city," Harris said over his shoulder.

"Our guides sure are a little jumpy in here," Ally said, keeping her gun up.

"If *they're* jumpy, we should be too," Jane replied.

The warriors continued and even sped up a little, perhaps wanting their allotted task to be over.

The new tunnels led for miles, and after another hour they noticed that the magnificently carved tunnel they started in, that after first turning more roughhewn, was now getting worse and beginning to be nothing more than raw cave.

"Getting hotter," Mike said.

"Closer to the Gadime well?" Jane asked, hopefully.

"I'm feeling confident," Mike replied. "Ulmina seemed to know what we were inferring."

"Makes me wonder whether they had ever tried to travel up there, and see what's on the surface. If they even knew about it," Jane said.

"Do you think they knew that those beasts in the caves were their long-lost kin?" Mike scoffed softly and glanced down at her. "I wish..."

"Don't even think it," Jane shot back. "Yeah, sure, it'd be nice to understand more about this race's history, and if Katya survives long enough to create some sort of language roadmap then who knows what secrets it could tell." She lowered her brow as she looked up at him. "But that's not our job now."

Mike nosed toward Harris and Ally. "But someone will be back. Count on it. Whether it's our team or someone else's. This hidden place offers too may riches and opportunities."

Jane just grunted.

Up ahead the warriors began to whisper and slowed them down.

"What's happening?" Nadia asked.

Harris and Ally picked up on the vibe and held their guns up ready.

"Something's got our guides spooked." Mike craned his neck to see as they caught up. "What is it?"

Their tunnel split into separate side caves, some small and some looking enormous. Most were ancient, but within a few of them, the rocks seemed newly broken and scraped.

One of the warriors turned and mimed putting his fingers on his lips to keep them closed. The motion was obvious: stay silent.

They continued on, slower, and keeping all sound to a minimum. Mike and Jane had used an old trick of hanging their crystals around their necks, but Mike reached for his flashlight and decided to use a bit of its precious battery's energy as he flicked it on and into one of the new caves.

He paused, straining his senses. Inside the cave he felt a humid and stinking draft on his face and moving his light around he saw it was dripping wet inside compared to the arid dryness of the tunnel they had moved along.

Up ahead the warriors stopped and urged him to follow. Mike nodded to them but turned back briefly. Jane was beside him peering in as well.

"*Shit,*" Mike whispered. "See that?"

Up against the rear of the cave were several ovoid shapes, pale and powdery looking. He turned to Jane who mouthed a single word: *eggs.*

"That's what I think," Mike whispered back.

The ovoids came to his knees and they looked leathery rather than the normal hardshell coating. Whatever had laid them must have been of considerable size.

One of the warriors prodded him with the butt of his spear. He scowled at Mike and put his hand to his face in front of his mouth, making the fingers like dagger teeth.

"I get it." Mike grabbed Jane's elbow. "Let's go."

They continued on for another few hundred yards and Jane tugged at his arm. "I wish we could ask them how much further."

"Yeah," Mike agreed. "But at least this route means we don't have to hack through jungle, climb mountains, or trek over desert. And by my estimation, we've covered most of the distance to the column mountain."

Mike's foot squelched in something, and he looked down. "Yech." His nose wrinkled. There was a puddle, or rather large blob, of some sort of jelly-like substance.

The caves they were passing through now were natural formations and looked to be extremely ancient stone. There was no single tunnel, and in some areas out to their sides there were no cave walls, just massive spaces or rips in the solid stone where everything just disappeared into darkness.

Columns held aloft the ceiling, most likely from stalagmites and stalactites joining up after countless millennia of mineral dripping.

The warriors gathered together near one of the columns and urgently whispered amongst themselves. After another moment they seemed to come to a decision and called the surface people in closer.

One of them held up his crystal and pointed to the column closest to them. On it was an arrowhead carved into it, pointing to one of the cave entrances.

Mike nodded. "That way, *huh*?"

The small red warriors gathered together with their leader at the front and bowed.

"They're leaving us," Jane said.

"I guess this is as far as they go." Mike walked forward and patted the leader on the shoulder. "Thank you."

The small red men bowed again and with that they turned silently back the way they'd come.

Harris watched them go for a moment more. "Was it something we said?"

Mike pulled out his flashlight again and shone it down the dark cave. "We stick to the cave with the direction-arrows and keep moving. Hopefully, it comes out at the Gadima gravity well."

"We follow the yellow brick road and then keep a look out for an 'x' marking the spot." Ally grinned. "Kinda would have liked the little guys to hang around until we got there. After all, one of them was kinda cute."

Mike scoffed. "But he was half your size."

"There'd be nothing left but a smoking loincloth." Ally laughed out loud.

"You've been down here too long," Mike chuckled.

"Lucky for you, Miss Jane is here, or you'd be mine by now." She winked at him, and Jane groaned.

"Quiet," Harris ordered. "Those locals know this place better than we do. If they were nervous, we should be."

Mike moved his light around. "They've been spooked ever since they saw those eggs."

"They didn't exactly settle my stomach either," Harris said and walked a few paces to the inky black cave exit. "We're on our own from now on. And the sooner we start..." he turned away, "...the sooner we're home." He led them onward.

They moved quickly but cautiously. Though the crystals gave off good light, they didn't throw it forward very far. It was like moving within a blue bubble of illumination. In fact, it illuminated you and your immediate surroundings more than it illuminated anything hiding in the dark ahead, behind, or beside you.

Harris slowed as he came to a cross cave and in to sniff. He fished in a pouch for his flashlight, held it up in his fist and shone it into the cave.

Harris bared his teeth and cursed softly. "More damn eggs." He spoke over his shoulder. "And these ones have hatched."

Jane moved in beside him. "Shit," she said softly as she stared. "And recently."

There were several eggs stuck to the wall and floor. They were open but not cracked, and instead had been ripped or peeled as if the occupants had simply grown too large and burst out of them.

The casings still leaked a glutinous fluid, as the atmosphere hadn't had time to dry them out.

"So, somewhere around this place there's several critters scuttling around, and one momma creature big enough to push those things out." Harris quickly moved his light around inside a little more. "You know, I'm kinda thinking we should up our pace." He began to withdraw.

"Works for me," Ally added.

They continued on for another ten minutes before Ally in the rear closed the gap a little.

"Guys," Ally said from the darkness. "Hearing some weird shit back here."

"You need help?" Harris asked from the front.

"Just a little more speed," she replied. "Think we might have picked up some followers."

Mike looked back to see Ally walking back for a while. She had switched on the barrel light from her gun that was illuminating the passage they had just come out of.

"Don't suppose it's our red people escort?" Jane asked.

"Maybe," Ally said. "But sounds like who or whatever it is, is trying to be re-*eeeal* quiet."

"Double-time," Harris said and broke into a jog.

Mike placed a hand on Jane's shoulder to steady himself as he walked and looked back to Ally. In the glow of the blue light from her crystal he saw that her brows were drawn together, and she constantly turned to look back the way they'd come. But for now there was nothing but the swallowing blackness.

Ally ran silently, probably hoping that if she couldn't see what was going on, she could at least hear what was happening behind her. She turned back momentarily and saw Mike watching her.

She shook her head. "Yeah, it's back there, and it's still coming."

Mike nodded and when they entered a long and straight section of the tunnel they were in he took out one of the smaller shards of crystal Ulmina had given him and let it drop to the ground.

Ally saw it and stepped over it, and they continued on. But this time as they ran, the cave behind them remained illuminated.

After a few seconds, Ally slowed. "Something."

Mike and Jane slowed to watch, and Nadia noticed and began to back up, but into Harris.

Harris spun and pushed her aside. "What the hell are you doing?"

"Here it comes," Ally whispered.

From a narrowing in the cave, just back from the illuminated section, a pair of human-like hands gripped the rocks to the top of the passageway. Then easing its way through came a pair of shoulders and head, still human-shaped, they thought.

But only at first because as it leaned in closer to the illuminating crystal they saw that the head looked smooth except for two holes high up on the front of the face that opened and closed wetly. It seemed these weren't eyes, but nasal holes for sniffing the air.

But there were more anomalies, as instead of a mouth there was a tight ring of crinkled muscle in the lower face that slowly stretched open and out showing rings of needle-like teeth. This hole was actually on the end of a fleshy pipe that extended outward for a few inches, waved in the air and then drew back in.

"Oh, fuck off," Ally whispered, lifting her rifle.

216

Any final semblance of the creature being human-shaped was shattered when it drew the rest of its body in closer to the light. As it appeared, they saw that the upper human-like torso was attached to something that was like a short centipede, with segments and multiple sharp-pointed legs that it carefully placed forward, obviously still working in stealth mode and not aware it had been seen.

Ally lifted her gun. "Anyone want to take a guess at what laid those eggs?"

"This is what the red warriors were afraid of. Probably for good reason," Jane said. "We need to back away, real slow."

From behind them a single gunshot rang out, making Nadia squeak and Mike cringe and turn. Ally just braced herself with her gun up.

Mike saw that it was Harris that had fired a single round into the thing, and snapping his head back around saw that his bullet had punctured the chest plate. The creature froze for a moment, but gave zero indication it had been hurt.

Jane shook her head. "With that weird symmetry we have no way of knowing where any of its vital organs are."

The creature lifted its blank face and its nostril holes fluttered for a moment and they could hear the sucking intake of air.

"It's tasting us," Jane said softly. "It knows we're here."

From beside it on all sides, smaller versions of the creature began to appear. Each of the mini horrors was about a foot long and clung to the walls and ceilings like elongated spiders.

"The hatchlings," Jane whispered.

The group began to back up. More of the smaller creatures appeared, now numbering about a dozen.

Harris breathed. "We're out of here, people." He walked forward a few paces to Jane and Mike, grabbed Jane's shirt and tugged on it, while keeping his eyes on the thing.

Ally began to back up, as Nadia got behind them all.

Then, as if being given a signal, the swarm charged. The huge creature barreled down the center of the cave, filling it, while the cave walls and ceiling became covered in the scuttling hatchlings.

"Run," Harris yelled and fired. Ally gave a burst and then turned as well, while occasionally firing back over her shoulder.

The upside of the single tunnel was it kept the creatures behind them. But the things were fast and Mike knew they'd be run down quickly.

In seconds the smaller creatures were among them, and each of the humans were fending off the tiny horrors as they tried to latch on with their sharp legs and attempted to burrow their long tube-like mouths into their flesh.

"*Argh!*" Ally reached down to grab one of the things that had attached to her leg.

Mike grabbed one from Jane's back and threw it hard against the wall. All that did was make it bounce, roll and get back to its multiple feet to scuttle after them all over again as if nothing had happened.

Mike then felt one on his calf and the pain was excruciating as the thing gripped and then burrowed in. The mouth end on the pipe seemed like a suction cap with the needle teeth when they stuck and then wormed their way into the flesh.

He pulled his knife blade and swept it down hard enough so that he chopped several of the legs from the body. It dropped away, scuttling lopsided back into the darkness. He turned to run on.

Ally screamed her fury and her gun went full throttle. The huge thing had caught up to them, and it had tried to pin Ally with one long pointed leg. She dived and rolled away and came up firing again as the group continued to be forced back.

Finally they were pushed into a larger cavern with multiple exits. The crystals only provided light in close and with all the confusion and panic, and gunfire, and encroaching darkness, the group was forced to different corners and spread out.

"*Hey*, this way," Jane yelled to the group and pointed to an arrowhead carved into a wall.

Mike followed her and together they ran hard, hearing the rapid footsteps and gunfire of the others close behind them.

In minutes more they came to a narrower opening and Mike and Jane stopped to get their breath as the others caught up. Harris and Ally burst in after them, and Ally fired off another few rounds, until her rifle clicked on empty.

"That's it, this baby is out." Ally pushed her rifle over her shoulder and pulled her handgun, holding it in two hands to aim back down the passage.

They waited, but nothing followed them.

"I think they've given up," Harris said.

"Why?" Jane asked.

Mike frowned. "Hey, where's Nadia?"

Harris scoffed. "That's why."

*****

Nadia ran, almost blindly down the passage. The blue glow of her crystal only gave her a split second notice for twists, turns, or outcroppings in the labyrinthine cave.

She could hear the mad scuttling feet of the things in pursuit, and she just hoped that Harris and Ally behind her would be able to hold them off.

Mike and Jane must have run far ahead as she hadn't caught up to them yet, but she was sure she'd see their lights any second.

The exertion of running was making her hot, but it was compounded by the rising humidity in the tunnel, and she clearly felt the heat on her tear-streaked cheeks. When she burst into the new chamber, she slowed and then stopped.

"Oh." Nadia turned slowly, mouth hanging open. There was no exit. "Oh no," she breathed.

All there was in the dead-end cavern was one wall covered with large leathery-looking eggs. She licked her lips, feeling her heart racing so hard in her chest it was making he feel ill.

From behind in the passage she had just emerged from, she heard a soft scratching sound. Nadia reached into the pouch the red people had given her, pulled out one of her spare crystal fragments and tossed it down the passage as she had seen Mike do.

As she watched it bounce along the cave floor, she saw a shape begin to be illuminated, but far enough back that it couldn't be fully discerned. However, she could see it was human-shaped, and large.

"Mike?" Nadia said, her voice trembling. "Is that you?"

There was no response. She backed up a step.

"Please be you," she sobbed.

The shape in the tunnel began to ease silently forward, moving into the pool of blue light.

Nadia began to cry. The man-shaped torso emerged and she saw it was attached to an insectoid body.

"No, no, no." She shook her head and backed up some more. Her heels were stopped against something and she reached back to steady herself. Nadia's hand touched one of the leathery egg casings, and horrifyingly, she felt it tremble beneath her hand.

For some reason the large creature didn't come forward and just stood in the cave mouth, its legs spread wide. *Maybe it's scared of the light*, she wondered hopefully.

From behind her she heard the eggs rattle, and she spun to see some of them begin to bulge and split as the things inside fought to be free from the skin of the casing.

"Don't," Nadia begged.

Now she knew why the great creature was blocking her path. Not because it wanted to avoid coming in; instead it was stopping her from leaving.

In seconds the swarm hatched, and they did what instinct had trained them to do: seek food.

Nadia screamed as the horde quickly covered her.

*****

"What was that?" Jane spun. "Was that a scream?"

Harris shook his head. "No idea." He turned away. "We should get moving."

"Wait a minute. What about Nadia?" Mike asked. "We need to find her."

"No we don't." Harris' mouth set momentarily in a hard line. "Let it go, Mike, she's gone."

"We go back," Jane said. "She can't be far. If it were me, I'd want you to come find me. And I'm sure you'd want the same."

Harris drew in a breath and let it out real slow through his nose. "Listen, those little ones were like greased lightning and I think we only winged a few. But the big sucker, we put dozens of rounds into it and didn't even slow it down. We only just made it here with our lives. We go back, we're going to run into it again, and maybe more of them. Bottom line, going back is suicide. Sorry, Jane, I can't allow it."

"Can't allow it? Bullshit with that; we're going back," Jane said, her jaw jutted out.

Harris let his eyes slide to Mike. "Mike?" He raised his eyebrows.

"Gotta find her," Mike said.

Harris shrugged. "Fine, but we're done here. My mission priority is now getting this device back to our experts." The soldier sighed. "Sorry, but all I can do is wish you luck."

Jane's left eyelid twitched a little. Perhaps not expecting Harris to give up on her and Mike so quickly.

Jane turned to Ally. "Ally, please. Come with us; we can't leave a fellow human being down here to die."

Ally looked down at her feet momentarily. "Jane, you're a real nice person. But I agree with the boss on this; we've got to complete our mission and get this tech back home." She raised her head. "Besides, she's probably dead already and going back means one or all of us could get skinned as well."

"Nadia can't be far away. We can do it," Jane urged. "At least to make sure…"

Harris' mouth turned down. "You guys do remember why those assholes were down here, and what they did, right?"

"So she gets what's coming to her?" Mike scoffed. "She was with the science team."

"Mike, forget it." Ally glanced at Harris and then shook her head. "Sorry."

Jane put her hands on her hips. "Can you at least damn wait for us?"

Ally nodded, but Harris bobbed his head from side to side. He turned back to the dark cave momentarily. "We'll push on to try and locate the base of the gravity well. If we find it, we'll wait at its base for three hours. That is, unless something changes our risk profile."

Harris adjusted his pack. "If the Russian woman is any further away than that, then, like I said, she's gone. And if you guys are longer than that, then you've run into trouble, and you're also gone. If we get attacked while waiting, we'll be making the jump then and there." He hiked his shoulders. "Best I can do. But I strongly urge you not to do this."

Jane pulled out her gun, ejected the magazine to check it, and slapped it back in. "Three hours, at the base of the well. We'll be there."

Mike looked from Harris to Ally. "If we don't see you again, good luck."

"And to you, Jane, Mikey." Ally gave them a small salute, and her eyes lingered on Mike's for a moment more. She looked like she wanted to say something else, but her lips pressed flat and she turned away.

Jane patted Mike's arm and when he looked down at her he saw that her eyes were glassy from fear. "We'll be fine. Let's go get her," Mike said.

"I know we will." Jane shared a fragile smile.

They turned and headed back the way they had come.

EPISODE 10

We were alone. Where, I could not say, or hardly imagine

— **Jules Verne**

CHAPTER 33

Harris saw the familiar carving on the wall and crept forward to examine it. It was the arrowhead mark, and he felt enormously relieved, but he also noticed the hairs on the back of his hands were standing on end.

"Some sort of charge in the air; a good sign I guess." He waved Ally on.

It wasn't long before they came to another solid-looking door set hard into the rock. There was a heavy bolt across it with a single keyhole at its center.

Ally pulled out the large iron key Ulmina had given them. "So now we know what this is for." She inserted the key in the lock and tried it, but it wouldn't budge. She gripped it in two hands and tried again.

"Don't you snap it," Harris said.

"Not a chance." Ally pressed her lips together and used a little more gentle force.

The key turned with a deep grinding and with it went the bolt sliding back into the wall. She stood back and allowed Harris to put his shoulder to it and give it a shove.

The door opened on squealing hinge-like mechanisms, and a draft of hot air blasted back at them. Harris immediately felt the work of gravitational forces on him that even made his back teeth tingle.

He held his gun and light up and entered the large cavern. This one, unlike the natural rock tunnels they had been moving through, had been adorned with carved images, statues, and columns. The small red race had obviously known what it was for.

"Like a church vestibule," Harris said and stopped before one of the artworks. It showed a line of white-haired people ascending in the air one after the other.

Ally joined him. "So this is why we never saw any old people amongst those little guys. They shuffle them all off here and send them up the pipe," she said.

"They thought they were going to heaven." He scoffed. "Poor bastards. All they were doing was feeding those dog-monsters." He turned. "Or that big bastard back in the cave."

"Think positive." Ally turned with raised eyebrows. "Maybe this section of cave doesn't have any of those ugly bastards."

"Let's hope," Harris said. "But if they come out to play, I'll be feeding them some Russian grenades."

"I heard that." Ally chuckled. "Hey, we've got three hours; got a deck of cards?" She dropped her pack.

"I'll settle for some peace and quiet." Harris dropped his several packs and squatted to the pulser box and also began to portion all of their remaining food supplies he had, plus ammunition into his pocket pouches and belt loops to try and lighten his bulk.

He paused to sip from his canteen and then held it up. "We've got to be sparing with our supplies and time now." He continued to work. "Not three hours."

"*Huh*, how long?" Ally frowned.

He looked up at her. "Fifteen minutes."

She blinked. "We said we'd give them three hours."

"We could wait three days and they still won't be back. You know that." He thumbed over his shoulder to the pulser. "Our mission is over."

"*Ah*, shit." Ally shook her head.

"Get ready to depart; that's an order," Harris said.

Ally snapped to attention. "Sir, permission requested to stay behind and wait for them."

"Request denied." Harris closed his pack.

"Boss, please, just give them their three hours." Ally stayed at attention. "Please."

Harris stared for a moment. "Negative, soldier." But then. "One hour."

Ally remained at attention and kept staring straight. "Two hours; we owe them that, sir."

Harris scoffed. "One and a half, because I'm in a good mood. Then we're going home. Conversation closed."

*****

Jane and Mike crept along the lightless passageway. Jane was in the lead, holding the flashlight in one hand, gun in the other, and crystal around her neck. Mike, who was taller, was holding his light over her head, giving them double the forward illumination.

They emerged from their tunnel into one of the larger caves that had multiple exits, and Jane shone her light down at the ground. She turned and spoke so quietly she was almost only mouthing her words to him and Mike had to concentrate on her lips.

"This is where the things attacked us." She pointed down.

The cave floor had a layer of disturbed dust. There were spatters of dark liquid.

Mike nodded. "Let's check the small exits. Maybe Nadia ran down one."

The pair walked along the perimeter, checking the cave dust at the smaller cave entrances.

Jane stopped. "This one. Inside there are boot marks."

Mike joined her. The footprints were fairly small. "Yep, that's her." He sucked in a breath. "Then let's take a look."

The tunnel was bigger inside than the main passages they had been moving along, and after a while Jane wrinkled her nose. "Stinks," she said.

They continued moving for another few minutes and Mike checked his watch. They'd been gone just over an hour. He wanted to be back on time as, though he didn't expect Harris to leave without them, he bet the guy wouldn't wait a second more than he had to.

"Light up ahead," Jane breathed.

Sure enough there was a blue glow emanating from just around the next bend. Jane lifted a hand and nearly smacked Mike in the face, he was so close.

"Hear that?" She tilted her head.

Mike concentrated and after a while he heard a soft sucking noise. "Yeah, weird."

"She might be hurt; come on." Jane moved forward.

Together they came out of the passage into a smaller alcove that was a dead end. At the far side of the cave was a wall crusted with open eggs, and at their base was Nadia, lying flat, surrounded by her crystals, and covered in the hatchlings.

The small monstrosities had their feeding tubes attached to her body and were greedily sucking the fluid from within her. Already she looked colorless and deflated.

"*Oof.*" Jane put a hand over her mouth and crushed her eyes shut.

"We're too late," Mike said. He grabbed her elbow. "We can't stay."

"Should we…?" Jane grimaced up at him.

"We can't do anything for her now. Let's go while those things are occupied." He dragged her back, and they both turned.

As both of their flashlights illuminated the passage behind them, they saw that it was fully blocked by the adult creature that had crept in behind them.

"*Jezus!*" Mike felt a bolt of fear run right through his body to even tingle his scalp. He lifted his gun, but his hand shook.

"It's a dead end." Jane looked quickly over her shoulder. "We're trapped."

Mike knew that the huge creature was armor-plated, and even Harris and Ally's rifles hadn't caused it any problems. Their handguns would be useless.

Going back is suicide, Harris had said. Suddenly Mike agreed.

Mike didn't know how long he and Jane stared into the blank face of the thing. But for now, all it seemed to do was block their path, and *inhale* them, as its nostril flaps gently flared open and closed.

After a while Jane spoke softly. "Does it know we're even here?"

Mike nodded. "Yeah, I bet it does. It's just keeping us here" He looked over his shoulder and shuddered. "Until its young finish with Nadia."

CHAPTER 34

Harris checked his watch and then got to his feet. "Ms. Ally Bennet, time to go home." He stood, shouldered the pulser pack and strapped it down hard.

She grimaced, but Harris just shook his head. "Forget it, they're gone; I can't save them, but I can at least save you. Now on your feet."

Ally rose, then walked to the mouth of the cave and leaned her head into it. She shut her eyes and concentrated, but there was no noise, nothing. She opened her eyes and gave the darkness a half-smile.

"Good luck you pair of fools."

She then followed Harris up the gravity well.

*****

Jane and Mike were frozen to the spot. The huge creature blocked the tunnel completely as its sharp legs were braced to the bottom and sides, creating prison bars.

We're screwed, Mike thought, but knew he'd never say it out loud to Jane.

Behind them the sound of liquid sucking was beginning to fade, and that meant the hatchlings were finishing their meal.

Mike lifted his gun and pointed at the spider-like thing in front of them. It didn't move an inch. He turned to point the gun at the hatchlings now beginning to climb off the shrunken body of Nadia. The effect was immediate; the massive creature surged forward several feet and then stopped.

Mike spun back with his gun. "I'm sure it can see us somehow."

Jane shook her head. "Some cave creatures have such acute scent and auditory senses they can create images in their mind as to what is occurring. It's seeing by sound and smell only."

"We don't have a choice," Mike said. "We've got to try something, and right now."

"It sees by sound," Jane repeated. She quickly dug into her pocket for the small jar containing the beetle that Ulmina had given her. She held it up and then opened it.

The shriek of the tiny thing made Mike and Jane wince, but the effect on the large creature was astounding. The pain and terror were immediate as its legs skittered insanely for a moment before it withdrew from the tunnel.

Behind them the small creatures threw themselves to the ground and went mad in their desire to escape the torture to their senses.

"Now!" Jane yelled and sprinted forward, holding out the small container.

Mike rushed after her, and together they navigated the side tunnel without challenge. The small beetle still shrieked and when they came to the main passageway, they turned a hard left and kept on going.

Mike glanced over his shoulder but nothing followed them, and after a few minutes sprinting their fatigue began to set in and Jane slowed. After another few minutes the shrieking began to die down.

"Oh crap." Jane peered into the small container. "He's running out of juice." She closed the container and the noise was immediately shut off.

"Hope we've got a big enough lead," Mike said.

"Well, I just hope this little guy recharges. He was supposed to be used in the upper labyrinths, against our cave dog people."

The pair jogged now, and within another twenty minutes they came to the huge door swung open.

"This looks promising," Mike said.

Then they found the gravity well. And the cave was empty.

"Those bastards." Mike looked at his wristwatch. "We haven't been three hours."

"Doesn't matter." Jane sighed. "I can't blame them; Harris thought we were as good as dead. And he was nearly right."

Mike went and pushed the heavy door closed and then stopped before the artwork showing the grey-haired people ascending one after the other.

"This confirms what we suspected as to why there aren't any elderly people amongst our red friends." He pointed. "They all ascended. Or were forced to."

Jane nodded. "To their ancestors."

"That's why Ulmina knew enough to give us the sonic beetle. Maybe they all took them to ward off the cave horrors." Jane shut her eyes. "I don't want to think about it."

"Let's get ready," Mike said. "We've got about twenty-eight hours of time in the gravity well. I'm looking forward to the nothingness."

"We need to be alert for when we get there," Jane said. She pulled out her gun. "We should reload, just in case." She looked up. "And hope our little beetle buddy is reloaded as well."

"Short bursts only when needed. We'll have a long climb," Mike replied and pulled a rag from his kit that he strategically tore into one long piece. He tied it around his wrist, and Jane smiled and held out her hand.

"Good idea."

He tied the other end around her wrist.

"There," Mike said. "You're not getting away from me again."

The pair went and stood underneath the gravity well and could feel the charge in the air. Mike leaned down to her and Jane lifted her chin. He kissed her gently on the lips.

"Whatever happens, it happens together," Jane said. "We're going to make it."

"And only a few thousand more miles to go." He smiled.

"Is that all?" Jane grabbed his hand and then bent her knees. "Count of three, two, one..."

They jumped.

CHAPTER 35

Dreams of endless blue water, golden sunshine, and the smell of freshly mown grass. Chocolate ice cream at the beach, glasses of chilled wine with beads of condensation running down their sides. Bunches of white roses in antique blue vases, full moons and shooting stars.

Jane smiled in her sleep and felt more content than she had in months. It was only the tug on her arm that roused her, and for a while she refused to let go of the wonderful dreams, moaning her displeasure.

"Hey, get ready," Mike whispered. "Something's up ahead."

"*Huh*?" She snapped fully awake, remembering where she was. "Shit." She fumbled for the small box containing the bug. Mike undid their hands, but held onto her.

Up ahead, there was a growing blue glow, and in the next seconds they began to slow, and then stopped to hang in space above the dark hole of the gravity well.

There was blood everywhere. Fresh blood.

There were also clothing fragments, shattered crystals, and some wooden possessions. Some of the items looked only months old and others looked centuries old.

Mike and Jane swam to the side. Mike sniffed. "Cordite."

"What happened here?" Jane held her gun and panned it around.

"I can only guess based on the gun smoke still in the air and fresh blood. The clothing and possessions must have belonged to the older red people who ascended to what they thought was their heaven to meet up with their spiritual ancestors. Instead, they had their real-life ancestors waiting for them, and they didn't get the welcome they expected."

"Horrifying. They found themselves in a nightmare instead." She turned to him. "These things, Harris' dog people, learned to wait here for a free and easy meal."

He nodded. "But then Harris and Ally turned up, a much more ferocious and formidable species. By the amount of blood, I'd say they put holes in dozens of them."

"But no bodies," Jane said. "And no Harris or Ally."

"No, and I hope that means Harris and Ally scattered them, and maybe later more of the creatures returned to carry away their dead." Mike did a quick walk around, picking up some of the larger crystals.

"We'll use these while we can. But remember, now we're away from the interior, they'll start to fade. So we have to try and save our flashlight batteries."

There was only one cave exit. "We need to start climbing and look for a way up into the Gadime cave system."

Jane turned to the dark cave mouth. "One more climb, one more climb." She turned and her lips were pressed flat for a moment. "Did I tell you I damn well hate caving now?"

"You and me both." Mike took her hand. "Come on."

Inside they immediately smelled the rank odor of acrid urine and knew what it meant.

They didn't want to, but both of them used their flashlights as well as the crystals, shining them in every nook, cranny, and crevice of the cave. *Just until we get out of this danger zone*, Mike promised himself.

Both Mike and Jane crept along, as silently as was humanly possible. They knew this was next to useless against something that hunted using sound and vibrations. But what it did do was allow the pair to pick up the faintest noises. And just ahead there was a skittering sound, and then the sound that filled Mike with dread.

Tock.

He grabbed Jane and they both froze to the spot. "Up there," he mouthed.

Jane turned to him. "We can't go back. No choice." She lifted her gun and put one foot in front of the other as she continued on.

The cave narrowed in a choke, and then the hollow echoes told them the cave probably opened up. It would be the perfect ambush spot.

"They're waiting in there; I know it," Jane said and pulled out the tiny wooden box that contained the bug. She placed a hand over the top momentarily.

"Please be alive," she said softly. And then lifted the lid.

The sonic squeal smashed out into the cave, and from inside the large cavern ahead of them there was an explosion of noise and movement. They heard dozens of bodies scrambling and falling over one another.

"Come on, while it lasts," Jane said and ran forward, holding out the shrieking beetle.

*****

After two more days, the beetle had died, even though they hadn't used it for many hours.

Then after four days, their crystals began to fade, and so too their halo of light.

Next day their food ran out, and their remaining water was now just a warm dreg.

On the route they'd chosen, they saw no more signs of the translucent, dog-like creatures, the ancestors, and worryingly, no sign at all of Harris or Ally passing this way.

Mike and Jane stopped momentarily when they thought they heard something like distant gunfire. The soft thundering went on for ages, but it was so far away and so defrayed by the billions of tons of rock and countless miles of labyrinthine tunnels that there was no way of knowing whether it was up, down, ahead, or behind them.

On the sixth day of ascending they came across a stream, clean and clear, and drank their fill. In its black depths tiny, blind fish like tiny neon lights flitted back and forth. With their food long run out, Mike's stomach growled. They were too small for a meal, and he couldn't yet bring himself to try and catch one of the living jewels.

"Look." Jane pointed.

There was something like a large cockroach with extremely long legs poised at the edge of the stream, also watching the fish.

She snorted softly. "*Damon Diadema*, the whip scorpion." She grinned. "Predator species; they live in caves, *but*, not always." She looked up at him. "Do you know what that means?"

Mike shook his head. "Something good I hope," he croaked.

"Oh yeah." She nodded. "They don't stay in caves, so we must be close to an exit."

Mike looked back at the weird thing all covered in spikes and with stilt-like legs. He pointed at it. "Count yourself lucky, buster. I was about to eat you."

They continued on, heading ever upward, along narrow paths on the edge of towering cliff walls, crossing stone bridges over bottomless dark pits, and through holes that narrowed so much they needed to wriggle on their bellies.

Soon their crystals were totally exhausted and only Jane's flashlight carried a weak orange glow. But they experienced something that they hadn't in months: a cool breeze.

Jane closed her eyes and filled her lungs. "Smell that?"

Even in the near-total darkness, Mike saw her broad white smile. He grinned and returned the smile. "Yeah, I do; smells like freedom."

After edging around a massive cliff drop, they followed another small cave stream for several more miles until it ended at a wall of rock that was dangling with long translucent pearls of some sort of lichen or waterweed.

"Shit," Jane said. "Dead end."

Mike came closer. "Lift up the light." Water seeped from behind it, but when Mike held up his hand, he felt the coolness of a breeze on his fingertips. "There's something behind here." He used the butt of his knife to pound against it. He turned to her. "Got any dynamite?"

She turned about. "We didn't come this far for nothing." She found what she was looking for: a stone the size of a bowling ball.

"Who needs dynamite?" She handed Mike the flashlight and then bent to pick it up and shakily lift it above her head. She then slammed it into the cave wall. It impacted and broke apart.

Jane nodded, satisfied by the dent it made. "Your turn, Hercules."

Mike found an even larger rock and used his upper body and shoulders to slam it forward so hard, it struck like a cannonball.

The rock wall dented and also cracked at the seep lines. More water flowed.

"Well done," Jane said. "Just a few more."

After several more, Mike held up a hand and turned back to the dark cave behind them. He waited and listened for a while after the echoes of their rock strikes died down. *Was there the sound of furtive movement?* he wondered.

After another full minute, he shook his head.

He lifted another boulder, slammed it against the wall, and then lifted another. He staggered a little. "*Phew*, I'm about beat."

"Want me to take over?" Jane asked.

"*Nah*, I got this." He turned away and closed his eyes for a moment to settle himself. After days of no food and general fatigue he didn't have many reserves left and he felt dizzy as all hell.

Mike shifted the rock in hands that were now rough and abraded. "We better be careful; there might be water behind there," he said and hefted the stone to his shoulder.

He threw boulders again and again, and on Mike's fourth throw, the wall exploded out at them, followed by a wall of dark water.

The freezing torrent pushed them back to skid and slide down the tunnel for hundreds of feet before its surge abated.

Mike thought that whatever waters were behind the cave wall must have come from a fairly shallow pool, and thankfully not a river. Otherwise they could be washed for miles, or over one of the towering cliffs they had just scaled.

"Jane," Mike said softly. He still had her flashlight, meaning she was somewhere in total darkness. "Jane!" Mike shifted, becoming panicked. "*Where are you?*"

She coughed wetly. "Here."

He turned the flashlight to her voice but the light was too weak to pick her out. He jumped to his feet and headed to where he thought she had called.

"Keep talking," Mike said. "And don't move."

"Here," Jane said again.

Mike found her just twenty feet from the dismal drop-off they had skirted not more than an hour ago. If the water's surge had been a little stronger, or Jane a few pounds lighter, she would have been washed over the edge.

Following his light, she came to him and held on for a moment. She was cold and wet, and shivered. She looked up at him. "Give me some good news; what did we break through into?"

"Let's find out." He held her hand and they quickly went back to the seeping cave wall. Now it was a gaping hole, and through it they could smell a faint odor of ozone; some sort of old arc lighting.

"Nearly there." He pulled her with him.

In another hour they found an ancient cage elevator usually used for mining, but still in use at the very bottom of the Gadime cave system.

He laid a hand on it, rubbed the rusting steel and then turned to her. "It's real." He lifted the cage door. "After you, my lady."

She entered and turned to him. "Top floor, please."

He closed the cage gate. "Going up; next floor, women's hosiery, haberdashery, and silk pillows." He pressed the button, and the elevator clunked and then responded by lifting off.

It ferried them to the upper levels of the Gadime, where tourists are usually allowed. Exiting, they continued by foot, and then in mere hours more they were walking up a neat, stone pathway.

The upper level of the Gadime cave was known as the Marble cave, and enjoyed by tourists during the summer months when it was accessible. Mike and Jane climbed the concrete ramp and came to a pair of glass doors, which seemed incongruous after what they'd been through after so many months.

Jane stopped before it. "It doesn't seem real," she breathed.

"It is." Mike pulled it open. "Your carriage awaits."

Jane laughed and went through. Inside the well-lit room there was a man in his fifties with salt and pepper eyebrows, probably a tour guide sitting at a desk. His eyes widened as he saw the unexpected and very disheveled pair of strangers emerge from the cave.

His mouth hung open momentarily as he looked them up and down; they were nothing but a pair of skin-and-bones strangers emerging off-season from the cave, dressed in rags, covered in dirt and open wounds.

Mike and Jane slumped into chairs, and Mike turned to the guard.

"Two cheeseburgers and coke to go. Plus a couple of bus tickets."

The man's frown lightened a little, and the Kosovan obviously spoke a little English. He straightened, still confused, but ever the professional.

"*Ah*, did you enjoy our cave tour?" he asked.

Mike and Jane looked at each other and then began to laugh. They continued laughing until tears ran down their cheeks, and then they simply leaned forward to hug each other, and continued to let the tears flow.

EPILOGUE

There came a single sob from deep within the impenetrable darkness.

Ally's arms and legs were broken, but still tied and spread wide. Raw meat had been stuffed into her mouth a while back and she immediately vomited it up knowing what it was.

"*He-eeeelp*! *He-eeeelp.*"

She sobbed again. But knew no one would come. She and Harris had been set-upon and besieged, for hours, until their ammunition had been exhausted. They had run and tried to hide, but the things found them. Probably the smell of their fear alone had been like a beacon in the darkness.

Eventually, Harris had gone down under the weight of their final attack, and then she was brought down, using her blade to slash one way and then the other at the pale and greasy bodies that flew past to strike and scratch at her, though just tormenting her, and not wanting to kill her.

But it was different for Harris. They had fallen on him with tooth and claw, and then dragged them both back to their lair.

She was stripped, hobbled, and bound, and then she was forced to listen to Harris' screams as he was torn limb from limb. The sound of ripping flesh, tearing tendons, and then breaking bones had sickened her soul. But it was nothing compared to when she heard the feasting begin.

Over the fetid smells of ammonia, body odor, and shit, she smelled the coppery tang of fresh blood.

They tried to stuff more food in her mouth but she kept her teeth jammed closed and turned her head away. She just thanked God she couldn't see.

How long would they keep her alive? she wondered. *Until she gave birth, again and again*, she knew.

"Kill me." She screamed. "*Kill me-eeee!*"

She heard them coming back and she called out for Mike and Jane, pleading with them to come for her, and begging forgiveness for not waiting for them.

Finally, she just called for her mother.

Another of the slimy beasts fell upon her to begin its frantic rutting. Ally wanted to die. But she knew her time in Hell had only just begun.

END

CHECK OUT OTHER GREAT DINOSAUR THRILLERS

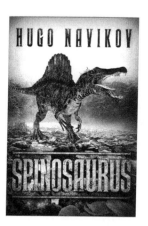

SPINOSAURUS
by Hugo Navikov

Brett Russell is a hunter of the rarest game. His targets are cryptids, animals denied by science. But they are well known by those living on the edges of civilization, where monsters attack and devour their animals and children and lay ruin to their shantytowns.

When a shadowy organization sends Brett to the Congo in search of the legendary dinosaur cryptid Kasai Rex, he will face much more than a terrifying monster from the past.

Spinosaurus is a dinosaur thriller packed with intrigue, action and giant prehistoric predators.

LAND OF DEATH
by Eric S Brown & Alex Laybourne

A group of American soldiers, fleeing an organized attack on their base camp in the Middle East, encounter a storm unlike anything they've seen before. When the storm subsides, they wake up to find themselves no longer in the desert and perhaps not even on Earth. The jungle they've been deposited in is a place ruled by prehistoric creatures long extinct. Each day is a struggle to survive as their ammo begins to run low and virtually everything they encounter in this land they've been hurled into, is a deadly threat.

HECK OUT OTHER GREAT
NOSAUR THRILLERS

WRITTEN IN STONE
by David Rhodes

Charles Dawson is trapped 100 million years in the past. Trying to survive from day to day in a world of dinosaurs he devises a plan to change his fate. As he begins to write messages in the soft mud of a nearby stream, he can only hope they will be found by someone who can stop his time travel. Professor Ron Fontana and Professor Ray Taggit, scientists with opposing views, each discover the fossilized messages. While attempting to save Charles, Professor Fontana, his daughter Lauren and their friend Danny are forced to join Taggit and his group of mercenaries. Taggit does not intend to rescue Charles Dawson, but to force Dawson to travel back in time to gather samples for Taggit's fame and fortune. As the two groups jump through time they find they must work together to make it back alive as this fast-paced thriller climaxes at the very moment the age of dinosaurs is ending.

HARD TIME
by Alex Laybourne

Rookie officer Peter Malone and his heavily armed team are sent on a deadly mission to extract a dangerous criminal from a classified prison world. A Kruger Correctional facility where only the hardest, most vicious criminals are sent to fend for themselves, never to return.

But when the team come face to face with ancient beasts from a lost world, their mission is changed. The new objective: Survive.

SEVEREDPRESS

facebook.com/severedpr
twitter.com/severedpress

CHECK OUT OTHER GREAT DINOSAUR THRILLERS

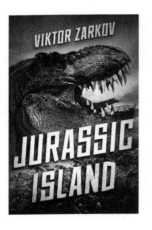

JURASSIC ISLAND
by Viktor Zarkov

Guided by satellite photos and modern technology a ragtag group of survivalists and scientists travel to an uncharted island in the remote South Indian Ocean. Things go to hell in a hurry once the team reaches the island and the massive megalodon that attacked their boats is only the beginning of their desperate fight for survival.

Nothing could have prepared billionaire explorer Joseph Thornton and washed up archaeologist Christopher "Colt" McKinnon for the terrifying prehistoric creatures that wait for them on JURASSIC ISLAND!

K-REX
by L.Z. Hunter

Deep within the Congo jungle, Circuitz Mining employs mercenaries as security for its Coltan mining site. Armed with assault rifles and decades of experience, nothing should go wrong. However, the dangers within the jungle stretch beyond venomous snakes and poisonous spiders. There is more to fear than guerrillas and vicious animals. Undetected, something lurks under the expansive treetop canopy . . .

Something ancient.

Something dangerous.

Kasai Rex!

Printed in Great Britain
by Amazon